Disaster was imminent . . .

Today's press conference was important to Abbie. She hoped to squeeze enough publicity mileage out of it so that her promotion campaign for the Seaport museum would get off to a good start. Her unruly hair was keeping itself in place, and she considered that an excellent omen.

Abbie reached the museum offices and saw Josie standing in front of the building. The older woman's eyes were wild.

"Something terrible's happened at the piers!" Josie cried.

"I'm sure it has," Abbie said gently, "but we'll have to talk about it later. I'm very busy now."

"No, no, this can't wait. You must get over to Pier 15 right away. One of the ships is sinking!"

ABOUT THE AUTHOR

Alice Harron Orr grew up in a small city. Now she lives in a big one and sometimes wishes she could go back to streets lined with maples. She shares her New York City life with Jonathan, her husband and best friend, the grown children she adores and a slightly neurotic cat. Alice has been writing seriously since the eighth grade.

SABOTAGE
ALICE HARRON ORR

Harlequin Books

TORONTO • NEW YORK • LONDON
AMSTERDAM • PARIS • SYDNEY • HAMBURG
STOCKHOLM • ATHENS • TOKYO • MILAN

To Jonathan—
always my romantic hero

Harlequin Intrigue edition published December 1986

ISBN 0-373-22056-1

Prologue

He could tell it was well after dawn because the rocking of the morning tide-change was long past. Still, there was no chink in the hull to betray the slightest glimmer of natural light. The copper ship's lantern cast its pinkish glow on the narrow, scarred desktop and open journal, but otherwise the cabin was all in darkness. He'd overstayed his time and was sure to be caught by the sun. Yet he made no move to flee, which he would have done on any previous morning. He was stronger now. Maybe even strong enough to withstand the day.

He set the quill down next to the journal page, which was nearly covered in fine hand-script, more than half faded, the rest fresh.

He had to be patient. It wasn't his time for daylight yet. There was a way each task should be done and a way it should not. That was why he'd come back, to remind these fools of the right order of things and to show them the wrath of the Captain at their forgetfulness. As for the other one, the less-than-being—was it man or woman, urchin or adult? He couldn't tell—it would be vanished soon.

Chapter One

Abbie Tanner was about to place the framed photograph next to the spanking new desk blotter when she noticed the envelope.

"Pretty fancy," she commented to her empty office.

The heavy ivory paper really looked elegant against the porous green of the blotter, and a shaft of morning sunlight gave it a luminous, beckoning quality.

"Must be an invitation to my first society ball."

She smiled at the thought. After only three weeks in New York City, she hardly knew a soul, much less any of what her ex-husband, Robert, would have called "the right people." More likely, this was a greeting from one of her new colleagues, welcoming Abbie to her first day on the job as summer program promotions consultant for the South Street Seaport Museum. Her assistant, Meredith Stanfield, seemed the thoughtful type. Maybe she had left the envelope.

Abbie set the photograph down and picked up the unsealed envelope. She pulled out a folder of the same heavy paper, like a wedding announcement minus the orange blossoms. Unfortunately, what she found inside had nothing to do with a happy occasion.

"You don't belong here," the message said. "Get out now, or I'll make you sorry you ever came." It was signed, "Your Sworn Enemy."

Abbie sank slowly into the swivel chair behind her desk and read the two typewritten sentences again. "This has to be a joke," she muttered.

Her thumb stroked the corner of the folder without really feeling it. She wanted to believe the note was just a prank by someone with a twisted but harmless sense of humor who would get his kicks out of shaking her up on her first day of work . . . sort of an initiation rite. Still, she wasn't convinced. She could almost feel the truly sinister intentions seeping from the expensive paper. She dropped the card as if her fingers had been burned.

The breeze from the open window was June soft and pleasantly warm, but Abbie shivered all the same. She'd been warned about moving to New York. "They've got loonies coming out of the cracks in the sidewalks up there," everyone she knew in Baltimore had said, and her Philadelphia friends had agreed.

She'd laughed at them. "Too much reading in the supermarket lines, that's what's wrong with you," was her answer. "Those are just tabloid exaggerations." She'd looked forward to living in a city where there were all kinds of people, including some unconventional ones. The cities she'd been in until now were on the conservative side. Manhattan would be a great adventure, kooks and all, she'd told the people she'd met at her last free-lance assignment in Trenton. Now she wasn't so sure.

Her glance fell on the eight-year-old freckled face in the photograph, and a gasp of fear escaped her throat. What if whoever had written this warning knew about Davey? Abbie's mind reviewed the morning in a flash. Her son was safe. She'd watched him climb aboard the day-camp bus and waved till he was out of sight. Still, what if this threat was real? The surest way to get to her would be through Davey. Nothing in the world mattered more to her than he did. For the first time since that ecstatic day when she'd been offered the New York City assignment, Abbie wondered if she'd been wrong to follow her dreams to this place.

A FEW MINUTES IN FRONT of the ladies' room mirror made Abbie feel better. At least, she looked the part she was supposed to play that morning. Her gray-and-white summer gabardine suit set the perfect professional tone; her makeup was just enough to brighten the natural pallor of her complexion and flatter her direct, green gaze without being too much for the office. Even her willful red-blond curls had decided to behave and remain tucked in their neat coil at the nape of her neck. Abbie latched on to that as a sign the rest of the day would be better than its beginning.

The sunlight in her office was even brighter now. It touched the frizzled, silver-gray hair of the woman who hovered behind the desk. "Hello there," she chirped as Abbie stood stunned in the doorway. "I'm Josie." She bounded around and thrust out her hand.

"What were you doing there?" Abbie asked, ignoring the proffered greeting. A moment ago this same hand had been on the drawer in which the ivory-colored card was hidden.

"I was looking for some paper to write you a note."

Or maybe you were checking on the note you left here earlier, Abbie couldn't help thinking.

Josie was still wagging her hand, and Abbie couldn't avoid it any longer. She shook the eager fingers briefly, then stepped behind her desk to glance at the drawer. It appeared undisturbed.

"I've been anticipating your arrival for days now. I came early so I'd be the first to welcome you to South Street." Josie plopped into the chair opposite the desk without waiting to be asked. "Of course, I'm always around early. Up with the birds, I say. It's the only healthy way to live."

By the looks of Josie, that must have been sound advice. She was probably in her mid-sixties, but her twinkly blue eyes and clear pink skin made her appear much younger. Only the fringe of frizzled gray hair betrayed her age. She wore a rumpled jacket and skirt of mismatched plaids that reminded Abbie of the frumpy, eccentric characters in Agatha Christie's novels, the ones who had often committed the murder no matter how innocent they might seem.

"Do you work at the museum?" Abbie asked, sitting down herself and trying to think how Miss Marple would handle this situation.

"Oh, no, but I spend most of my time in the neighborhood, and I try to keep up with whatever's going on. Right now you're the big news around here. Everybody's been gossiping about what you'll be doing this summer. In fact, that's one of the things I want to discuss with you . . . but at the moment, I can't recall exactly why." Her gaze seemed to click off into the distance for an instant before it returned to Abbie. "This is a great place for gossip, you know."

"You couldn't be more right about that, Josie."

The voice from the doorway was deep with throaty undertones. Its owner was standing not quite inside the office in a casual pose, one hip cocked above the other and his hand resting on it. Tanned fingers trailed into the pocket of his pleated khaki trousers. The man looked more California than New York despite the slight lilt of Brooklyn in his words. In fact, it occurred to Abbie, he looked like the kind of man one didn't see very often any place these days: physically imposing, decidedly masculine and in control, as if he should be leading a wagon train or striding the deck of a tall ship.

"I'm Calhoun Quinn, and you must be Abigail Tanner. Am I interrupting?"

"No, of course not. Please come in."

Abbie was only a little startled to have such an attractive man appear at her door so early in the morning. He crossed to the desk and held out the hand that wasn't in his pocket. His grip was as solid as the rest of him and quite warm.

"Won't you sit down?" Abbie released his handshake, but she could still feel the warmth of him along her fingertips when he lifted the remaining chair from its spot by the wall and set it next to Josie's.

"Don't you think he looks just like Errol Flynn?" Josie whispered gleefully, leaning forward as if to confide a delicious secret.

"Well, I . . ."

Calhoun Quinn rescued Abbie from groping for an answer by throwing his head back in a rumbling laugh that resounded from the navigating charts and the prints of ships at sea on the office walls. A lock of dark, sun-streaked blond hair fell across his forehead, and he gestured toward it. "Errol had curly hair, Josie, remember? Look at this. Straight as a rigging wire, as you old salts would say."

"Oh, Cal, you're such a kidder." Josie giggled, her eyes twinkling brighter than ever.

Abbie was beginning to wonder if she'd been favored with a visit from the neighborhood vaudeville team when

Quinn turned toward her. "Has Josie told you about her project?"

"No, she hasn't."

"She has a theory about the sea gulls."

"I can't say that I'm surprised."

"Keep listening. You may be."

His eyes were medium blue with facets of a lighter shade. The straightforwardness of his gaze would have been impertinent if not for the smile that lit his tanned features. He ran a hand through his brown-gold hair to smooth back the wayward lock.

"Tell us about your project, Josie. I think Mrs. Tanner would be interested."

"Yes, I would." Abbie suppressed the urge to clarify that she might be a Mrs., but she was no longer married.

Josie bounced forward to the edge of her seat. "We have to stop what they're doing to the ships. Don't you agree?"

"I don't think I understand," Abbie said.

"The mess, of course. The sea gulls make a terrible mess, all over the spars, on the decks, everywhere. It's a disgrace." Josie snorted her disgust. "But I have a solution." She inched forward even more, until it looked as if she were about to fall off the chair. "Plastic."

"What?"

"Plastic, silly. Don't you see? We stretch clear plastic over all of the ships. Then the sun can shine through, but no more mess."

Josie appeared to be totally serious about this. Abbie was tempted to grin at the thought of the museum's small fleet of antique sailing vessels swathed in plastic.

"I know it can work," Josie went on. "And the ships would look just lovely, like presents wrapped in cellophane." Her cheeks glowed at the prospect.

Quinn had watched her with affection in his gaze as she spoke. "Josie's been working on her plan for quite some time," he said gently. "She knew you'd want to hear about it."

"Thank you, Josie—and you, too, Mr. Quinn," Abbie replied.

"Please call me Cal." He was looking directly at her again with those eyes that could probably pin a person to her chair if he wanted them to. He turned back to Josie. "I'm sure Abbie will study your proposal very carefully."

"Unless she's one of them." That thought wrought a surprising change in Josie. Her twinkling eyes suddenly became hard, and her general air of flightiness stiffened into something much more stern. She reminded Abbie of a schoolteacher who wielded a long stick with which she rapped desks and cracked hands. Then the moment ended, and Josie was bouncy and bright again. "But, of course, you aren't one of them, are you?" she chirped.

"One of whom?"

"Josie, isn't it feeding time?" Cal prodded.

Josie gazed vaguely up at him, as if trying to translate what he'd just asked her. Abbie felt equally confused.

"Oh, yes," Josie chimed in at last. "It's feeding time."

"Josie feeds the gulls every day. Several times a day, in fact."

"That's right. I do it down South Street, away from the piers. It distracts the birds from the ships, at least for a little while."

"And it gives you something to do." Cal took Josie's arm and eased her out of the chair. She stared vaguely at him again. Then a happy smile crinkled her rosy cheeks.

"Yes, that's right," she agreed. "It gives me something to do." She seemed very pleased about that.

Cal was guiding her to the doorway when she stopped short and whirled back toward Abbie. "There's something I had to talk to her about. Something crucial." Josie furrowed her brow as if straining to remember. Her manner had altered from breezy to urgent this time, and she'd planted her feet in firm opposition to Cal's attempts to move her into the hall.

"You can see Mrs. Tanner another day," he said.

"I know what it was I wanted to say. It's about the crowds. She's going to bring crowds of people down here, isn't she?" Josie was looking at Abbie but speaking to Cal.

"That's what I've heard." He glanced toward Abbie. Then, unexpectedly, he winked, and for an instant that wink fluttered inside her as if his long lashes had triggered the response.

"No crowds," Josie protested, belligerent now. "They'll make more of a mess than ever. No crowds."

"As I said before, you can talk with Abbie about that some other time."

Even Josie's firm stance was no match for Cal's determination. She had no choice but to let him maneuver her through the door.

"Don't let her do it." Josie's voice rose to a whine as he led her out of sight. She repeated her plea several times down the hall.

Abbie sagged back in her swivel chair and stared at the empty doorway. It was only a little past ten, and she'd already been confronted with a threatening letter, an eccentric old woman whose moods shifted all over the lot and the most attractive man she'd run into in a very long time.

"What a morning," she said with a sigh.

She got up from her chair and walked to the open window. Below, on Front Street, a houseplant vendor had left his empty display cart overnight. A few lumps of soil remained in the corners of the brightly painted wooden box, and as Abbie leaned forward against the sill, a rank odor of fertilizer drifted in. She shook her head. That was hardly what she'd expect to smell on the New York waterfront, but she was beginning to think the city specialized in the unexpected. She glanced toward the desk, in which she'd hidden the anonymous card and by which Josie had sat before being led away, protesting vehemently. Obviously the surprises this place had in store wouldn't all be happy ones.

A flash of movement brought Abbie's attention back to the street. Cal Quinn and Josie had emerged from the shadow of the building. He was patting the older woman's shoulder, though she appeared perfectly calm now and no longer in need of coddling. He bent to say something Abbie couldn't hear. Then he reached into his pocket, pulled out some bills and gave them to Josie. She took them and grinned widely before hurrying off toward Schermerhorn Row, at the next corner.

"I wonder what that was all about?" Abbie asked herself aloud.

"All what?"

The experiences of the morning had left Abbie a little jumpy. She spun around toward the voice in the doorway, and her elbow struck hard against a small pane of the window. The glass shattered more loudly than she would have thought it was capable of and tinkled down into the street. Cal Quinn glanced up toward the sound, and Abbie stepped instinctively back from view, embarrassed to have done something so stupid. She barely noticed the surprise he displayed at having discovered her watching him. Meanwhile, her assistant, Meredith Stanfield, had entered the office and was approaching the window to survey the damage below.

"No corpses in sight," she said. "You can look now."

Abbie's humiliation was compounded by having been caught cringing out of sight. She'd seen Meredith only once before, at the interview for this job. Their meeting had been friendly, but Abbie didn't know her well enough not to feel pretty foolish right now.

"I'll take your word for it." Abbie went back to her desk, wishing she could crawl under it instead of sitting behind it.

"Just first-day jitters," Meredith said. "Happens to the best of us. I'll have this mess taken care of for you."

A few minutes later she'd done exactly that and brought them two cups of coffee besides. Abbie was beginning to suspect that Meredith might be the godsend that would make up for everything else that had happened so far. She rubbed her bruised elbow and thanked her lucky stars.

Meredith brushed the last glass splinter from the windowsill and pushed the bottom sash upward so the broken pane would be less visible. She had a look of sober concentration about her, as if she took everything very seriously, especially her work. Yet her manner of speaking was offhand, even flippant sometimes. Her coloring was decidedly neutral, in all shades of beige: beige hair, beige skin, beige lips. Only her eyes varied from the monochrome of her face. They were gray and watchful. She was also unusually thin. The material of her linen suit dropped from her shoulders and waist in straight lines, unimpeded by so much as a hint of curving flesh anywhere.

"Let's take a walk," she said. "You look like you need a break."

Abbie agreed, and the two women left the office and went down the stairs to the street.

"I can remember when this street was nice and quiet this time of day," Meredith remarked as they strolled onto lower Fulton Street, now known as Schermerhorn Row. "Then the developers took over, and nothing's been the same since."

"You were here before the restoration started?" Abbie asked.

"Long before, and I wouldn't call what they did here restoration. That word implies a return to the original. The only place these buildings ever looked like this was in some architect's imagination."

The storefronts that lined the street were painted in pastels, their wide display windows facing the cobblestone walkway. Abbie was reminded of an urban Williamsburg.

"Quaint. That's how I'd describe it," Meredith said. "All scrubbed up clean and neat and, most of all, quaint."

"You sound like you don't approve."

"Go with the flow, as they used to say. I can't change it, so I might as well accept it. Wave makers tend to get drowned."

"At least the ships are authentic "

"That's why I stay here."

"Well, if I do my job, their future will be a lot more secure at the end of the summer than it is now."

Meredith snapped her head around so abruptly her pale hair swept back from her face. "We've managed to survive without you till now," she said in a tone as cool as the June morning was warm.

Abbie's first instinct was to blurt out an apology, but she kept herself from doing that. "I didn't mean to suggest you hadn't," she said with a conciliatory smile. "I was simply referring to the fact that I was hired to increase public awareness of the ships so more people will visit them and there'll be more revenue for taking care of them."

"You won't hear me argue with that." Meredith had started walking again, and her manner was reservedly friendly once more. "But take my word, it's not easy to compete for attention with happy-hour bars and bathing-suit sales."

The touchy moment had passed, yet Abbie still felt uneasy. At first she thought that was the reason for the creeping sensation at the back of her neck. They'd gone through the gate to the museum piers. The long, graceful hull of the four-masted *Peking* dominated the scene just ahead, but Abbie's attention was drawn suddenly to someone behind her.

"There's a man watching us," she said. "He's crouching down in back of the kiosk with the tour boat posters on it."

Meredith glanced over her shoulder. "That's just Nathan Mallory. He probably followed us from the office. He does things like that."

"Who is he?"

"One of our faithful volunteers. Too faithful as far as I'm concerned."

"What do you mean?"

"He's a pest. He's constantly hanging around the volunteer office. That's right next to yours, by the way, so be careful what you say. The walls are very thin, and they definitely have ears—small pointed ones like Nathan's."

Abbie looked back toward the kiosk once more. Nathan Mallory had moved forward several yards and was cowering in the shadow of the round, windowed booth where tickets were sold for harbor sails aboard the schooner *Pioneer* and the paddle-wheeled *Andrew Fletcher*. She couldn't tell if the man actually did have pointed ears, but his appearance was eccentric enough without them. She guessed he'd be fairly tall if he stood up straight. Instead he hunched in on himself, as if he were trying to pull his head into his chest cavity and hide it there.

His clothes looked like thrift-shop purchases meant for someone much larger, and he tugged compulsively at the lengthy overlap of the belt that cinched his trousers into bunches at his waist. His limp dark hair was unevenly cut, and a shock of it fell over his eyes. Abbie was reminded of another man whose hair had a tendency to stray across his forehead with a much different effect. It wasn't the first time Calhoun Quinn had popped into her thoughts since she'd last seen him beneath her office window.

Nathan appeared to have noticed Abbie watching him, and he slipped away behind a group of tourists.

"There was another interesting character in my office this morning," she told Meredith. "Her name was Josie."

"The sea-gull lady?"

Abbie laughed. "Is that what you call her? I can understand why."

"You say she was in your office?"

"She was there when I arrived."

That wasn't exactly true. Abbie had been there earlier, when she'd found the threatening note; but she'd decided not to mention that particular incident to anyone just yet. How would it look if her colleagues knew she already had a sworn enemy, in writing no less, her first morning on the job? She was determined to make a much more favorable initial impression than that.

"I'm surprised," Meredith said. "Josie knows the offices are off-limits for her. I've never seen her go up there without being invited. Did you invite her?"

"Of course not. I don't even know her."

"Was she by herself?"

"At first she was. Then a man named Calhoun Quinn came in."

"I see." They'd reached the second long gangway to the deck of the *Peking*. Meredith stopped and leaned against it, one thin finger stroking the black-painted metal absentmindedly. She seemed deep in thought for a moment before she went on. "That might explain what Josie was doing in your office."

"How?"

"Maybe Quinn sent her there."

"Why would he do that?" Abbie squinted against the brightness of the sun in order to see Meredith more clearly. The older woman looked perplexed.

"You must have noticed how Josie comes on fairly sane at first, then veers off into left field."

"Yes, I noticed. She was talking about some scheme of hers to wrap the ships in plastic."

"Well, that kind of thing can be a little unnerving, wouldn't you agree?"

"I have to admit I was rather confused by her."

"Maybe that's what Quinn was after, to confuse you."

"Why would he want to do that?"

Meredith sat down on one of the metal steps to the gangway and stretched her lanky legs out in front of her. She laced her fingers in her lap and sighed. "You're bound to find this out eventually, so I might as well tell you. Cal Quinn and some of his cronies had their own boy in mind for the job you're in now."

"Who is Mr. Quinn anyway? His name isn't on the museum staff roster." Abbie was beginning to feel uncomfortable, and not just from the warmth of the sun through her long-sleeved suit jacket.

"He's a member of the museum advisory committee. They're big business guns who volunteer their time to the museum. They're not paid staff. Still, they have a lot to say about what goes on around here, and Cal Quinn has more to say than most.''

"Then why was I hired for this assignment instead of the man he was promoting?"

"Some of the committee members think Quinn's getting too powerful. They backed you as a challenge to him, and he conceded. My guess is he's putting off the fight till the permanent promotions spot opens up in the fall."

"What permanent spot?" It was clearer by the minute that there was more going on at the South Street Seaport than Abbie's research materials had told her.

"Public relations director. Don't tell me you didn't know about that!"

"This is the first I've heard of any permanent position."

Meredith appeared almost as confused as Abbie felt. "I was sure you were after that job, too."

Abbie shook her head. She hated office politics, and it seemed she'd stepped into a hotbed of them. Meredith looked skeptical, as if she didn't quite believe Abbie's denial. "The job opens up in September, and Quinn definitely wants his boy in it. He's already salted the staff with a number of flunkies who were hired because he was behind them. This P.R. guy would be one more he'd have in his pocket."

"So you think Quinn might have sent Josie around to knock me off balance my first day on the job?"

Meredith nodded. "Just enough to get you started on the wrong foot, unsettle you a little."

Abbie was feeling unsettled, all right. "Then it seems like they should have hired his man instead of me." She thought for a minute. "I saw him give the sea-gull lady some money after they left the building. Do you think he might have been paying her for coming to my office to rattle me?''

"I'm not sure what I think about any of it. This might be the first step in some kind of campaign of his to get to you, or it could be nothing." However, Meredith's gray eyes revealed more certainty of the former than she had expressed. "All I know is Calhoun Quinn comes from a long line of wheeler-dealers, and he usually gets what he wants. Right now, unfortunately, he may want your job."

ABBIE HAD A NERVOUS HABIT. When things were going badly, she'd push at her hairpins. She'd done that ever since she was a little girl, and her mother had tried to tame her springy curls into a ponytail. By the time Abbie had got back to her office, she was pushing the hairpins so hard she'd scraped her scalp red in several places.

"Why don't you cut it if you're worried about keeping it neat? Your hair is much too beautiful to be tacked down like that anyway?"

Abbie had walked straight to her desk without noticing there was someone waiting in the chair near the door. She dropped her hands from her curls, feeling suddenly self-conscious, as if she'd been caught in an act too private to be observed, especially by Cal Quinn.

"It seems like everybody's cut his or her hair off these days," he went on.

"I'm not everybody."

"Yes, I noticed." His blue eyes with their pale lights suggested he'd noticed a lot more than that about her.

"Was there something specific you wanted, Mr. Quinn?"

She made a show of going through some junk mail on her desk so she wouldn't have to look at him. After what Meredith had told her, Abbie didn't feel like being very friendly to this man who'd apparently been against her even before she arrived.

"You're hurt," he said.

"What?" She certainly was, but she hadn't expected him to bring it up. Who wouldn't be hurt to find out that someone had tried to maneuver him out of a job?

"Let me look at that." He sprang up from the chair and was at her side before she could think to step away. He took the envelope she was holding and dropped it on the desk. Then he began pushing her jacket sleeve up.

"What are you doing?" she protested.

"The question is, what have you done? You have blood on your elbow."

Just as he said that, Abbie felt a sting of pain. She turned her arm and looked down at the sleeve. He was right. A small red stain, stiff and dark, marked the gray gabardine. She'd apparently cut herself on the glass when the window broke but hadn't noticed it till now.

"We'll have to get this jacket off. The sleeves are too tight to push up. Are you wearing something underneath?" His question was so matter-of-fact and clinical, he might have been a doctor.

"Yes, I..."

But, of course, he wasn't a doctor. Abbie felt suddenly more self-conscious than ever.

"I'll try not to hurt you any more than you already have been," he said.

Abbie looked up at him. She was aware of the irony of his words in view of what Meredith had said, but at the moment she was even more aware of his fingers unfastening the top button of her suit jacket. He continued downward to the next button and then the next. Abbie's arm was stinging noticeably now where the jacket material had been pulled away from the small wound. She convinced herself it was the distraction of the stinging sensation that kept her from stopping Cal and unbuttoning the jacket herself.

When he'd slipped open the last button, he slid the jacket gently from her shoulders and down her arms. He folded it once and draped it over the back of her swivel chair. Neither of them spoke, and Abbie hardly moved a muscle. She would've thought that being this close to someone so attractive and at the same time so distrustful would be an upsetting experience. Instead she felt very calm. No one had fussed over her like this since she was a child, especially not her ex-husband, Robert. For a moment she could hardly believe how good it made her feel.

"I had a slight accident," she said, finally pulling her arm away from him. "It's nothing."

"Oh, yes, with the window. I saw that."

Cal made no effort to resume his fussing. He walked back around the desk and was about to sit down in the worn leather chair Josie had occupied earlier.

"I asked if there was some specific reason you came here, Mr. Quinn." She spoke in a tone that wouldn't encourage someone to take a seat and stay a while. He remained standing.

"Actually I came to explain about Josie," he said. "We've gotten used to her around here. You might say she comes with the territory, but I can understand how she'd confuse a newcomer."

"What makes you think I was confused?"

"When I walked by and heard Josie babbling away in here, I got the impression you didn't know what was going on."

"I'd have figured it out eventually."

Abbie was standing, also. She had no intention of sitting in the desk chair with him towering over her. He was several inches taller than she, but this way she could look him almost straight in the eye.

"I'm sure you would have," he said after a pause. "I just assumed you could use some help."

"Do you make assumptions often, Mr. Quinn?"

"I thought you were going to call me Cal."

"Do you always make such assumptions, Cal?"

"You said 'often' the first time. Now it's 'always.' I seem to be a bigger bad guy by the second."

He was smiling and obviously trying to be friendly, but Abbie couldn't manage anything warmer than politeness at the moment.

"I apologize if I sounded critical, Mr. Quinn."

"Cal."

"Cal," she said, suppressing a sigh.

"It's your first day on a new job. I can see why you'd be a little touchy."

"Mr. Quinn, I'm not touchy. I am not confused. I am not in need of help. In fact, I'm doing just fine, thank you very much."

He stepped backward in one long stride toward the door, perusing her as he might have done with some curious exhibit in a glass case. "I see," he said in a voice now as cool and impersonal as her own. Then Cal inclined his head slightly in what looked like a parody of a respectful bow, turned and left her office. He didn't shake her hand as he had when they'd met, nor did he repeat his insistence that she could call him by his first name.

Abbie watched him go. She'd wanted to put him at arm's length, and that was exactly what she'd done. So why did she suddenly feel sad?

She yanked open the bottom drawer of her desk and pulled out her shoulder bag. She'd had enough of this. She was going to lunch.

In her haste, Abbie didn't notice that the bag wasn't in the same spot where she'd left it earlier.

Chapter Two

A friend from Philadelphia had once told Abbie that if she was going to live in New York City, she should practice her subway face—a blank expression that telegraphed the message "hands off" in no uncertain terms. Practice wasn't necessary tonight. Tired as she was, blankness came naturally. After the strain of her first full day on South Street, she barely had energy left to look around.

Her arm had begun to ache from clinging to the metal strap above her head. She might be five-eight-and-a-half, but she wasn't tall enough to hang on to one of those things for very long. New Yorkers must grow special muscles for this, she thought. She'd have to do the same if she planned on becoming a New Yorker herself.

She spotted an opening in the pileup of hands along the vertical pole at the center of the car and edged toward it. The subway train, packed tight with homebound travelers, was speeding under the East River from Manhattan to Queens, where Abbie and her son had an apartment on Thirtieth Avenue in the Astoria section. She liked it there, and until this morning she'd been certain she'd come to the city to stay.

After all, she'd worked five years to get here. Almost from the day she'd started in this business, Abbie had known she had to reach New York. The most prestigious public relations firms in the country were based in the Big Apple, and she intended to be on the staff of one of them eventually.

She'd hardly had any background in the field when she first got into it, but very soon she'd figured out the fallacy of beginning at an entry level and following the gradual route up. That could be an extremely long-term process, especially for a woman, and Abbie couldn't afford to take that long. She was already more than twenty-six by the time she got her first P.R. job, and it was a business in which you made your success when you were young or else you were left behind.

Back then she had no contacts who could help her along. Robert knew everybody of importance in D.C. and Baltimore, and he made certain none of them offered so much as a flattering word in her behalf. She had to do it entirely on her own. She decided to free-lance, going from one assignment to the next, learning as she went along, striving as hard as she could to make a reputation for herself in the field. She'd succeeded and had moved up fast. Then, just a month ago, she'd landed the New York position.

The Seaport museum was a nonprofit, public institution. Abbie's true goal was corporate public relations, but this job could be a way in. A stellar performance at the museum would look great on her résumé. In fact, the permanent staff position of public relations director, which Meredith had mentioned, would be a good place for Abbie for a year or so. She could learn the city and check out other job possibilities. Meanwhile she'd produce the kinds of results that would really get her noticed. She had no doubt she was capable of doing that. But after today, she wasn't sure she could take more than a couple of months on South Street.

Abbie let the swell of the crowd propel her out of the subway car at her elevated stop; then she trudged wearily down the stairs to street level. She hated to admit it, even to herself, but the thing that frustrated her most about today was what had happened with Cal Quinn. She'd decided the poison-pen note was probably a one-shot dirty trick by some crank she'd never hear from again. Cal, however, was something much more serious than that, and for more than one reason.

Hopping from one free-lance assignment and city to another had kept her from getting embroiled in office intrigues. It had also kept her from getting very involved with men. At least she'd thought that was the reason—until this morning. Now she realized she simply hadn't met anyone with that special something to which she could respond strongly. Cal Quinn was definitely in possession of that special something.

She'd felt it when she first saw him in her office doorway. Still, she told herself, that was just his good looks and didn't mean a thing. After all, Robert was handsome, too—and look how that relationship had turned out! Then, later on, she'd returned to her office and found Cal waiting. Remembering how his fingers had traveled, button by button, down her jacket made her shiver even now. Under other circumstances Abbie might have been intrigued, but it appeared she could hardly have picked a less appropriate man to find so attractive.

According to Meredith, Cal Quinn was a dangerous adversary. He'd tried to maneuver Abbie out of the most important job assignment of her career, and he might very well be at it still. He could even be the one who'd left the ivory-toned envelope on her desk blotter. Yet she didn't really think so. She'd bet a week's salary that wasn't Quinn's style.

However, playing little mind games with Josie as pawn was another story. Abbie had watched Robert do things like that many times during the six years they were married. Such manipulations were stock in trade in Robert's world of politics, and the world of business was no different. That meant Calhoun Quinn, very possibly, was not a man she should trust.

She was standing in front of the small supermarket near the elevated station. The sign above the window said Trade Fair.

I could use a little of that right now, she remarked to herself in a wry inner voice before going inside.

A half hour later she was walking down Thirtieth Avenue once more, with a plastic grocery bag hanging from each hand. She'd planned to pick up only a few items. But as she'd wandered through the narrow aisles of the market, boxes and jars seemed to leap into her cart. "Never shop when you're tired and hungry," her mother used to say. "You'll buy everything in sight." Her mother was apparently right, because the plastic bags were stretched thin from the weight of her purchases.

Between her exhaustion and the heavy bags, Abbie wasn't walking as fast as she usually did along the bustling city streets. Besides, she'd noticed that people moved at a less frantic pace in Astoria than they did in Manhattan. That was one of the things she liked about this neighborhood. In fact, she was beginning to relax already, despite the terrible day she'd had.

Meanwhile she could feel the handles of her shopping bags narrowing as the plastic stretched thinner. She had to get home fast, before her groceries erupted all over the sidewalk. She quickened her pace, and by the time she reached her corner, she was nearly running; the bag on the right threatened to give way any second. She fumbled for her keys as she heaved open the ornate, ironwork door of the entryway to her building.

The lobby door took several twists to get it unlocked, as usual. Then she was inside. She lived on the first floor and was only a few feet from her apartment when the inevitable happened. As if by magic, the right-hand bag grew suddenly lighter, and Abbie's supermarket purchases tumbled across the polished tile floor. At least nothing was broken, she thought as she bent to retrieve an orange that had rolled onto her welcome mat. Then her shoulder touched the apartment door, and it moved suddenly open.

Abbie sprang to a standing position as if catapulted there. The door was unlocked. She was sure she'd locked it this morning on her way out with Davey. He wasn't due back home from camp for another hour. Her heart skipped faster. How could the door be open now? She could see nothing through the opening except a corner of the hall carpet.

"Davey," she called, though she knew he wouldn't answer. Her arrangement with the camp bus driver was that he wouldn't be left here unless she was home. She'd paid an extra fee for that assurance.

She leaned through the doorway and listened. Everything was silent. Even the sounds of the street she'd just left were muffled by two heavy doors. Abbie pushed cautiously against her door with a palm turned suddenly damp. The opening widened, and she stepped quietly over the threshold to peer into the kitchen. All was as she'd left it, including the dishes she'd been too rushed to wash, still stacked in the sink.

Then she remembered something. She'd been in a hurry that morning. Davey had taken longer than usual to get dressed and she had been keyed up about her first day on the job, so she'd kept dropping things. Because of that, they'd been later getting out of the apartment than she had planned. Maybe she'd been careless about the door. Still, that would be out of character for Abbie. She prided herself on being cool under fire. Unfortunately, she wasn't feeling very cool right now. She set the second grocery bag on the hallway floor and eased the door shut behind her. Then she began walking very slowly toward the living room, shifting her weight carefully from one foot to the other so the floorboards wouldn't squeak.

The living room was as undisturbed as the kitchen. The clockface on the bookshelf seemed to mock her for being silly as she crept past it toward her bedroom. Several creaks of the floor shattered the silence along the way, and Abbie's heart beat louder with each one. She gave the bedroom door a quick shove, then jumped back out of sight around the jamb, just as she'd seen on TV. She peeked into the room and found it as empty as the others.

She decided to abandon the stealthy approach and walked straight into the bathroom. Once again, everything was in order. She'd scared herself half to death for nothing. There was obviously no one here but her, and no sign other than the front door that anyone had been there since she and Davey had left hours ago. She simply must not have locked the front door. But she'd look in Davey's room just to be thorough.

The breeze hit her the minute she opened his door, and for an instant its cool touch froze her to the spot. The window was open, the bottom sash raised as high as it would go. The window had been shut this morning when she'd closed the door to Davey's room. She was positive of it. She might have her doubts about the front door but not about this window. As far as she was concerned, Davey's room was a part of Davey himself, she'd never leave either of them so vulnerable.

She hurried across the room and peered out the window, which faced a courtyard that was empty now. There was no sign of disturbance in the shrubbery below the window, no indication that anyone had gone in or out. Abbie pulled her head back through the opening, lowered the sash and locked it tight, then tried to push the frame up hard twice to make doubly certain it was secure. All the while she kept herself very calm, but that was only possible on the outside. She couldn't stop her imagination from conjuring one startling image after another of what might have happened here today.

She wandered back through the living room and into the hallway, thinking about what she should do next. She might be able to make light of threatening notes on her desk at work, but someone's invading her son's room was another thing entirely.

The sound of movement outside the apartment door brought a clench of fear to her chest, and she held her arms tightly around her for a moment. Then she reached forward, grasped the doorknob and pulled it toward her.

The silhouette was tall and thin against the overhead light of the lobby. Because of the dimness of the hallway, Abbie, her hand still on the doorknob, could not discern the person's features. A dozen thoughts passed through her mind before she noticed a pair of hands full of groceries.

"I found these on the floor out here, Mrs. Tanner. Did you drop them?" The voice of Abbie's visitor was small and feminine, in contrast to her height. "I'm Rachel Steiner. My daughter, Sarah, is in day camp with your Davey. They became fast friends today, and Sarah's invited him to stay over with us tonight if that's all right with you."

"Where is he?"

"Mommy, Mommy," her son's voice rang out in response to Abbie's abrupt question. He was running across the lobby from the entry door. A little girl with short blond curls skipped along in his wake. "Can I stay at Sarah's? They've got a VCR!"

His green eyes, so much like his mother's, were bright with eight-year-old enthusiasm. They shone through the tension Abbie had been feeling ever since she arrived home.

"I realize you don't know us, Mrs. Tanner," Rachel Steiner said, "but we live just a few blocks away, and you can call the day camp to verify who we are."

"Oh, no. That won't be necessary." Abbie was a little embarrassed that her suspicions were so obvious. Mrs. Steiner, in her polo shirt and Reebok sneakers, couldn't have looked more the Queens housewife. "It's just that we're new in the city, and Davey doesn't know his way around yet. I worry sometimes."

"I certainly understand that. I worry myself."

Abbie took the groceries from Mrs. Steiner's arms and invited her and Sarah inside while Davey hurried off to pack his pajamas and toothbrush. Abbie followed him to his room.

"Do you remember if your window was open or closed when we left this morning?" she asked.

"Closed, I think," he answered half attentively as he stuffed comic books into his fluorescent, orange backpack.

"I need you to be sure."

The seriousness of her tone caused Davey to look up from what he was doing. His green eyes were a bit bewildered above the round cheeks ridged in freckles. "Why?"

"Just think back for me. Was your window open or closed?"

Davey thought for a moment. "I remember. It was closed."

Abbie's heart fell.

"Then I was out in the kitchen," he went on, "and I decided I wanted to take my Transformer helmet to camp with me, so I came back in here to get it. Then I saw the greatest thing. There was this lady outside, across the way, and do you know what she was doing, Mom?"

"No, Davey, I don't. What was she doing?"

"She was putting out food, and a whole bunch of cats were waiting to eat it. That's when I opened the window." He looked suddenly sheepish. "I think maybe I forgot to close it back up again."

"Are you sure of that?"

"Pretty sure. I'm sorry, Mom. I know that was a dumb thing to do."

"Just be careful not to do it again," she said, and smiled with relief. It was the best news she'd heard all day.

A few minutes later she was back at the front door, waving goodbye to Davey and thinking she probably needed an evening alone to calm herself down and stop imagining things. Suddenly something occurred to her. She picked up the keys she'd left on the kitchen counter and stepped out into the lobby, pulling the heavy firedoor shut behind her. She fitted the proper key into the keyhole and twisted it back and forth, then took it out and put it back in several times.

She'd decided before that she must have pulled the key out of the lock that morning without ever turning it. She remembered having the key in her hand and inserting it in the keyhole, so that was the only explanation she'd had for the front door being open. Now she saw that couldn't have happened. The lock was designed to take hold of the key and release it again only after the lock mechanism had clicked into place. She couldn't have pulled the key back out without turning it. Then she remembered something else. She distinctly recalled having turned the knob and pushing on the door to make certain it was secure before she'd hurried out to the street after Davey.

She'd definitely locked the front door that morning. Someone else had opened it again sometime between the time she'd left and her return from work a while ago. Abbie had no doubt about that now. Instantly she was on her knees, scooping up two apples Mrs. Steiner hadn't noticed in the corner. As fast as she could move, Abbie was back inside the apartment with the door slammed shut and locked behind her. She leaned her forehead against the smooth, cool surface of the painted metal.

What was going on here? Could all of this really be happening to her? But why?

An urge came over her so strongly it almost sent her flying into the bedroom to pack their bags and get her and Davey out of the apartment, maybe even out of the city altogether. She took a deep breath instead. She couldn't run away. She had to face whatever was happening, calmly and logically.

She put the apples on the kitchen counter, put the groceries away and went into the living room. On top of the television console sat the ashtray Davey had made for her when he was in the first grade. It was crude and chipped, with a long crack meandering across the bottom, yet it was more precious to Abbie than all the Waterford crystal in Ireland could ever be.

What if he'd touched it, whoever had been there today? What if he'd picked up this precious thing and handled it?

Abbie grabbed the ashtray and clutched it tight to her heart for a moment. Then she went to the telephone table, opened a drawer and put the ashtray inside. She sat down on the couch, very near the edge, just as Josie had sat on her chair that morning. But Abbie wasn't feeling either eager or enthusiastic. She was feeling exposed. Until now she'd harbored the illusion that she'd always be able to keep herself and her son fairly safe and private. Now she sensed all of that shattering, as surely as Davey's hand-made ashtray would have shattered if her unwelcome visitor had chosen to sweep it from its place of honor. Abbie had never thought of herself as a violent person. Yet if that intruder was here right now, she'd pick up the first heavy object she could lay her hands on and pound him with it—just so she wouldn't feel so helpless.

Abbie wasn't sure how long she sat there before the phone rang, but one thing she was certain of. The last person she wanted to talk to was Robert Tanner.

"Is my son there?" he asked without so much as a greeting.

"He's staying overnight with a friend."

"What friend?"

"A little girl from day camp."

"What do you know about the family?"

"Look, Robert, I'm not in the mood for one of your interrogations. Davey is having a good time, and he's just fine."

"You don't know a thing about those people, do you? You let my son go off with strangers."

Abbie sighed. "He's my son, too, Robert. Believe me, he's fine."

"This is just another example of how irresponsible you are. You were immature and irresponsible when I met you, and you haven't changed."

"I was nineteen years old when you met me."

What had she found so appealing about him back then? She couldn't imagine what it had been. Of course, he'd been tall and handsome, but she hadn't known that wasn't enough to build a marriage on. He wasn't even handsome any more. He'd let himself get too fleshy, and his formerly strong features were now merely coarse. She'd noticed the same thing in a portrait of his father, which showed all the years of hardness imprinted on the man's face.

"Why are you suddenly so interested in Davey anyway?" she asked. "You've seen him exactly twice a year since we got divorced—less than a dozen visits. Now you're calling all the time. Why?"

"I want David to come to Tannersfield for a long visit this summer," he said, ignoring her question. "Maybe I'll even take him to Europe."

"We'll have to talk about that." Abbie would have liked to believe Robert wanted to be a real father to Davey. Heaven knew, he never had been. He'd always been too busy, working his Washington deals, making things happen the way he wanted them to. That was the problem. Robert was a manipulator. He never did anything without having an angle, a hidden agenda. She didn't want Davey manipulated.

"In the meantime, I don't like the way you live," Robert continued in that cold, superior tone of his. "You're like some kind of gypsy, working in one place and then in another, moving around all the time."

"I'm not a gypsy, Robert. I'm a free-lance consultant."

"I don't care what you call it. That's not a proper life for my son."

Abbie sighed once more. "As I said, he's my son, too."

"Then why don't you settle down and act like a mother for once?"

She could almost see Robert standing there in his usual gray pin-striped suit, looking stern. She couldn't help fantasizing how good it would feel to grind one of her high heels into the toe of his Italian leather shoe. Of course, she'd never be foolish enough to antagonize him so openly. Under his severe exterior lurked a temper of dangerous dimensions. She knew that better than anyone, and she found it wise to appease him whenever possible. Maybe that was why she said what she did next.

"As a matter of fact, I am settling down. I'm in line for a staff position at the museum."

"Really? What position is that?"

"Public relations director."

"Is that so?"

"What's the matter? You don't sound happy. Isn't that what you wanted? Every time you call lately, I have to put up with a lecture about settling down. I thought you'd be more enthusiastic."

"I simply find it hard to believe."

"You just wait and see."

Once she was off the phone, she couldn't imagine why she'd said that. She was just so tired of listening to Robert, she'd wanted to shut him up. He'd also made her feel defensive. The trouble was he had a point. All this moving around wasn't good for Davey any more. It had been all right when he was younger, but now he needed some permanence. So did she. For five years she'd been constantly on the lookout for the next assignment, something to move her another notch up the ladder. She'd made that plan of action work for her, but she had to admit she was tired of the strain. She really would like to stay at one job for a long time. The museum would be the perfect spot if it weren't for—

Abbie was interrupted in midthought by another jangle of the phone. She sighed. Robert was probably calling back to toss a few more barbs her way. She'd managed to surprise him for once, and he couldn't bear to let anyone else have the last word, especially not her.

"Yes?" she answered, sounding more than a little impatient.

"Did you guess it was me calling, or is there someone else you're fed up with this evening?"

She'd been with him only twice, but his voice was already unmistakable to her. It caught her completely off guard.

"Mr. Quinn, I thought you were somebody else."

"Can't we come to terms about this name thing? You call me Cal, and I'll call you anything you please."

"Abbie will do," she said, rapidly collecting her cool.

"It's a deal."

She wished she knew what other deals he might have up his sleeve that he wasn't mentioning.

"You're probably wondering why I called."

"As a matter of fact, I am."

"We started off on the wrong foot today at the office. I can tell by your tone just how wrong it was. So I propose we change feet."

"That's not really necessary, Mr. Quinn."

"I think I'm going to have to make you put a quarter in the kitty every time you call me that. At this rate, we'll have enough for a trip to Tahiti in no time."

"I'm sorry. Cal. I was simply trying to say a phone call wasn't necessary. I'm sure we'll be able to work amiably together." Abbie was amazed at how controlled she sounded. In reality, she was wishing she could get off the phone and prepare herself for this conversation before resuming it.

"Well, I want to make certain of that, because I'm looking forward to our relationship with great anticipation." He paused, then added, "Our business relationship, that is."

"Of course." Abbie was feeling less prepared by the second.

"I concede I made a few too many assumptions this morning. I do that sometimes. You might say it comes with the territory, like Josie does. Still, I'd like to make up for it if you'll let me."

"You don't have to do that."

"I insist. I want to take you someplace very special as a peace offering. That's why I had to call you tonight."

Visions of candlelit hideaways jumped into Abbie's mind, along with an awareness that she wasn't at all ready for such a scene with this man. She raced through a mental list of excuses, searching for one to fit the situation.

Meanwhile Cal was still talking. "I want to take you on a tour of the Fulton Fish Market."

This was so far from what Abbie had been imagining that she almost laughed out loud.

"The fish market is one of the few surviving traces of what the waterfront is really all about. I'd like to share it with you. Besides, it will give you a chance to find out all about me, and what could be more enticing than that?"

His tone was joking, but Abbie took what he said seriously. If Cal truly was her adversary, then the more she knew about him the better.

"It sounds like an interesting excursion," she replied.

"You'll have to get up early in the morning."

"I think I can manage that. Tell me when and where we should meet."

"Tomorrow morning, unless there's a problem about your boy. I could pick you up in Astoria."

Abbie was silent for a moment. "How do you know where I live and that I have a son?"

"I looked it up in your personnel file."

Since he was a member of the museum advisory committee, it wasn't surprising that he had access to those files. But Abbie couldn't help thinking that the person who had entered her apartment might have found her address in the same way. Could it have been Cal Quinn? Somehow the act of breaking and entering didn't strike her as being his style, any more than the writing of threatening notes would be. Yet how could she be sure?

"I guess I'm guilty of an assumption again," he said when she didn't respond right away. "Or maybe it's more of a *pre*sumption this time. I shouldn't have presumed to read your file."

"As long as it was done in the line of duty, I have no objection."

There was a pause on the other end of the line. "Mostly in the line of duty," he finally said.

Abbie was glad they were talking on the phone and not in person, because she could feel her face growing warm with a redhead's easy blush.

"The offer stands to pick you up at your apartment in the morning."

"I'd rather meet you down there." She thought that seemed less personal, and she had the definite feeling that getting too personal with Cal Quinn could be dangerous.

"All right, then. How about the corner of Front and Beekman, outside Carmine's Restaurant at five-thirty?"

"Five-thirty?" Abbie couldn't help sounding shocked.

"Okay, six. But we can't make it any later than that or there won't be anything left to see. Fish-mongering is an early morning business."

"Six is fine. In front of Carmine's."

"Rain or shine?"

"Rain or shine."

CAL MUST HAVE BEEN TUNED in to the weather forecast, because when Abbie rolled herself out of bed the next morning, it was dark and drizzly outside. She considered calling him to cancel out but decided against it. She'd promised to be there rain or shine. It would be bad office politics to give him the impression she could be stymied by a little precipitation. Besides, she couldn't deny a certain curiosity to see what Cal Quinn was like so early in the day. Consequently, she found herself walking up Thirtieth Avenue while the streetlights were still shining.

The wide sidewalk was empty except for a few early risers hurrying along under umbrellas. Most of them, like Abbie, were headed toward the subway station. An occasional straggler passed more slowly in the opposite direction, probably returning from working the night shift. The shops lining the streets hid behind burglarproof gates, except for the twenty-four-hour diner on the corner. Abbie was tempted to go in and have a fast cup of coffee, but she wasn't sure how regularly the trains ran at this hour. If she missed one, it could be a while till the next one came along, and she didn't want to be late.

In fact, she didn't seem to want to do anything that would make a bad impression on Calhoun Quinn. She'd even dressed with special care. She'd spent so much time in the damps of Baltimore and D.C. that her wardrobe was well stocked with foul-weather gear. Her long, lavender rain poncho reached halfway down her shiny, black, calf-high boots and was the perfect complement to her strawberry-blond hair and pale pink skin. In this weather there was no preventing the froth of wispy curls that framed her face, and the early morning coolness nipped her cheeks to a dewy rose. She had to admit she was looking forward to being with Cal, adversary or not.

Still, nagging worries plagued her, shadows of what had happened the day before and pangs of guilt that Robert might have been right about Davey. Maybe she shouldn't have let him go with the Steiners. She'd called there last evening and learned he was watching old Roy Rogers videos and eating popcorn. Yet she was beginning to realize that you could never be too cautious here. Everyone was so separate and anonymous, you could have a maniac living right next door and never know it.

Luckily the people on the subway platform looked fairly normal. She'd been there only a couple of minutes when the train arrived, snaking out of the gray predawn, over a rise in the tracks and into the station. The cars were more sparsely populated than they would be in a couple of hours, so Abbie easily found a seat among the silent riders.

Her downtown connection at Fifty-ninth Street was as fast as the one in Astoria had been. She hadn't realized that the trains would run more rapidly with their lighter load at this hour, and she arrived at her Fulton Street stop much sooner than she'd anticipated. The streetlights were still on when she climbed up from below-ground and walked east toward the river. Unfortunately, their shimmering glow did little to brighten the rainy gloom. The tall buildings and the narrow street made it much darker here than it had been on Thirtieth Avenue. At the bottom of this gray-walled canyon, it was still nearly night.

The street was deserted. The business district wouldn't come to life for hours yet. Not even the corner newsstands had opened to display the headlines of the day. Abbie walked fast along the rain-slick sidewalk. The sleepy lull she'd fallen into aboard the train was being replaced by something more in tune with the murky darkness around her. She wouldn't say she was exactly afraid, but she definitely didn't care to be out by herself in this part of the city.

The lighted window of the John Street Diner beckoned, but she hurried past, anxious to get to Front Street and more familiar territory. She crossed the main artery of Pearl Street and was relieved to see cars speeding back and forth. Far ahead, where John Street met the waterfront, she could make out the shapes of parked trucks crowding the roadway. The moving traffic receded into the distance as she walked away from Pearl.

Then, not far behind her, she heard the sound of scuffling footsteps.

Chapter Three

Abbie turned just in time to see a dark-clad figure disappear into the shadow of a doorway. She quickened her pace, glancing over her shoulder as she hurried along. The street was empty and silent now, yet she was sure she hadn't imagined that dark figure. Probably just someone coming home from night work on the docks, she told herself. There were apartments above the commercial properties that were at street level along here.

Nonetheless she walked quickly after turning the corner onto Front Street, her shiny boots smacking through the puddles in long strides. The bright lights of Schermerhorn Row were less than a block ahead. She had almost reached them when she sensed rather than heard someone behind her. Another glance over her shoulder confirmed that sensation. The dark figure had moved from the shadows nearly a block away and was advancing rapidly, keeping close to the buildings, so that it was difficult for Abbie to see him. He might be someone in a hurry to get wherever he was going. Yet Abbie's instincts warned her of sinister intentions, just as they had done with yesterday's threatening message. She faced forward and began to run.

She was halfway across the cobbled promenade of Schermerhorn Row, headed for the block in which the museum offices were located, when she considered changing direction and going toward the sounds of South Street. But the offices were closer. She continued forward. She'd already slung her shoulder bag around in front of her and was fishing in it for her keys while she ran. Her fingers touched metal just as she reached the doorway with the small sign announcing the office of the South Street Seaport Museum. She'd never in her life seen more welcome words, but her relief was shortlived.

Abbie's trembling fingers fumbled for the right key on the ring. There were several, some from old apartments and offices. She'd intended to take those off but had never got around to it. Now they all felt the same; they even looked alike in the dim light of the charmingly quaint but impractical nineteenth-century streetlamps. She couldn't tell which key fit the office-building door. That realization made her heart beat even faster than it had while she'd been running.

She peered back along the street. Her pursuer was now in the light of Schermerhorn Row. Abbie could see he was wearing a long, dark coat and a dark cap pulled around his face, but since he'd lowered his head, she couldn't make out his features. He was still too far away for her to do that anyway, but he was near enough so she could tell he was definitely after her and getting closer by the second. She didn't have time to fumble with the keys.

Instead, she was going to try something daring. She backtracked a couple of buildings, knowing her stalker was bound to follow. She had to throw him off her trail. That was the purpose of her plan—if it worked. Abbie ducked into Cannon Walk, the shopping arcade that had been created out of the alleyway between the buildings. She pulled a scarf from her pocket and dropped it ahead of her on the walkway, then backtracked once more and retreated into a deep doorway.

She couldn't see very far out into the arcade, but she heard him enter it and then hesitate a moment. Her breath stopped, and she thought her heart might have too. She pressed back so hard against the wall that she felt as if she could push right through it. Would he take the bait? Or would he look into these shadows and see her cowering here? She tensed herself to run again, right over him if necessary.

Then he was moving once more. Scuffle, scuffle, scuffle...past her doorway and down the walk. The scuffles broke off, which had to mean he was picking up the scarf. Moments later he was off around the corner and into the adjoining wing of the arcade. He'd fallen for the bait, but Abbie couldn't take the time to congratulate herself now. She ran, as noiselessly as possible, out of her hiding place and back to Front Street.

For the first time she noticed, straight ahead, the lights of Carmine's Restaurant and the night gates lifted. She never would have imagined they'd be open at this hour. She ran faster, sprinting flat-out with no thought of being quiet any longer. Panting from both tension and exertion, she reached the corner. To the right and left, the block was deserted. Her pursuer would be back out on Schermerhorn Row by now, diverted in the wrong direction by the one-way alley she'd deceived him into taking. It wasn't likely he'd brave this corner anyway, with people just beyond Carmine's smoky windows. Even so, Abbie decided to go inside. She'd had enough of deserted streets for the moment.

Once through the swinging doors, Abbie understood why Cal had said to meet him on the corner. The bar and a number of tables were crowded with men in work clothes. Several of them turned and stared as she hurried in. There were calls of overfamiliar greetings and even a long, low whistle, but Abbie didn't take offense, which she might ordinarily have done. In fact, she'd never been so glad to hear a whistle in her life. It confirmed that she was inside and safe and that whoever had been chasing her was on the outside.

She slid into the booth nearest the door and kept her head down. Soon the comments died away, and her admirers returned to their beers and breakfasts with only an occasional glance in her direction. A waiter appeared at her elbow with a mug of steaming coffee, which he set down in front of her along with a menu. Abbie smiled up at him. She couldn't remember ever being so happy to be anywhere in her life.

She had no idea how long she sat there, staring at the time-deepened wood grain of the table and sipping the strong black liquid. She usually drank her coffee light with sugar, but this tasted wonderful to her just the way it was. The morning chill was long forgotten. She was even feeling a bit too warm in her poncho, after all that running and her agitation, yet she didn't move to take it off. She was absorbed in what had just happened to her out there on the street.

Who had been chasing her? Could it have been a random mugger hoping to grab her purse and do heaven knew what else? She didn't think so. Except for some occasional shadowy spots, this area was too open and well lighted to be a likely haunt for street thieves. Besides, the incident wasn't an isolated one. A threatening note yesterday morning, someone breaking into her apartment yesterday afternoon, and now this. There was a pattern here of someone out to get her.

Yet if whoever it was really wanted to hurt her, why hadn't he? Why hadn't he been waiting inside the apartment when she got home last night? Why hadn't he made less of an effort to stay hidden earlier and more of an effort to catch her? Maybe he didn't want to do anything directly to her after all. Maybe he was just trying to scare her.

That was it. She slapped her mug down on the table so hard that two men seated nearby turned to stare at her, but she hardly noticed them. She was onto something now, and it was so astonishing she couldn't think about anything else. She'd finally figured out what was happening to her. The note, the break-in, the chase—all had been for one purpose. Somebody was trying to scare her off. These weren't random acts. It was a concerted campaign to get her out of the museum.

Then she shook her head in disbelief. The idea seemed so farfetched. Why would anyone go to so much trouble to get rid of a promotions consultant, especially one who was free-lance and supposed to be leaving in a couple of months anyway? It didn't make sense. But then ever since she'd arrived on South Street, many things hadn't made sense.

"I thought we were supposed to meet outside on the corner." Cal's voice broke through her bewildering thoughts.

Abbie was about to blurt out how glad she was to see him, when she looked up and the words stopped in her throat. What actually came out of her mouth was a gasp. Cal was wearing a long, dark trench coat. She was tempted to ask where the cap that went with it might be.

"Are you all right?" Cal asked with what passed for sincere concern.

"I'm fine."

"You don't look fine." He slid into the seat across from her. "Your cheeks are bright red, and the rest of you is as white as a sheet."

"I thought you men loved the blushing, pallid look." Her tone was less than friendly.

Cal leaned back against the grained oak of the booth. "You certainly aren't a morning person, are you?"

Abbie had avoided looking at him. Now her glance jumped to his face. "There's just one thing I want to know from you," she said.

"What's that?"

"Did you tell anybody we were meeting here this morning?"

"Not a soul."

Abbie's heart plummeted. If only the two of them knew she'd be at the Seaport at this hour, and if the man who chased her had been after her specifically, then there was only one conclusion. Cal had to have been that man...unless her pursuer was indeed a random mugger. She grasped at that possibility, but somehow she knew it wasn't true. Her keenest instincts told her she'd been a deliberate target that morning, just as she had been the day before.

"Why the interrogation?"

How could he sound so amused?

"If you're worried that people will gossip about us, set your mind at rest," he went on. "They'll gossip about us no matter what we do, so you might as well not concern yourself with it. Coffee-break scuttlebutt has me linked with every woman at the Seaport, from Josie on up."

"How nice for your ego."

"Look, I didn't say anything to anybody about meeting you here, and if they're nosy enough to have read the note I left on your desk, then—"

"What note?"

"Late yesterday afternoon you were in a staff meeting, so I left a note inviting you down here this morning."

"I didn't go back to my office after that meeting. I went straight home. I didn't see any note."

"I assumed as much when I called you last night."

"Tell me something, please. Was my office door unlocked when you left?"

"Of course. Nobody ever locks offices up there. Now, you tell *me* something. Why are you asking so many questions?"

"No reason," Abbie fibbed with a relieved smile. "Just idle curiosity."

She couldn't have been happier. Anyone at all might have walked into her office yesterday afternoon and seen that note. It wasn't necessarily Cal who had chased her earlier. In fact, now she was sure it hadn't been him at all. Sitting across from him, looking into his direct gaze, she was more convinced than ever that he would never do that kind of thing.

Suddenly it dawned on her how surly she'd been acting and how strange that must seem to him; for some reason, that thought struck her as uncommonly funny. She started to laugh. The laughter bubbled out of her like a fresh spring washing away bad feelings. Finally she had to clamp her lips tight together to calm the flood.

"I'm sorry," she managed at last.

"Don't mention it. I like to start my day with a little manic-depressive outburst."

His remark threatened to set Abbie off again. She sipped at her coffee. "I think I must be overtired. I don't usually act like this."

"Too bad. A touch of insanity is very becoming to you." He stood up and dropped some money on the table for her coffee. "Now, how about some air?"

Outside, Abbie sucked in deep breaths of the cool, moist morning and felt in control of herself again. The laughter had been a release of tension, not from tiredness. She'd just said that to explain her behavior to Cal.

"By the way, how is your arm?" he asked as they walked toward the river and the hubbub of activity on South Street.

"Oh, it was only a scratch."

"I saw you turn around and smack right into the window. Do you tend to be accident-prone?"

"Lately I tend to be incident-prone."

"What do you mean?"

"Nothing really. Just a private joke on myself."

"Maybe you'll share it with me someday."

"Maybe."

The remark had slipped out. She hadn't meant to say it, but now she longed to tell him everything, which she'd wanted to do last night on the phone but known she mustn't. The cautionary feeling was still with her. She had to be very careful in this situation, perhaps more careful than she'd ever been before. Reminding herself of that made her tense up again. She pushed nervously at the pins that were attempting to hold her hair in place.

"That's a habit of yours, isn't it? Playing with your hairpins," he said. "I'll have to keep watch and figure out what it's a signal of."

Abbie dropped her hand from her curls, just as she'd done the morning before. Again she felt more exposed by his perceptiveness than she cared to be.

"In the meantime, on with the tour. You're about to experience one of New York's most colorful traditions."

They turned onto South Street and were greeted by the sounds of lusty voices, trundling handcarts and truck engines. Abbie was grateful for the change of mood. The entire width of tne street was taken up by the business of fish-mongering on a grand scale. In open, brightly lit stalls men wearing white aprons reduced long silvery fish to neat fillets with a few thwacks of the knife. The fillets were weighed in metal scale baskets suspended from the rafters, then packed in crates of ice and stacked to be carted away. Net bags crammed with shellfish were heaped in bins nearby, and the air was tangy with the pungent odor of the sea.

"This has been going on since the middle of the night," Cal said.

"Really?"

"I come down to watch it quite often." His eyes shone an even brighter shade of blue.

"I can see you like it here."

"I used to do heavy work like this when I was a kid." He gestured toward a burly man hefting huge crates as if they were almost weightless. "I was a porter on construction jobs. That's basically a beast of burden in steel-toed boots. I liked it. You push your body so hard you forget your mind even exists—almost the opposite of the work I do now."

"What is it you do now exactly?"

"I buy and sell things."

"What kind of things?"

"Businesses mostly, but let's not talk about that now. What's going on here is much more interesting."

Abbie tried not to be too concerned about his reluctance to discuss his work. She wanted to forget doubts and suspicions for a little while and concentrate on his deep, soothing voice washing over her.

"The tractor trailers start coming in around midnight, full of seafood from up and down the East Coast. Most of the big trucks are gone by now, but they're really something to see when the street is jammed with them." He looked over at her. The glow from a nearby burning trash barrel flickered in his eyes. "Do you think you'd like to see them with me sometime?"

"That might be interesting." She didn't let on the tremble of excitement his eyes made her feel. "What happens then, after the trucks come in?"

"They unload all along here, piles of fish, right in the middle of the street. Then the trailers leave, and smaller trucks start pulling in from the local restaurants and fish markets. They park all the way down to John Street and around the corner."

Abbie remembered seeing them there earlier, just before she had started running for her life.

"Then the haggling begins," Cal continued. "That's really something to watch. You shouldn't miss it, so keep my invitation in mind."

He was staring at her again. He'd taken off his trench coat, and he was just as handsome in his faded jeans and open-necked shirt. The charge of action in the air had ruddied his cheeks. Just looking at him made Abbie draw her breath in fast.

"But right now I'm starving," he added. "How about breakfast?"

Abbie suddenly realized she was hungry herself. Being in the brisk, waterfront air and in the midst of so much activity had put an edge on her appetite. She was also enjoying this time with Cal, probably more than was wise; but, wise or not, she didn't want it to end just yet.

"Breakfast sounds wonderful," she said. "Where shall we go?"

"There's a diner up the street that serves great steak and eggs, and I have to confess I'm a diner man."

Abbie didn't answer. They'd reached the corner where ner early morning stalker had hidden in the shadows. He seemed far away and unreal now that she was here with Cal; it was almost as if that terrifying chase had never happened. But, of course, it had. Seeing this dark doorway again brought back its reality.

"Maybe you don't feel like eating right now," Cal said in response to her hesitation. "The smell of the fish market can turn off the appetite sometimes."

"No, I'm really very hungry."

"Maybe you'd rather go someplace else, then. The John Street Diner isn't exactly four-star."

"Actually, I'm a diner woman myself. I've spent too much time in four-star places." She was thinking of her years with Robert and, before him, with her mother. "When I was a kid I used to sneak out on my parents and go looking for the greasiest hamburger in town."

"Then this place should be right up your alley. It has wonderfully greasy hamburgers as well as steak and eggs."

"I'm so hungry right now, I may just order both."

They were about to cross Pearl Street, and Cal took her arm. Abbie reminded herself it was only a gentlemanly gesture to guide her past the traffic. Still, she liked the feel of him gripping her elbow and holding her at his side as they hurried toward the lighted windows of the diner.

She was true to her word about her appetite. Not only did she wolf down steak and eggs, but orange juice, home fries and two cups of coffee, as well. It made her smile to think how much Robert and her mother would disapprove

"Next time we do this you should bring your son along," Cal suggested as they relaxed over the steaming mugs.

"He's not too fond of getting up early these days. He used to be running around at the crack of dawn, but he seems to have outgrown that. It takes forever to get him out of the house in the morning."

"Where is he right now?"

"He stayed overnight with another day camper."

"It's good that he's making friends, being as new in town as he is."

"Yes, I was pleased about that myself."

Abbie remembered wanting to talk about this with Robert on the phone last night, but she'd known he wouldn't understand. Making friends had never been high on his list of priorities. He always said that making contacts was much more important.

"I grew up in Brooklyn, and I know city kids aren't always very quick to accept the new boy on the block," Cal told her. "I'm glad to hear your son's settling in so well. Do you have a picture of him?"

"Only a walletful." Abbie rummaged through her bag, then handed her photo holder across the table.

"He's a cute little guy." Cal set down his coffee mug for the waiter to refill. "Does he get to see his father very often?"

Abbie didn't answer until the waiter had left. "Often enough," she said.

"How does he handle all that anyway?"

"All what?"

"His family breaking up." Cal handed the photos back to her.

"Are you asking about Davey or his father?"

"Both, I suppose."

"Davey handles it just fine, and I wouldn't presume to speak for his father." She tucked the case back into her bag, then took a deep breath before going on. "Remember what you said about getting off on the wrong foot?"

"I remember."

"Well, you're in danger of doing it again."

"Why's that?"

She looked into his steady gaze. "Because this is a sensitive subject for me. I don't discuss it casually."

"I wasn't being casual. I'm never casual about what they used to call the broken home. I grew up in one."

Something in his tone told Abbie he hadn't asked about Robert and Davey out of idle curiosity. Cal's interest seemed more sincere than that.

"Sometimes I wish I'd grown up that way," she said. "Then maybe I'd understand what it's like for Davey." She hesitated, but Cal's openness encouraged her to continue. "What was it like for you at his age?"

"Bad at first." Cal shifted his lanky body in the booth, and she realized the subject wasn't an easy one for him, either. "I missed my father constantly, but that wasn't the worst part of it."

"What was?"

"I was very aware of being caught in the middle between my mother and father. I was sure someday I'd have to choose one or the other, and that possibility tormented me. I reacted by withdrawing. I even stopped talking for a while."

Abbie's heart reached out to the unhappy little boy he'd been.

"To make matters worse, I got it into my head that the divorce was somehow my fault and that made me withdraw even more. I was pretty confused for a long time." He fingered the paper place mat. There was a far-off look in his eyes, as if he'd drifted back in time. Then his broad smile returned. "But, as you can see, I'm completely rehabilitated. In fact, there are people who think my mother did too thorough a job and that now I talk too much.'

"It was your mother who got you through it? How did she do that?"

"She just kept saying the right things till I finally started believing them."

"I've talked with Davey about its not being his fault that Robert and I broke up. I think he felt like you did for a while. It's strange how that happens."

"Children tend to think they're to blame for everything. Just keep reassuring him."

"I do."

Abbie hadn't discussed Davey and the divorce very much with anyone. Moving around the way she did, she hadn't made many of the kind of friends she could share such things with. Now she realized how often she'd needed to do just that. She felt a sudden warmth toward Cal for giving her the opportunity.

"There was one thing my mother didn't handle very well," he said. "She couldn't seem to hide how much she resented my father. I think she wanted to, but she just couldn't. Her feelings ran too deep. That made my relationship with him difficult later on."

"In what way?"

"She kept me away from him as much as she could, and she was always talking about the terrible things he'd done to her. When I grew up and finally got to know him, I felt guilty for having listened to all of that, as if I'd betrayed him. I thought I had to make up for it. I leaned over backward to be fair to him and ended up making far too many compromises." Cal smacked his palm down on the table. "But enough of that subject. I only brought it up because I have this thing about kids in these situations seeing both parents regularly.''

"I try to encourage Davey to get to know his father, but Robert hasn't really been very interested. He was always too busy for family things.''

"I see you have the father cast as the villain of your scenario, too.''

Abbie's reaction must have telegraphed instantly across the table, because Cal put up his hands in a gesture of appeasement.

"Too many assumptions again,'' he said. "Forgive me. Your son's situation is probably nothing like mine was. I shouldn't compare them.''

"No, you shouldn't.''

"I consider myself justly chastised.'' He lowered his hands and smiled. He was very appealing when he smiled.

Abbie softened immediately. She couldn't help liking Cal, and not just because of his good looks.

"So how did you get into the hit-and-run racket?'' he asked.

Abbie laughed at the expression. "I'm afraid I don't understand.''

"Free-lancing. You know what I mean. Here today, gone tomorrow.''

"Like a gypsy?''

"Right.''

She could hardly believe this man. She'd just decided she really liked him, and now he was sounding like Robert.

"I've always free-lanced,'' she said. "It's been very good to me.''

"You actually enjoy that kind of life?''

"I love it,'' she overstated with emphasis. She didn't like being put on the defensive.

"I see," he said, then paused. When he spoke again, he seemed distant. "Well, I've studied your résumé, and we're lucky to have someone of your caliber handling the assignment."

"Does that mean you intend to keep me on through the summer—till the job is finished?" Abbie sensed that things had turned suddenly very businesslike between them.

He was looking at her with a curious expression on his face. "Of course," he said. "And I wish you well with it." He stood up quickly and extended his hand for her to shake. "I'm glad we had this opportunity to get to know each other better. It helps to make things run more smoothly in the office." He shook her fingers briefly. "Now, you just sit here and relax. Have some dessert. I'll tell the cashier to put it on my bill."

Dessert at eight o'clock in the morning? Abbie thought that must be his way of saying he didn't want her to leave with him.

"I enjoyed this morning," she said, taking his lead, "and I look forward to working with you." She smiled cordially to cover her disappointment. For a while there, she'd fancied a mutual interest in something more than just business. Obviously she'd misunderstood.

Cal nodded graciously, took his trench coat from the hook next to their booth and was gone. Abbie stayed and stared into her coffee mug long after its contents had turned cold.

THE CANDLE GUTTERED where he'd secured it by its own wax to the tin plate. It was long past dawn, and though he'd been out during the night attending to preliminaries, he didn't feel weak. The quill lay on the yellowed page, next to the last, fresh entry. All was clear to him now. He understood what he must do. He'd written it down. His long fingers stroked the gold-crested scabbard that leaned against the scarred desk. He had only to gather strength to perform the small element of the next phase of his plan that required his being exposed to daylight.

Chapter Four

That night Abbie hardly slept at all, and not only because of her disappointment over Cal. She was afraid for Davey. So she stayed in the living room on the couch, on guard against whoever had been plaguing her these past two days. By morning she'd decided. She had to report the incidents to someone in authority at the museum, and that person couldn't be Cal.

She'd spent at least part of the night searching her memory, trying to remember whether she'd revealed how attracted she was to him. She wasn't sure. Also, she was no longer so convinced that he couldn't be her tormentor. Anybody who switched from open and friendly to cool and distant as rapidly as he had yesterday morning wasn't as predictable as she'd thought. Consequently she'd made up her mind to go to the museum director, Lester Girard, with her story.

Now she was sitting opposite Girard's sleek, lacquered desk, feeling slightly unnerved by how much he reminded her of Robert Tanner. His dark good looks were highly polished, like the expensive piece of furniture that separated them, and his smile seemed more diplomatic than sincere. Abbie waited through chitchat about the weather for him to ask how she was faring in her new job. That was to be her signal to tell him what had been going on. However, he didn't ask that question. Instead, his voice took on a sneering tone.

"You know, it wasn't my idea to hire you," he said. "As far as I'm concerned, we need a promotional consultant about as much as we need more dead fish in that river out there."

Abbie noticed a vagueness in his gaze and a loose quality to his movements, that could indicate he'd had a drink or two, even though it was still morning.

"I told them we could handle the problem with the staff we had," he went on, "but they insisted on bringing you in to show me up."

"That's hardly my intention. I—"

"That damned advisory committee runs this place like it was their private sandbox, especially Quinn. Of course, he wanted his own flunky as consultant. I managed to scotch that for him. In fact, the only good thing about your appointment, Ms. Tanner, is that you're not one of Quinn's henchmen, though I won't be surprised if he cons you into his corner eventually. If I know him, he's started already. Is that right, Ms. Tanner? Have you already been favored with an application of the Calhoun Quinn charm?"

The question made Abbie more uncomfortable than Girard's venom could ever have done. "Mr. Quinn has been very gracious to me," she said, choosing her words carefully.

"I'll just bet he has."

Meredith had told her that the reason Girard had this job with the museum was due more to his impressive Yankee roots in an old New England family than to anything else. Abbie could see now what her assistant meant. Lester Girard certainly didn't act like a professional administrator, and he definitely wasn't someone she could confide in.

"Well, Mr. Girard, I'd better get back to work now. I simply wanted to touch base with you."

Abbie hated expressions like "touch base." They were so phony and contrived, they distanced people from their true feelings. But that was exactly what she wanted—to put as much distance as possible between her and Girard.

She stood up from her chair and was walking across the lavishly decorated office toward the door when it opened and Cal walked in.

"Mrs. Tanner, you look lovely today," he said in response to her stare.

Abbie remembered that her mirror had shown unmistakable signs of her lack of sleep. She'd put on a rose-colored suit because she was looking even paler than usual, and she'd hardly describe herself as lovely right now. She was reminded of Girard's reference to Cal's charm and its manipulative purpose. She moved closer to the door, wishing she didn't have to pass so close to Cal to get through it. She almost jumped when he reached out and put his hand, gently but firmly, on her arm.

"Don't leave on my account," he said. "I just stopped in to confirm an appointment Les and I have this afternoon."

"Cal! Wonderful to see you, as always." Girard was out from behind his desk in a flash, pumping Cal's hand. He gave the impression of welcoming a favorite colleague rather than someone he'd been attacking only minutes before. "Mr. Quinn is thinking about buying my sports car," he told Abbie with a slick smile. "I've decided it no longer fits my life-style, but Cal must still have some wild oats to sow, because he wants to take it for a test spin. Isn't that right, my friend?" Girard clapped Cal on the back.

"Something like that."

Cal was watching Abbie as he answered. She could feel the impact of his direct gaze even though she'd been deliberately avoiding his eyes.

"Wait a minute," Girard said. "I have a brilliant idea. Cal, why don't you take Ms. Tanner along on that test run instead of me? She's new to the city—and what better a way to see Manhattan than with the top down on a beautiful summer day!"

What was Lester up to? Abbie wondered. A moment ago he was venting his paranoia about her being taken in by Cal's charm. Now he was pushing them together.

Cal nodded. "I'd love to take Mrs. Tanner for a ride."

The possible double meaning of those words wasn't lost on Abbie. "I'm afraid I have a full schedule this afternoon," she said.

"Nonsense!" Lester boomed with overflowing good will. "I'm your boss, and I insist. I'm sure we can stumble along without you for an hour or two."

He'd made it impossible for her to refuse. "Well, if Mr. Quinn agrees."

"I can't imagine anything I'd enjoy more." Cal said those amiable words in a tone that was even cooler than the one he'd used yesterday morning at the diner.

BY THE AFTERNOON, Abbie was nervous as a cat. The last thing she wanted was to go for a joy ride with Cal Quinn. Or maybe it was really the *first* thing she wanted, and *that* was the reason for her agitation. To make matters worse, Meredith had come back from lunch with unwelcome news. Word of Abbie's impending drive with Cal had hit the rumor circuit, and romantic speculations were being bandied about. Abbie remembered with dismay that after Cal had walked in that morning, Lester's office door had been left open. With everything that had been happening to her recently, Abbie didn't enjoy being the subject of gossip, too.

She'd agreed to meet Cal in the parking lot outside the pier gate. The day was beautiful, just as Lester had said. A pale yellow sun touched the light streaks in Cal's hair as he crossed South Street. In the instant before he spotted her waiting, Abbie felt a tremor of response to him ripple through her. It suddenly occurred to her that she was going to feel the same type of response every time she saw him—until this unfortunate attraction wore off, whenever that might be. The thought made her even more uneasy.

"You don't have to do this if you don't want to," Cal said, his hand on the door of a midnight-blue Jaguar XKE.

Something in his voice eased her tension a little. "Lester was right. It's a beautiful day for a drive."

"Then, since Lester's so seldom right about anything, we should probably take advantage of this rare wisdom of his."

Abbie returned Cal's brief smile and stepped into the low-slung car while he held the door open for her. "Are you really thinking of buying this?" she asked.

Call settled his considerable height into the bucket seat beside hers. His long legs stretched the limit of the recess below the dash. "The last thing I need is another car, though this one is a beauty." He turned the key, and the hand-tooled engine rumbled to life. "But Les hasn't taken very good care of it. I have a feeling it needs a lot of work. I'd only buy it to help him out."

"Does he need help?" Abbie asked as they turned into South Street and roared off north, along the block where they'd walked through the fish market.

"Everyone knows about it, so I suppose there's no harm in discussing it. Les likes to play the stock market, but he hasn't done very well the last few innings. You might say he has cash-flow problems.''

''So he isn't really selling the car because it doesn't suit his image any longer?''

''That's just his cover story. A lot of people have one of those.'' Cal shifted his gaze from the road to Abbie for a moment. ''What's yours?''

He asked the question in the same friendly, noncombative tone of voice he'd been using since they got in the car. Yet Abbie sensed the challenge in his words. She was deciding whether to answer or evade when he turned back to the road and accelerated around a curve. Now South Street bordered the river, with only a wide stretch of asphalt separating the flow of traffic from the water's edge.

Abbie heard the engine race on the curve, whining higher and louder as the long, bullet-shaped car suddenly picked up speed. Cal began to pump the brake. Abbie looked down below the mahogany dash and saw the problem immediately. The gas pedal was all the way to the floor, even though Cal's foot was no longer on it. Meanwhile, the powerful car surged ahead.

''The accelerator's stuck,'' Cal shouted over the roar of the engine.

The XKE was barreling out of the curve now. To the left, traffic streamed toward them along South Street. Several car lengths ahead, a truck was moving at normal speed. But they would overtake it very quickly, and there'd be no way to pull around it with the traffic moving steadily in the other lane. To the right was the asphalt and then the river. Abbie realized Cal had no choice even before he veered in that direction. The brakes hadn't slowed the car's burst of speed long enough to make a difference. The Jaguar was roaring headlong toward the East River.

Abbie felt herself being lifted in one powerful swoop up out of her seat. At first she thought the car must have hit something and that she was being catapulted out of it by the force of the impact. Then her stunned senses became aware of Cal's arm in a tight grip across her back. He'd swept her upward and now clamped her close against him as he vaulted over the side of the car.

Cal got his other arm around her and managed to twist his body somehow before they hit the asphalt. Abbie found herself on top of Cal, captured in his protective embrace. The impact of their landing jarred her, but otherwise she was unhurt. She looked up to see the XKE strike the line of railway ties that marked the end of the asphalt. They'd been placed there to keep parked cars from rolling into the river. There were no parked cars today, and the usual barrier didn't even slow the streak of midnight blue as it left the scrub of dry grass at the shore and sailed, in a long, gradual arc, straight into the river.

Cal pulled Abbie to her feet, his hands touching her hair, her face, her arms. He didn't seem to notice or care what had happened to the car. "Abbie, are you all right?" The words tumbled out fast, and his voice was thin with worry.

"I think I'm fine."

He drew her close to him and held her tight. She could feel his heart hammering beneath his business suit and shirt. He'd been very much afraid, and she knew that his fear hadn't been for himself. His face was in her hair now as he rocked her soothingly.

"Thank God," he whispered. "Thank God you're safe."

Abbie didn't stir or lift her head from his shoulder until she heard the siren.

"The police are coming," he said, loosening his embrace only a little. "Someone must have called them about the accident."

Abbie moved backward in his arms and looked up at him. All this time her heart had been pounding as hard as his. Now it seemed to have lodged in her throat, and she had to gulp the words out over it.

"Oh, Cal," she cried, "I don't think this was an accident!"

ABBIE TOLD HER STORY TWICE, first in rapidly erupting syllables to Cal, then more calmly to the police officers when they arrived. All the while Cal never let go of her hands, nor did she pull them away. She could feel his strength urging her on through his fingertips, and she could see the caring in his eyes. She'd never felt so close to anyone or so protected. Even after the questions and answers were finished and they stood watching the diver go down with the grappling hook into the river, Cal kept his arm around her. They hadn't been more than inches apart since he lifted her out of the hurtling car and saved her life.

The officers had listened without much reaction. They'd taken notes and asked for details, but Cal had listened in a different way. Abbie could tell he was deeply troubled by what she'd said. He'd pressed her fingers harder when she told about being chased through the streets of the Seaport. Just from the sound of his breathing, Abbie understood that he wished she'd turned to him for help after she'd found the threatening note. But he didn't scold her for it. He only repeated how glad he was that she was safe.

A small crowd had gathered by the time the car was hauled up, pouring water from a sprung-open door and clotted with mud.

"This should work out pretty conveniently for Les. I bet he had this baby heavily insured."

The skeptical edge in Cal's voice made Abbie glance at him quickly. She realized what he was inferring, though he didn't spell it out. He didn't have to. She'd already thought something alarmingly similar herself. Except that she'd been concentrating on the angle of Lester's obvious resentment of Cal and his fear that she'd make him look bad as the museum director if she succeeded where he'd failed. Neither she nor Cal said anything about their suspicions while the police were around. They called Les several times at the office, but he wasn't there.

Finally Abbie decided to go home. Her stockings had ripped in the fall, and the heel had broken off one of her shoes. She didn't look or feel fit to return to work that afternoon. Cal wanted to drive her to Astoria, but she insisted on taking a cab so he could stay with the Jaguar while it was towed to the police garage for a thorough investigation. He didn't release her hand till she was in the back seat of the taxi and it was pulling away.

Soon after Abbie arrived at the apartment, Rachel Steiner invited Davey and some neighborhood children for supper and a movie at her place. Abbie couldn't have been more grateful. Rachel had heard nothing about the car going in the river, and Abbie didn't mention it. In any of the cities where she'd lived before, the accident would have been all over the six-o'clock news, but here her near drowning was just another incident in a metropolis full of incidents. She was relieved that Davey didn't know what had happened. It would scare him, and she didn't want that. Also, a long discussion would have been necessary to calm his fears, and right now she needed to concentrate on other things.

She understood, in a way, what had taken place between her and Cal this afternoon. They'd shared an intense and shocking experience that had brought them very close to each other very quickly. She'd heard of that happening among people who had survived a near tragedy together. The difference was that it had happened to her with a man to whom she was already strongly attracted. Being in his arms, holding his hand, staying at his side all afternoon had accelerated that attraction into something she was a little afraid to give a name to.

After all, she had no reliable indication of what Cal felt toward her. Until that car had gone plunging off toward the river, he'd been polite at best and cold at worst. His subsequent behavior might be nothing more than a natural protective reaction brought on by feelings of relief and of responsibility because he'd been driving the car. After the emotional impact of the incident had passed, he could go back to acting impersonal once more.

Abbie was attempting to resign herself to that possibility—or probability—when the doorbell rang and Cal's voice boomed through the intercom in the front entryway.

She buzzed him into the lobby, then waited to hear him on her threshold before opening the apartment door. She spent the intervening seconds trying to settle herself emotionally, but when she saw Cal silhouetted against the lobby light, she was far from feeling calm. She remembered how he'd looked standing in the doorway of her office. She'd thought some kind of optical illusion must be happening, because nobody's shoulders could possibly be that broad. Seeing him standing before her now, Abbie realized in an instant that nothing about Calhoun Quinn was an illusion, especially not the way he'd been with her that afternoon.

Then he was through the door and had shut it behind him. She knew what was going to happen even before his arms circled her and his lips touched hers. She stretched up toward his kiss as instinctively as flowers reach for the sun. His warmth engulfed her. A small moan rose in her throat as she leaned into his strong body and surrendered herself to the awakening inside her. Then suddenly he pulled away, and she felt as if she'd been thrust from a warm nest into a wintry chill.

"I shouldn't have done that," he said. "Your son might see us."

"Davey's at his friend's house."

Abbie moved back into his arms, and they stood there in the hallway holding each other for what seemed a long time, but not long enough.

"We have to talk," he said finally.

With their arms still around each other, they went into the living room and sat down on the couch. Neither seemed willing to let go of the other for even a moment. It occurred to Abbie that she had never had that feeling about anyone before.

"The police went over Les's car very carefully," Cal said. "Their conclusion is that it was definitely an accident."

"Are they sure?"

Cal nodded. "Les simply didn't take very good care of the car. The police contacted his mechanic, who said he'd recommended work on the accelerator cables long ago, but Les never bothered with it—probably because he couldn't afford to. What happened this afternoon was a mechanical malfunction, nothing more."

Abbie felt only partially relieved. "What about the rest of what I told the police? Did they say anything about that?"

"They'll be in touch with you again, but they don't seem to think there's any pattern of harassment. They believe it was just some crackpot who put the note on your desk and that you must have left your apartment door unlocked. As for a man chasing you down Front Street, they don't think that's so unusual when a woman walks alone on a dark, deserted street in New York."

"They think I'm a crackpot myself, don't they?"

"I wouldn't say that."

"Do you believe me?"

Cal looked into her eyes. His fingers slipped up her back to the tumble of hair she'd let down and brushed out before he arrived. "Yes, I believe you," he said.

"Then I need your help."

"Anything. Just name it."

"Help me get Davey ready, then drive us to LaGuardia. I'm putting him on the shuttle for Washington tonight."

THE LAST THING Abbie wanted to do was to send her son away. She regretted it even before she saw the plane take off, but she had no choice. Something dangerous was going on, she was sure of it; and that danger might harm Davey. She'd do anything to keep that from happening. So she'd led Robert to believe that the pressures of the new job had forced her to send Davey early and on short notice to Tannersfield for his summer visit. She'd been afraid Robert might protest. Instead he'd seemed pleased, even triumphant, about the change of plans. Abbie didn't share his pleasure. She and Cal stood at the airport window long after the plane had vanished into the night.

The next few days at work were difficult. Abbie's story to the police about being harassed was common knowledge; sarcastic remarks about paranoia were made regularly within her hearing, followed by laughter and pointed looks. Rumors about her and Cal were also running rampant. The fact that he was in Boston for a couple of days, tending to the interests of a shipping business he owned there, didn't quiet the talk any. His absence made Abbie feel lonely twice over, from missing both her son and the man she'd come to care for so much in such a short time.

Luckily she had lots of work to preoccupy her. She'd scheduled a press conference to highlight the museum's summer program, and careful preparation was essential. She and Meredith worked long hours to make certain that the media would have a well-oiled, efficient operation to report on. Abbie thanked heaven for her assistant. In a week's time Meredith had taught herself enough about Abbie's project plans to take over when necessary. Abbie was doubly grateful that Meredith never mentioned the gossip, especially the derisive talk about Abbie's claims to being chased through the streets and otherwise terrorized. Nothing unpleasant had happened since then, and she was beginning to think the police were right.

The night before the press conference, she and Meredith worked even later than usual. It was past ten when Meredith plopped her stapler down with finality on top of a neatly stacked pile of press packets. "What do you say we blow this pop stand?" she asked.

Abbie smiled. It amused her to hear that kind of talk coming out of someone as proper looking as Meredith Stanfield. "At the last minute like this, I always get the feeling I've overlooked something really crucial that will end up ruining everything."

"I can't imagine what that could be. It looks to me like everything's in perfect order for your public debut. You're just coming down with backstage jitters." Meredith gathered the remains of the hamburgers she'd run out for earlier and dumped them in Abbie's wastebasket. "There's nothing more we can do tonight, except maybe check once more what we've checked three times already. Personally, I'd rather go home and get some sleep, and I think you should do the same.''

"You go ahead. I'll be out of here shortly."

"Promise?" Meredith said, already at the door.

"I promise. I'll go home and sleep like a baby."

"No more backstage jitters?"

"Not a one."

Still, a half hour later, as Abbie took one more look around the office before clicking off the light, she couldn't shake the feeling that something was terribly wrong.

Chapter Five

Her vow to Meredith didn't keep Abbie from sleeping badly. She had to dab extra makeup under her eyes to hide the shadows she found there in the morning. It was important that she look her best today, even though she expected only a few reporters to show up. An orchestrated press conference like this one was what media people referred to as a "nonevent event." Abbie's public debut, as Meredith called it, wouldn't be a high priority for New York newspapers and TV stations. But if it was possible to get at least a photograph and some filler space in a couple of places, that alone would be worth the trouble she and Meredith had gone to. Whatever publicity mileage she got out of today could mean a boost to the museum program.

Abbie wore her navy-and-white silk print dress with the matching navy linen jacket for the big event. There was an outside chance one of the local television channels would send a crew to shoot some footage for the tag end of the news. In that case, she had to be as photogenic as possible. She lined her eyes a little darker than usual for contrast against her pale skin and was pleased with the effect, despite the shadows underneath. When even her unruly hair fell obediently into place, Abbie considered it a favorable omen for the day ahead.

The morning dawned clear and bright, and by the time Abbie had reached the Seaport, sunny skies promised beautiful weather for the conference, scheduled to take place on one of the museum piers. Then Abbie turned onto Front Street and saw Josie waiting in front of the museum office, her frizz of hair sticking out in all directions and her eyes wildly brilliant.

"Something terrible's happened at the piers!" she exclaimed. Her fingers flew nervously in front of her, reminiscent of the seabirds she'd made her crusade.

"Yes, Josie, I'm sure it has, but we'll have to talk about it later. I'm in a hurry now." Abbie was trying her best to be patient, but she really didn't have time for Josie's babbling.

"Oh, no, this can't wait. You have to get over to Pier 15 right away."

Something in Josie's eyes told Abbie she should listen this time.

"Right away," Josie repeated, her hands soaring into a beseeching gesture. "One of the ships is sinking."

ONE STEP PAST the pier gate, Abbie knew Josie hadn't exaggerated. Something was very wrong here. The museum docks were usually quiet at this time of the morning, but today the waterfront crew was out in full force, dashing back and forth to the sounds of shouted commands and roaring motors.

"It's the *Lettie*."

Abbie almost didn't hear the soft voice at her elbow. She turned to find Nathan Mallory matching her rapid steps as she hurried toward the area of loudest confusion.

"She's docked over here," he said, slouching along. "I hope she doesn't sink. So much history would go down with her."

Abbie spotted the *Lettie G. Howard* through the crowd of scrambling workmen. The usually graceful, wooden fishing schooner rocked awkwardly in the agitated docking slip while the river lapped dangerously close to her gunwales. Josie had been right. The *Lettie* was sinking.

"Refill the gas tank on that second pump!" Sam Denicola's Hell's Kitchen nasality rang above the pandemonium.

He was at the dock's edge, hauling on a noisy pump at his feet. He bent his compact frame over the pump as he wrestled a kink out of the heavy, black discharge hose. Then the gurgle of water from the nozzle turned into a stream and shot over the side of the pier into the East River. Sam straightened up and wiped the back of his hand across his brow. His tank undershirt had probably been white when he got here. His wife, Phoebe, would have insisted on that. Now it bore the evidence of hard, greasy work. He also had a habit of scratching his head when he was perplexed. From the looks of his tousled brown hair, he must have been very upset this morning.

Sam was head man down here. He'd been given a formal title—waterfront director—but the desk-job sound of it was deceptive. He worked side by side with his crew, and Cal had said more than once that Sam Denicola was the best man on the docks. Abbie assured herself that if Sam was in charge, everything must be under control. Then she glanced up at the *Lettie*. At close range the old ship looked pathetically helpless as she listed sharply to one side in the churning water. Abbie thought that maybe her optimism was premature.

"What happened?" she shouted to Sam above the clamor of the pumps.

Sam's usual friendly gaze was dead-serious now behind his wire-rimmed glasses. "She must have been shipping water most of the night. I'm not sure exactly how it happened. Maybe the pump cut out for a while, but it was back on when I got here. I just don't know." He'd begun scratching furiously just above his left temple.

"The *Lettie*'s wood is so old her seams must have sprung right open when they got wet," Nathan said quietly, like a prompting advisor, at Abbie's ear. She'd forgotten he was there. "An electric pump is kept running twenty-four hours a day belowdecks just to keep her afloat."

Abbie might not be an expert on antique ships, but even she could see that, for some reason, the pump hadn't done its job last night. The South Street Seaport Museum was in danger of losing one of its star attractions.

In the early years of this century, these piers would have been crowded with schooners like the *Lettie*, unloading tall baskets of cod and haddock from the Massachusetts shore, then loading up again with salt for the trip home. Nowadays, however, the *Lettie* was the last of a disappearing breed, and even she needed a round-the-clock pump to keep her alive.

"Maybe they'll listen to me now." Abbie was surprised to hear good-natured Sam speak in such a bitter tone. "More attention has to be paid to what's going on over here and less to that carnival across the street." He shook an angry fist in the direction of the shops and chic restaurants of Schermerhorn Row and lower Fulton Street. "All those three-piece suits care about is the almighty buck. Meanwhile, I'm trying to hold these ships together with spit and chewing gum. I swear, if this town doesn't appreciate what it's got down here, then it doesn't deserve to have any of it."

Abbie nodded. Sam had a right to be angry. He'd dedicated himself to the old vessels, and sometimes he must feel as if he were all alone in his dedication. She couldn't claim to feel as strongly as he did for the same reasons, but she was determined to do her job the very best way she could. She'd been hired to accomplish exactly what Sam was shouting about—to spotlight the museum ships so brightly that everyone would notice both them and their value to the city.

"Is there anything I can do?" she asked, gazing around at the hectic scene.

"If you've got any pull with Neptune, you might try putting in a word for us. Short of that, I'd say we're at the mercy of the pumps right now." The wisecrack was more typical of Sam than his anger had been, but he didn't smile as he squinted up at the schooner's double masts. "She's the last of her type in the water," he said.

"Yes, I know," Abbie answered softly. She could tell he was grieving for an old friend.

"We'll save her, Sam. You've got my personal guarantee on that."

The deep voice seemed to resonate out of Abbie's imagination, where she'd heard it so many times these past few days. Cal was walking toward them, wearing faded gray coveralls with the collar turned up rakishly against his suntanned neck and the zipper open halfway to his waist. Abbie had never seen so much of him exposed before; it was a compelling sight. She had to remind herself not to stare too obviously at his broad chest and bronzed skin.

"How's everything on board?" Sam asked.

"I think the patient will live," Cal said.

Abbie suddenly realized that Cal had come from the *Lettie*. His overalls were wet past his knees.

"Hallelujah," Sam exclaimed as he grabbed Cal's hand and pumped it enthusiastically. "The mighty Quinn has been running the on-deck crew," he told Abbie.

"I see." Abbie's reply was calm and steady, but she actually felt like exclaiming along with Sam, and not just because of the *Lettie*. She hadn't known when Cal would be back from Boston. Seeing him now was a bright spot in an otherwise distressing morning. That brightness shone from his eyes as he smiled warmly at her and winked, just as he had the first day she met him. The same flutter trembled through her in response, but this time it was much stronger.

"So how do you like it down here with us river rats?" Sam asked Cal.

"I like it a lot. In fact, I just might change professions. Do you have any openings on your crew?"

"I'd start you out at the bottom like everybody else, sweeping and swabbing."

"I wouldn't have it any other way."

"This crazy fool's been out here all morning," Sam told Abbie with comradely pride.

"Has he really?"

Abbie was feeling rather proud herself right now as Cal beamed so admiringly at her. She returned his smile, and since Sam's attention was on the *Lettie* for the moment, this time she was the one to wink. Then she noticed Meredith staring at her from across the pier. Almost immediately Meredith's glance darted off toward the schooner, as if she hadn't really seen Abbie standing there at all.

"Meredith—over here," Abbie called.

"Yes, I'm coming," Meredith answered, still gazing distractedly at the floundering ship. "Isn't this the most terrible thing you ever saw?" she said as she wandered up to them. She sounded as if she was in a daze.

"Cal says he thinks the *Lettie*'s going to make it," Abbie reassured her. She'd never seen Meredith be anything but calm and in control. In fact, until this moment Abbie had marveled at her assistant's ability to be right on top of things, no matter what happened. However, she was hardly on top of things now. A black smudge smeared her flushed cheek, and a hank of beige hair hung in her eyes.

"We're giving it our best shot." Sam added his reassurance to Abbie's. "And we'll keep it up for as long as it takes."

"I'm afraid this is going to disrupt your press conference," Cal told Abbie.

"Yes, I know." She'd almost forgotten about it. "What do you think we should do?" she asked Meredith.

"About what?" Meredith was still staring at the *Lettie* again and barely paying attention to the conversation.

"The press conference. It's scheduled to start in less than two hours."

Meredith's gaze leaped from the *Lettie*'s listing hull to Abbie. Her gray eyes were suddenly so cold they chilled Abbie to the bone. "To hell with your press conference and your project, too! I couldn't care less about either right now!" Her words seemed propelled by near hysteria. Then she turned abruptly and marched away, her flat heels slapping angrily against the pier.

For a moment Abbie was too startled to respond. She wouldn't have thought cool, professional Meredith capable of such behavior, and she wasn't sure whether to follow her or not.

"She just needs to be by herself for a while." Cal's hand was on Abbie's arm. "You have to understand Meredith. These ships mean everything to her—maybe too much, as a matter of fact. I suspect they may be all she has to care about."

"What about her family in Connecticut? She told me she's from there."

"From what I've heard they take more from her than they give. So she's made the ships her family."

"That's not exactly professional."

"No, but it's understandable."

Abbie thought that Cal was being very compassionate toward someone who'd had nothing but critical things to say about him.

"I suffer from a touch of that same mania where these old tubs are concerned," he went on. "I can guess how she's feeling. I'm sure she didn't mean what she said to you. Just give her a little time to cool off, and she'll be telling you she can't imagine what came over her."

"All right. I'll leave her alone for a while." Meanwhile, Abbie had a crisis on her hands. "Is there any chance the *Lettie* could still sink?"

"Not as long as these pumps keep us one step ahead of Old Man River," Sam answered, running his fingers through the thatch of hair he'd scratched to wildness. "The problem is she went down deeper than the waterline. The wood above that line was even drier than the wood below, so the seams opened fast and wide. That's what we're up against now. I'd say we're running about neck and neck with the leaks at the moment. I don't think she'll sink any deeper anyway, unless her hull gives way altogether. That can always happen with a ship this old, but it's not very likely." He crossed his fingers and raised them toward the sky. "Did you hear that up there? Don't make a liar of me!"

"What's it going to look like around here at eleven o'clock?" After Meredith's outburst Abbie felt a little guilty about asking that, but she had to know.

"I'd say it will look just about the same as it does now," Sam said.

"I was afraid of that."

Abbie surveyed the frenzied activity going on around ner. Coils of hose and rope twisted every which way along the pier, which was covered with endless puddles of water. Grimy workmen tended the noisy pumps, and the whole place smelled of gasoline fumes from the pump motors. She had no doubt how a bunch of reporters would react to all this. They'd see disaster and chaos, and that was exactly what they'd report. It was hardly the upbeat, full-speed-ahead image she'd planned to project this morning.

Cal had stepped away to talk with a couple of the crewmen. Now he was back. "Is there any chance of postponing the press conference?" he asked her.

"It's too late for that."

"Maybe you could move it over to the offices."

"I don't think I'd better. They'd smell a rat for sure Reporters are like that."

Abbie rubbed the toe of one navy-and-white spectator pump back and forth across a splintered board on the dock. The press was supposed to gather on the next pier, behind the long hull of the *Peking*. But even so, there'd be no way to hide what was going on over here.

"Thank heaven there won't be a very big turnout," she muttered, half to herself.

"I wouldn't count on that," Cal said.

He was smiling as hopefully as the situation would allow. His caring made the whole mess a little easier for her to bear. Yet she sensed he had some bad news to deliver, and she wished she didn't have to know what it was.

"What do you mean?"

"Nathan's been running messages from the office. The *Daily News* called. They heard about the *Lettie*, and they're sending somebody. That means the *Times* and the *Post* won't be far behind, maybe the TV stations, too. It's not every day a fishing schooner nearly sinks in New York harbor.''

Abbie might have laughed at the irony if the joke hadn't been at her expense. An hour ago she'd have given almost anything for this kind of press coverage. Now she was going to have it, and she didn't know what to do with it.

"I think I'm getting bitten by that old Chinese proverb," she said in a wry tone.

"Which proverb is that?"

"The one about not wishing for something for fear you might get it."

"I'm not sure what that means, but I think your attitude is commendable."

He slipped an arm around her shoulder. It didn't even occur to Abbie to wonder whether anyone was watching. Instead she felt an almost overwhelming urge to lay her head on his shoulder, right there in front of everybody. His arm was strong, and she longed to hide under its protection for a while. Then she noticed Sam looking at them with a quizzical twinkle in his eye. She eased herself out of Cal's half embrace, suddenly reminded that a lot of gossip was going around about her and Cal already. She didn't want to encourage any more.

"By the way, I came ashore to tell you I'm going below to locate the leaks," Cal was saying to Sam.

Sam rubbed his chin instead of scratching his head. "I'm not sure the ship is safe enough for that yet."

"We'll never get ahead of the water she's taking in unless we do some serious caulking pretty soon."

"She's still riding a little low for you to take a chance on going into the hold. One of those old timbers could decide it's had enough and give way. Then she'd go down like a stone."

"The *Lettie*'s got too much fight left in her for that."
Cal ran a hand through the brown-gold of his hair. "Captain," he said, "I think you should order me below to caulk the seams."

The lightness of Cal's tone was belied by the serious expression on Sam's face. "If anybody's going to take that risk, it should be me. As you said, I'm the captain here."

"And the captain has to stay topside and in charge. Listen, Sam," Cal urged, just as serious now, "you're needed up here. Somebody's got to coordinate this operation, and you're the one who should do it. I'll handle the caulking, and I promise not to take any chances."

Sam squinted toward the *Lettie*, then back at Cal. "All right," he said reluctantly. "But you be careful, and that is an order. I don't want you going down with the ship. The East River's polluted enough already." Sam's usual wise-cracking style had returned, but it only partly disguised his concern for his friend.

"Don't worry, my captain. I have no intention of being lost at sea two yards from the dock. How would that look in the next issue of the yachtsman's journal? They'd send me straight back to landlubbing!"

"All right, all right. I've heard enough. Still, I could send one of my regular crew to do the caulking. It's not a very pleasant job, Cal."

"And rob me of the opportunity to root around in cold, dirty water when that's one of my favorite ways to spend a beautiful morning? Not on your life."

"Okay, you're the boss."

Technically, that was true. As a ranking member of the powerful museum advisory committee, Cal could do whatever he wanted around the piers.

"Of course, Quinn only pretends to be an executive," Sam said to Abbie. "He's really just a dockhand at heart."

She'd been listening with growing concern to the exchange between the two men. She didn't like the idea of Cal's being in possible danger. In fact, she was amazed at how worried she was for him. She hadn't felt that way toward anybody but Davey in a very long time.

"Would you care to join me below, Mrs. Tanner?"

Abbie wished she felt as much at ease about this as Cal sounded. "I think I'll be needed dockside." She made herself mimic his light tone.

"You're probably right about that. In fact, at the moment I'd rather have my job than yours. Those newshounds will eat this up. I can just imagine the headlines and the caption under your photograph: 'The face that launched a thousand ships—straight to the bottom.'"

"Well, do be careful belowdecks," she said. She'd decided, if teasing was the general response to what was going on, she might as well join in. "I agree with Sam about not polluting the river."

Cal dipped his head in a mock bow, and that same wayward lock fell across his forehead. Abbie's fingers itched to brush it gently back into place. As he turned and walked off down the pier, she whispered a silent prayer for his safety.

"They don't come any better than that guy," Sam said.

"I think I agree with you," Abbie replied so softly Sam didn't hear.

She watched Cal stride up the gangway to the deck of the *Lettie*. He stopped near the hatch that led to the lower deck. Then he slid the zipper of his coveralls downward and dropped the faded gray from his shoulders. Abbie found herself staring at the most perfectly proportioned torso she'd ever seen. He was wearing only a pair of white running shorts now. The side slits revealed hard-muscled thighs covered with a soft pelt of golden hair. Abbie's fingers were suddenly itching more than ever, and not just to push Cal's hair back from his forehead.

"What's your plan?" Sam asked.

"My plan?" Abbie's attention returned reluctantly to the dock as Cal ducked through the hatch and out of sight.

"For this morning's rapidly approaching fiasco."

"Oh, that." Abbie sighed. Cal had said he could imagine the headlines. She could do the same with the report on the evening news, billing her project as disaster of the week. She looked across the slip to the long sweep of the *Peking*'s black hull. Maybe she could have Sam erect some kind of wall to keep the press from coming over to this pier. She sighed again. There wasn't a chance that would work. Reporters had short attention spans. They'd be sure to get restless and start looking around. Then she remembered something Sam had said during his outburst earlier

"Maybe that's just what I want them to do," she mumbled.

"What you want who to do?"

"Sam, I think I might have a plan after all. Could you spare some of your crew to put up a platform right here with the podium high enough so the TV cameras can get a good shot of it?"

"You're going to have the press conference over here?"

"That's right."

Sam was scratching his head again. "Are you sure?" He glanced skeptically from Abbie to the listing *Lettie* and the turmoil on the pier.

"I haven't time to explain now. It's a long shot, but with the help of your crew, it just might work."

"All right, then. You'll have your platform if I have to build it myself."

''Thanks, Sam. Now I need somebody to open the souvenir shop early for me.''

Sam looked even more puzzled as Abbie hurried off toward the gate.

Chapter Six

An hour later the press had begun to arrive, but by then Abbie was ready for them. Sam had balked at first when she asked him to have his crew wear souvenir-shop T-shirts with "South Street Seaport" printed on them. He said they made serious workmen look like counselors at summer camp. Abbie had had to talk fast to convince him it was for a good cause. He'd relented finally and even sent his men to the head in shifts to clean up for the cameras. And he'd been true to his word about the platform. It stood, complete with podium and microphone, directly across from the *Lettie G. Howard*.

Abbie's attention had been somewhat distracted by the old schooner till she saw its list gradually correcting itself and she knew Cal was safe. Then she'd thrown herself with fervor into preparation for her slightly revised press conference. Now that effort appeared to be paying off. Photographers' shutters were clicking, and the television cameras had begun to roll. The pumping operation took center stage. Sam piped orders in his best sea captain's drawl, just as she'd asked him to do. She'd been right about the T-shirts. They gave the crew an organized, official look that would photograph well.

Abbie allowed herself her first moment of relaxation in more than two hours. "Maybe I can pull this off after all," she said aloud to herself.

"I'd bet my nickel on it."

Abbie hadn't seen Meredith since she ran off. Now she stood there smiling as if nothing had upset her in months.

"Sorry about my tantrum earlier," she went on. "I got a little carried away."

"I understand," Abbie said. "By the way, have you seen Sam? I'd like an update on the *Lettie* in case the reporters ask for specifics."

"I don't know about Sam, but I saw Cal Quinn. He might know. He was over by the pier gate talking to Josie a couple of minutes ago."

"Oh, no. Is she here?"

In answer to that, a nearby speaker began to hum, and Abbie looked up just in time to see Josie standing on the platform in front of the microphone. She was holding a long piece of paper and grinning down at the crowd.

"I have a matter of the utmost importance to bring to the attention of the members of the press." Her cheery voice crackled through the sound system Sam and his men had set up along the pier. "I have a petition here of the greatest urgency. Everyone in this city must be urged to sign it." Josie waved the paper over the heads of the reporters who'd turned to listen.

"I don't believe this," Abbie groaned and began elbowing her way toward the platform.

Josie appeared to be perfectly lucid, just as she had been at first on that morning in Abbie's office. The press was taking her seriously. A couple of photographers were already focusing on her, and television reporters' mikes were thrust up at the podium. Abbie was still pushing her way through the crowd when she saw Cal mount the platform in a single leap. He'd changed his running shorts and coveralls for a trim, tan suit; Abbie couldn't help noticing how his thigh muscles flexed beneath the fine tailoring as he bounded upward.

He clasped Josie's hand, the one holding the petition, and lowered it gently but firmly. "Thank you, Josie," he said.

Abbie could tell he was trying to maneuver Josie away from the mike, but she refused to budge. She just stared vaguely up at him. Then a flash of recognition spread her grin wider than ever.

"Errol," she exclaimed. "It's you."

"Tell everybody welcome to the Seaport," Cal said, loud enough to be heard over the sound system.

Josie looked down at the people as if surprised to see them there. "Oh, yes," she said. "Welcome. And have a nice day."

Scattered laughter rose from the crowd. Cal had begun to ease Josie across the platform, away from the mike, when she pulled out of his grasp and dashed back to the podium. "If no one is going to protect these ships, then they'd all be better off sunk, like this one almost was!" she shouted, wagging her petition in the direction of the *Lettie*.

"She may have a point," Sam said. He was leaning against the platform steps as Abbie hurried up.

She didn't comment. She was watching Cal. She preferred to let him handle this alone. The two of them up there wrestling with Josie would be too juicy a "photo opportunity" for the press to pass up. Even now they were snapping shots of him trying to persuade the older woman as gently as possible to remove herself from the center of attention.

"You don't really mean that, do you, Josie?" he said in the most silken, charming tone Abbie could ever remember hearing from a man.

Josie gazed up at him. The charm appeared to be working. She batted her eyelashes coyly, like a young girl with her best beau. "No, of course not, my dear," she said.

The laughter from the crowd was more general now as Cal handed Josie into the charge of a staff employee who'd followed him onto the platform. Cal stepped back to the podium. "We do have a somewhat more official welcome planned for you," he said into the microphone with a dazzling smile.

"He certainly has a way of showing up just in time to save you from the sea-gull lady, doesn't he?" Meredith had come up behind Abbie to whisper in her ear.

"What do you mean?"

"Oh, I don't know. I've just never trusted the savior type myself."

"Here with that official welcome is one of our newest and most valuable additions to the museum staff, Mrs. Abigail Tanner."

Cal's voice reverberating through the sound system tore Abbie's attention away from Meredith's troubling remark. She couldn't think about it now. After taking a deep breath and walking up the steps to the podium, she smiled softly at Cal, mouthed a silent thank-you, then turned to the faces and lenses below.

"I'd like to add my welcome to those of Mr. Quinn and, of course, Josie," Abbie began in a tone that dismissed the sea-gull lady as just another of New York's many colorful characters. She noticed Nathan at the edge of the gathering, backed up against the chain link fence with his head hung down nearly to his chest. Crowds probably aren't his thing, she thought. She'd run into him briefly a few times since the day he'd followed her and Meredith onto the pier. Whatever else might be true about him, he loved these ships. Somehow seeing him there banished Abbie's last inkling of stage fright. It was for people like Nathan that she was doing this.

"What you see behind me this morning is an example of the South Street Seaport Museum at work," she said in her most confident voice. "It is also an illustration of how much we need the people of this city to support our program. The funds that program can raise will make it possible for Sam Denicola and his crew to continue what they've been doing since dawn…keeping history alive and intact right here in New York Harbor."

Taping mikes lifted toward her while pencils flew across notepads and television cameras whirred. Her strategy was working. Sam had given her the idea to call attention to the needs of the ships. Instead of the full-speed-ahead image, she'd opted for sympathetic publicity. The press appeared to be eating it up. There was only one problem now. Les Girard, as museum director, was supposed to be here to introduce the rest of the people on the agenda, but Abbie hadn't seen him all morning. She looked around for him one more time, then glanced over at Cal, who was still standing near the platform steps.

"Now," she said after turning back to the microphone, "I'd like to introduce you to the gentleman who was up here a few moments ago. In the absence of our director, who has been unavoidably detained, Mr. Calhoun Quinn of our advisory committee will tell you something about the background of the museum."

"Thanks a lot," Cal whispered to her in mock exasperation as he took her place at the podium. He slipped his fingers over hers and squeezed briefly.

Abbie knew she could relax now. The rest of the morning was in Cal's strong, warm hands, and he wouldn't let her down.

WHEN ABBIE ARRIVED HOME that afternoon, she headed straight for the shower. She'd left the Seaport and its problems back on South Street, and now she could relax at last. Of course, she did plan to watch the TV coverage of her press conference. She'd even left the office early to get home in time for the six-o'clock news.

As the water warmed to just the right temperature, she unbuttoned her dress and let it slide to the floor in a tumble of navy-and-white silk. Then she stepped past the flowered shower curtain and stood, absolutely still, beneath the soothing cascade. It washed over her like liquid velvet, dissolving the tensions of the day and carrying them off into swirling currents around her feet.

The shocking chill came without warning. In an instant the soothing cascade had turned icy cold, and Abbie let out a small shriek of surprise. The hot water had gone off. She exited the shower at a much less leisurely pace than she'd entered it and grabbed a towel to rub her shivering body back to circulation once more.

Her mood of restful homecoming had shattered. Even the luxurious green silk of her favorite caftan, whispering down over her body, couldn't restore the atmosphere of haven and sanctuary that she'd promised herself for this evening. She waited impatiently now for the six-o'clock news to begin.

In the meantime she couldn't help thinking about Davey, and that brought a quiver to her heart. She missed him terribly. She'd tried to reach him at Tannersfield before she left the office, but the butler had answered the phone and told her that Davey was in Washington with his grandmother. Abbie hadn't been surprised to hear that. Robert generally tired of his son very quickly, then sent him off to Victoria Tanner's brownstone in Georgetown. Abbie didn't mind. She loved her kindhearted mother-in-law and knew Davey was better off with her than with a father who had no time for him.

She snapped on the television set but didn't turn up the sound. The news had begun. She kept herself only half attentive as scenes of crises and problems flickered across the screen. At the moment she didn't feel like listening to the troubles of the world. Finally a familiar skyline of masts and spars flashed into view, followed by—with a shock to her as unexpected as the cold water in the shower—the face of Cal Quinn smiling at her in brilliant TV colors. She was stunned for a moment by how handsome and at ease he looked on film, maybe even more so than in real life, if that was possible. Josie's comparison of him to Errol Flynn wasn't far from the truth.

He was dressed in the same trimly fitted tan suit he'd worn that morning. The usual errant lock of hair lifted from his forehead in the waterfront breeze. It occurred to Abbie that, whatever else might turn out to be true about him, there were some things she could definitely depend on where Cal was concerned. His eyes would always flash a piercing blue, the sun would always touch the gold in his hair with a special fondness, and she would always be startled anew, each time she saw him, by how absolutely wonderful he looked.

She turned up the volume.

"We have everything under control now," he was saying.

The camera panned to the old wooden schooner behind him. It was nearly upright in the water now. Then the picture changed to a shot of an earlier scene of the *Lettie* listing precariously. There was Cal again, emerging bare chested from belowdecks, his hair sexily disheveled as he lifted a muscular arm to wipe his brow. Then there was another shot of Cal in his suit, talking about the need for public support and funds to maintain the ships. He was paraphrasing exactly what Abbie had said on the speakers' platform that morning.

When the camera finally shifted its focus, Abbie saw why Cal was getting such exclusive attention. The shot was of the female reporter interviewing him. She was looking up into his eyes with a softness in her gaze that was hardly an example of journalistic objectivity. Before Abbie could stop herself, she began to wonder what might have gone on between Cal and this attractive woman after the interview was over. Had they gone out to lunch? Had he made a date with her for dinner? Maybe they were watching this telecast together right now. Abbie hadn't seen Cal since the press conference. Maybe that was why.

She pulled herself up short before the next worry could form. She had no right to be thinking like this. Cal was free to do whatever he wanted with whomever he wanted. She had no hold on him. There'd been a kiss and a few embraces between them, nothing more. That certainly didn't constitute an exclusive commitment of any kind. Still, she couldn't stop the twinge she felt watching the woman gaze fondly at Cal.

Abbie turned off the set with an impatient twist of her wrist just as the phone began to ring. She snapped up the receiver and said, "Hello," with some of that impatience evident in her voice.

"I'll bet you've been tuned in to the news."

"Oh, hi, Meredith. Yes, I've been watching Channel 7. How did you know?"

"You sound about as pleased as I feel."

"What do you mean?"

"Quinn hogged the whole segment. That's what I mean."

"It was good coverage." Abbie heard herself defending Cal when she wasn't entirely sure she wanted to.

"You call that good coverage? We needed publicity for the ships, and we ended up with a promotion piece starring my least favorite blue-eyed boy. I have half a mind to call up the station and tell them what I think."

"Don't do that. We can't afford to alienate the media."

"Well, I already tried calling Quinn, but he wasn't in his office or at home."

Abbie felt that twinge again. Maybe he was with the pretty TV reporter after all. "You can't blame Cal for the way the piece was edited," she said, still defending, but less wholeheartedly now.

"Are you kidding me? Did you see that woman practically throw herself at him? Don't try to tell me he didn't encourage that. There's more than one way to skin a reporter, and I'll bet our Mr. Quinn charmed himself right into the spotlight."

"Don't you think you're being a little hard on him?"

"Don't you think you're being a little easy on him? I told you this morning. He's a bit too Johnny-on-the-spot with the savior act for my skeptical tastes, and now he's doing it on TV, no less." Meredith made a snorting sound that was obviously one of disbelief. "Didn't you notice how he made it sound like he saved the *Lettie* single-handedly?"

Abbie didn't answer, because she knew Meredith had a point.

"Mark my words. He wants everybody in town to think he's the only person at the museum with a handle on things."

"Why would he want that?"

"I'm not sure, but isn't it interesting that he did the interview that would ordinarily be given by the director? That's why none of the press cared a fig about talking to Girard when he finally got there."

"It's not Cal's fault that Girard was late." But Abbie's defense of Cal was becoming less heartfelt by the moment. A fleeting question crossed her mind about how much her weakening faith in him might have to do with plain, old jealousy.

"I know our dear director is no prize, either," Meredith said. "I hear he stayed away till he heard catastrophe had been averted. He didn't want his good name besmirched by anything like that." Her sarcasm was unmistakable.

"So Cal didn't have any choice but to fill in for him with the press."

"Why didn't he share the spot with you or Sam or even me? I'll tell you why. Image is everything these days. Image and visibility are the highway to power. Nobody knows that better than someone in your racket, and Cal Quinn knows it, too."

"But why would he want power over a small maritime musuem?"

"That's a good question. And while you're figuring out an answer to it, think about this. Why is a high roller like Quinn so damned interested in the Seaport in the first place? He's hardly the yacht-basin type that usually gets involved down there. What's his angle?"

Abbie didn't try to answer that, and she didn't put up any more defense of Cal, either.

"Oh, to hell with it." Meredith sighed to release some of her frustration. "If I talk about Quinn any longer, I'll start chewing on the phone. Don't worry. I won't call

Channel 7, or anybody else. I guess I'll have to content myself with revenge fantasies.''

"I think that would be best."

A few moments later Abbie hung up and sank down onto the couch. Cal really had monopolized the television spot. There was no denying that. She wondered if he'd managed to do the same with the other channels and the newspaper people. He could be trying to give the impression he was in control at the museum, just as Meredith had suggested. Abbie understood business politics well enough to know that one of the best ways to help yourself to power was to make everybody think you already had it—but why would Cal want that power? As Meredith said, what could his angle be?

Abbie was still pondering that disturbing mystery when the buzzer sounded, the one next to her apartment door, not the one in the lobby. Obviously whoever was buzzing was inside the building rather than beyond the locked outer door. Abbie's attention leaped back to the here and now. Who could it be? Only people living in the building had keys to the lobby door, and she didn't know any of her neighbors.

The buzzer rang again, more insistently this time. Abbie crept out into the hallway, being careful not to make a sound, and peered through the peephole in the door. Someone was standing there, but he was too close for her to see up to his face. All she could make out through the thick, bleary lens was black leather and a zipper. She didn't like the looks of that. She pressed the listening button on the intercom panel next to the door and put her ear flat against the receiver. She could hear someone moving restlessly around, but nothing more.

"Abbie, are you in there? It's Cal."

His shout bellowed through the small box on the wall, and she jumped.

"Something's come up. I have to talk you."

"How did you get into the building?"

"I followed one of your neighbors through the front door."

Some security system, she thought.

"Are you going to open the door, or do I have to talk through it all night?"

She couldn't very well make him do that. She lifted the chain lock from its track and turned the knob that released the bolt on the second lock beneath it. Cal was wearing black leather all right—a motorcycle jacket—and he was carrying a helmet. She'd never have guessed he rode a motorcycle. She wondered how much more there might be about him that she'd never guessed.

Since she hadn't stepped aside or invited him in, he said what he'd come to say right there in the hall.

"That bilge pump didn't go off by itself last night. Somebody tried to scuttle the *Lettie*."

Chapter Seven

Abbie was the one who'd insisted they go to the Keystone, the twenty-four-hour diner near her subway stop. She'd said she was hungry, but what she really wanted was not to be alone with Cal. Her willpower wasn't strong enough for that. The mere thought of his warm hands caressing her through the whisper-thin green silk caftan had set her pulses leaping, and she was determined to keep her pulse rate as normal as possible with him till she had answers to a few questions. So she'd thrown on some clothes and marched him up Thirtieth Avenue.

They were in the diner now, speaking softly across the table to keep their conversation from being overheard.

Cal had already explained that he'd gone over the *Lettie*'s pump mechanism himself several times, turning it off and starting it up again. Abbie had been reminded of herself, trying the key to her apartment over and over, searching for the truth about why her door had been unlocked. Cal's conclusion about the pump was that it had been deliberately disconnected sometime last evening, then reconnected early this morning before Sam got to the pier. In between that time, the *Lettie* had sunk so deep it was a miracle they'd been able to save her.

"What does Sam say?" Abbie asked.

"He insists it was equipment failure." In response to her skeptical look, Cal reached over and took her hand. "You have to understand that just about everybody down there has his or her own special ax to grind. Sam's is the equipment and how obsolete and out of repair it is."

"Well, isn't it?" On the pretense of taking a drink of coffee, she eased her hand from his.

"Yes, but old equipment isn't necessarily the fall guy for everything. Sam won't let himself see that, because it doesn't support his campaign to get more maintenance funds for the ships."

"So you think you're right about somebody deliberately trying to sink the *Lettie*, and Sam refuses to go along with that for his own reasons?"

"Right."

"What are your reasons?"

"I'm not sure I know what you mean." Cal looked genuinely puzzled. He also looked extraordinarily handsome. He'd taken off the leather jacket, and his white T-shirt left nothing to the imagination concerning his broad chest and muscular arms.

As she waited to answer until after the waitress had put down their plates and moved away from the table, Abbie vowed not to be swayed by the way she felt just sitting across from him.

"If everybody at the Seaport has his own ax to grind, what's yours? Why is a very busy, successful businessman like you spending so much time and effort on a few old boats?"

A forkful of pasta paused halfway to his mouth while he regarded her curiously for a moment. Then he set the fork down on the edge of his plate. "It's a long story," he said.

"I've got all evening." She'd almost said she had all night but thought better of it.

"It started with the neighborhood I grew up in, an area of Brooklyn that wasn't much different from the way the Seaport district used to be—old buildings, narrow streets, lots of character. Most of the families on our block had lived there all their lives, some for generations. Nobody had much money, but it was a place you could feel you belonged to. I felt that way growing up there."

Abbie nodded. She'd missed that feeling in the insulated Maryland town she came from, with its proper lawns separating proper houses and the equally proper lives inside them.

"I imagine where you're living now is that kind of neighborhood," Cal said.

"I hope so."

He smiled at her, and that smile warmed her more than the hot coffee had done.

"Well, we moved away from there," he went on. "That's what prosperity does to you sometimes. You leave behind the things that really matter, then spend the rest of your life trying to get back to them. Unfortunately, by the time I realized that, the old neighborhood was gone. They'd torn it down and put up a shopping mall. I remember the first time I went back there and saw that." His chuckle had a rueful sound. "I felt like somebody had ripped out part of my life and stuck a K-Mart in its place. The experience made a powerful impression on me."

"What does that have to do with your involvement at the museum?"

"We'll have to flash a few years ahead in the story of my life for the answer."

"I'm listening."

Cal leaned closer and looked deep into her eyes. "You're sure I'm not boring you with all this?"

"Of course not." The truth was, nothing had ever bored her less than listening to Cal Quinn.

"Well, I was all grown up and in business for myself by then, and my office overlooked the Seaport. Staring down at those old buildings got me through many a dull business conference. I'd become very attached to the place. Then I heard somebody was making a move to grab a number of those properties, tear them down and put up condominiums. I couldn't sit there and let another part of my life be destroyed in the name of commerce. So I stuck my two cents in and never took them out again."

"And you kept the property deal from going through?"

"That's right."

"How?"

"That's another long story, and I'm tired of talking about myself." He had his elbows on the table and his hands clasped against his square chin. Sinew ran tautly beneath the golden gloss of fine hair on his forearms. "Now, you tell me something," he said. "Why this third degree?"

"I just had a few unanswered questions."

"What else?"

"Did you send Josie up to my office that first day?" Abbie had spoken quickly and in one breath, for fear she might say nothing otherwise.

"Of course not. Why would I do that?"

"To shake me up and get me off to a bad start."

"Whatever for?"

"Because you'd already handpicked someone you wanted in the job instead of me."

"Oh, that." Cal settled back in the booth with a sigh. Abbie's heart fell. She'd hoped he would deny that, also.

"It's true," he said. "I had someone in mind for the summer consultant spot, but that was before I met you.

Now I'm glad we hired you. As for my being against your appointment before, you'll have to accept it and forget it, just like I've decided to accept the fact that you're a dedicated free-lance type and will be out of our lives in a few more weeks, maybe never to return.''

Abbie had the feeling he'd wanted to say this before.

"That's why I walked out on you that morning in the John Street Diner. I realized you were just a short-timer at the museum, one of the summer people who come in for the season and then move on. My more cautious instincts told me to get away from you fast. I'd already begun to care more than was wise under the circumstances. Then I saw you the next day in Les's office, and caution went out the window.''

Abbie opened her mouth to respond, though she wasn't certain what to say. But before she could utter a word, Cal reached across the table and placed a finger gently against her lips. "We'll talk about that another time. Till then, just think about it. Right now I'd like to know if there are any more doubts you have about me.''

"Just one.''

"And what might that be?''

"Did you deliberately monopolize the news spot on Channel 7?''

Cal's laugh rumbled forth as it had that first day in her office. The waitress was passing by and glanced at him with a definitely appreciative smile.

"Let's just say the young lady who did the interview had more than professional interests at heart.''

"Did you satisfy those interests?'' The question popped out before Abbie could stop it.

"No, I didn't. She's not my type.'' He spoke the next sentence so low Abbie could barely hear it. "You should know what my type is.'' Then he was leaning across the table again, clasping her hand and looking very intently into her eyes. "It's crucial that we trust each other, because we're going to have to work together to figure out what's going on. You see, I think it's all connected."

"What do you mean?" Abbie's voice, like his, had dropped to an urgent whisper.

"What's been happening to you and this thing with the *Lettie*. I strongly suspect it's all being done by the same person."

"But why?"

"That's what you and I have to figure out."

"Shouldn't we go to the police or somebody?"

"They'd never believe us. They'd take Sam's word over mine about the pump on the *Lettie*, and they'd think I was just as paranoid as everybody says you are for believing someone's harassing you."

"That's true." Abbie sighed. This situation was getting too complicated for her. Her first impulse was to quit the Seaport altogether and find another assignment. Then she remembered what Cal had said about her being a short-timer and the look in his eyes when he said it. "Do you really think the incidents are connected?"

"I don't believe in coincidence, and it's too coincidental that these crazy things are all happening at once."

"What can we do?"

"Just think about it for now and try to come up with some possible explanation." He was still holding her hand. He closed his other palm over it. "You're going to have a lot to think about tonight, aren't you?"

THE NEXT NIGHT there was a party aboard the *Peking*. All of the museum staff was expected to attend, including the volunteers. The idea was to encourage good working relationships for the season ahead. Meredith had begged off, saying she had to drive to Connecticut to do something for her mother. So Abbie was on her own. Neither she nor Cal had mentioned the party the night before, though she'd wanted to ask if he was going. After the Keystone, they'd parted in front of her apartment building without the embrace or kiss she sensed was on his mind as much as both were on hers. She understood that, before they got any more involved with each other, he wanted her to think about what he'd said earlier.

She'd hardly been able to think about anything else since. He said he'd been worried about caring for her more than was wise. She'd been remembering those words off and on all day, and they'd sung through her heart every time. She knew she'd cared more about Cal than was wise from almost the first moment she'd seen him. Somehow, wisdom didn't seem so important where her feelings for him were concerned.

No one knew better than Abbie how painful it could be to fall in love. She'd watched relationships come apart for as long as she could remember, from the silent impasse of her parents' armed truce to her own divorce to many friends with ill-fated love affairs. Still, she couldn't seem to help what she felt for Cal, and what was more, she didn't want to. She believed what he'd said last night. She trusted him, and nothing else mattered.

It was past dusk as Abbie walked down Pier 16 toward the second gangway of the *Peking*. The sky showed a deep, dark blue through the crosshatch of shrouds and spars above the ship's deck, and the breeze carried a welcome hint of coolness after the heat of the late-June day. Sweeping cables along the Brooklyn Bridge laced a filigree of light across the river. The sounds of the city were muted by the darkness, and the Seaport had taken on a hushed beauty very much unlike the brightly colored spectacle of the day.

The long, upward slant of the gangway was lit by a spotlight mounted in the ship's rigging. Its rosy beam caught the sprinkle of sequins among the white chiffon layers of her skirt and set them sparkling as she climbed the gangway toward the deck. The bodice of her dress was plain, white chiffon draped Grecian style across her breasts; she wore a crystal pendant on a delicate silver chain. High-heeled turquoise sandals matched the clips in her hair that held the tumble of red-blond curls at the top of her head.

She heard murmurs of approval from along the ship's rail and tried not to be visibly excited by the thought that Cal might be among those watching her. Her heart skittered faster for an instant when a tall, broad-shouldered man in a white dinner jacket reached up to take her hand as she paused at the top of the gangway. Then he moved into the spotlight, and she saw he was no one she recognized. She took his hand in her gloved fingers and let him assist her down the few steps to the deck, while she smiled graciously to disguise the sting of disappointment she was feeling.

The *Peking* had been transformed into an exclusive waterfront salon for the night. Pink-and-gold lanterns strung overhead cast the wide deck in a twilight glow. Guests in evening dress clustered among white-clothed tables circling a dance floor. The women in filmy gowns and the men in dinner jackets reminded Abbie of a movie scene, too elegant to be real in the soft, intentionally flattering light. But her gaze didn't rest too long on anyone as she searched the deck for Cal, becoming more convinced by the moment that he wasn't there.

She maneuvered through the crowd and climbed the narrow stairs to the bridge deck to get a better view of the guests below. A bar had been set up on the bridge; a handsome young waiter flashed her an inviting grin and asked what she would like to drink. Abbie accepted a glass of mineral water, just so she'd have something to hold in her hand, then retreated from the waiter's appreciative gaze.

The deck was dominated by a large cabin known as the Chart House. Abbie wandered up to the doorway and saw Nathan Mallory bent over one of the glass display cases, staring intently at its contents. Since he was very shy, he was almost the last person she'd expect to find at an event like this. He didn't look as if he belonged here, either. His dark suit was rumpled and too large for him. His wide trouser cuffs fell in folds that nearly covered scuffed, brown shoes, and he'd buttoned his shirt fastidiously to the collar, though he wore no tie.

"Hello, Nathan," she said.

She hadn't meant to startle him, but apparently that wasn't difficult to do. He jerked suddenly around, his sleeve upsetting a plastic cup on the corner of the display case.

"Oh, no. Look what I've done!" He dragged a large graying handkerchief from his pocket and bent to mop up the spill, letting his bountiful cuffs trail in the puddle.

Abbie smiled sympathetically at his befuddlement. "What are you looking at?" She turned her attention to the case, pretending not to have noticed his awkwardness.

"That's a sextant," he said, straightening up and stuffing the drenched handkerchief back in his pocket.

"What is it used for?" Abbie might not be an expert on ships, but she already knew the answer. She was also aware that Nathan's one apparent accomplishment was his knowledge of the ships, and she thought he might be put more at ease if he could display some of that knowledge.

"They used the sextant to navigate by the stars back when sailing ships were the common mode of sea travel." He spoke so stiffly he sounded a little like a tour-guide manual. Then he leaned toward the case once more, as if transfixed by the polished brass instrument. For an instant he seemed different, almost poised. "It's very beautiful, isn't it?" he said.

Abbie nodded. "You know a lot about these old ships, don't you, Nathan?"

"What? Oh, well, you might say they're sort of a hobby of mine. That is, in a way I guess you'd call it that." His moment of poise had passed, and he was as agitated as ever. "Did you know the *Peking* used to carry an acre of sail?" He was sounding like a tour manual again.

"It seems to me I read that somewhere."

"Oh, yes, I suppose you did."

He'd set the cup back on the case, and his sleeve was flailing dangerously close to it. Abbie moved it out of harm's way to the windowsill.

"I bet you'd have liked to live in those days," she said, searching for some topic that would distract him from his nervousness. "Maybe you could have been a sailor on this very ship."

"Oh, no. I get terribly seasick, even in a rowboat. And then, well, I'm afraid of things."

"What things, Nathan?"

"All kinds of things." He made a small laughing sound and looked at her sheepishly. He seemed very pleased that she was interested, even in his neuroses. "For instance, high places. I'm very afraid of high places. In fact, would you like to know a secret?"

"Yes, of course, if you'd like to tell me."

"I had a hard time just coming up the gangway to get aboard this ship. I have to look straight ahead and recite the alphabet to myself so I won't think about the water being down there under me." He took a deep breath and let it out, then looked away from her, his eyes darting frantically around as if he were afraid someone else might have heard his revelation.

Abbie couldn't help smiling with affectionate compassion. He reminded her of a particularly awkward puppy in need of special protection.

"Everybody has fears like that," she said, trying once again to set him at ease.

"Really? What are you afraid of?"

"Well..." Abbie knew she'd better come up with something. "Parties like this one." She'd said the first thing that came to mind.

"Crowds, you mean. You're afraid of crowds." He sounded almost gleeful to learn that someone else was as phobic as he. "That's why you're up here on the bridge deck. You're hiding from the crowd."

Abbie smiled a little uneasily. She didn't want her small pretense to get out of hand. "But I love to watch. Let's go outside and watch the crowd."

Nathan followed her reluctantly. He didn't talk about phobias any more once they were out on the bridge deck, which made Abbie feel relieved. She understood that it was a subject he could warm to readily, but she didn't want to deceive him, even in a little way.

After they'd stood at the rail for a while, looking down at the deck, Nathan said, "He's not here. Cal doesn't come to things like this."

Abbie was so startled to have her thoughts read that she nearly toppled her own drink over the rail. "What makes you think I'm looking for Mr. Quinn?"

"Please, I didn't mean to make you mad at me. I just thought you might like to know."

"That's all right, Nathan."

"You see, I saw you together at the *Lettie*, and I could tell you were really good friends. So I just thought..." His voice trailed off.

"You were absolutely right about that, Nathan. Mr. Quinn and I are really good friends."

A band had begun to play directly across from them on the poop deck, which thrust out toward the river. The strains of a ballad drifted over on the evening breeze.

"I don't imagine you'd like to dance?"

Abbie was sure her ears had played a trick on her.

"We don't have to go down where the crowd is," Nathan added. "We could dance up here."

She couldn't refuse, of course, though she did think for a moment of her satin sandals at the mercy of his scuffed toes. Fortunately Nathan had another surprise in store for her. He guided her in a circle on the empty deck with an ease he certainly didn't possess ordinarily, and he didn't step on her feet once. She considered the venture a great success and applauded enthusiastically when the music stopped.

"Thank you, Nathan. That was very nice."

He managed a shy smile and darted his gaze up into the rigging. His interlude of social grace hadn't extended beyond the dance floor. In fact, Abbie suspected he might be about to retreat into another dissertation on the *Peking*'s acres of sail.

"Would you mind getting me something to drink?" she asked, to rescue them both from his awkwardness.

"Oh, yes. I mean, no, I wouldn't mind at all. Do you like champagne? They have champagne down on the main deck. I'll get you champagne."

Before Abbie could tell him that she'd just as soon have a glass of club soda, he was off across the bridge toward the steps leading to the deck below.

"You must be a miracle worker. Nathan usually spends evenings like this cowering in a corner."

Abbie turned to find Cal standing next to her. "Where did you materialize from?"

"I came up the other gangway." He gestured toward the bow of the ship, which jutted over the apron of the pier.

Abbie was only partially prepared for how incredible Cal looked in evening clothes. His dinner jacket wasn't white like most of the others, but deep blue with an iridescent lighter blue thread laced through it. The lapels were navy satin, and his shirtfront gleamed a shimmering white in the lantern light. A matching satin tie sat jauntily between the small points of the shirt collar at his throat. No doubt about it, Cal Quinn was definitely the most dapper-looking man on board.

"I'd have been here earlier, but I was checking on the deployment of troops." He flashed a smile at her.

"What troops?" Abbie smiled back at his whimsical tone.

"Extra security. I hired them myself. They're mingling with the crowd. I thought the additional protection would be a wise precaution."

"I haven't noticed any security guards."

"They're in evening dress, so they won't be conspicuous. There's one of them now." He pointed down over the rail at the broad-shouldered man who'd assisted Abbie off the gangway.

"He certainly doesn't look like a policeman."

"That's the secret of good undercover work. You must be new to the cloak-and-dagger business."

"Yes, I'm glad to say I am, but you seem to be an old hand at it and enjoying it, too."

"Not really, but I'll tell you what I would enjoy." His glance slid over her, and his amused smile softened into something more intimate. "I'd like to dance with you. If you haven't promised them all to Nathan, that is."

"I hope you aren't making fun of him," she replied a little sharply, rising to the defense of the helpless puppy once more.

"I'd never do that."

"Actually, he's quite a good dancer."

"I'm not surprised. That blueblood family of his probably sent him to dance classes before he could walk, whether he wanted to go or not."

"I would never have thought Nathan came from that kind of background."

"Back Bay Boston all the way. I know his family. In fact, that's why I'd never make fun of him. They ridicule him more than enough already."

"Nathan's family does that?"

"Mercilessly."

"But why?"

"Because they're pinch-faced Yankees, and Nathan hasn't lived up to the Mallory tradition."

"How cruel of them."

Abbie's protective instincts toward Nathan were stronger than ever. She was glad she'd spent time talking with him before. She was even glad she'd told him that fib about hiding up on the bridge deck because she was afraid of crowds. Anything that made such an unfortunate person feel more comfortable was justified in her estimation.

"How do you know his family?" she asked.

"One of my interests is shipping, especially through Boston. The Mallorys are in the shipping business, and I have some dealings with Nathan's brother, William. He's a powerful man who gets just about whatever he wants in Boston. And one thing old William wants is his black-sheep brother out of his hair.''

"Don't they have anything to do with Nathan at all?''

"I understand they keep him on an allowance. He has to show up periodically to collect so that William can keep an eye on him, but between collections the family doesn't want to know Nathan's alive.''

"Poor Nathan.''

"I'd feel sorry for anyone who had William for a brother. I've never heard him say a kind word about any-one or anything. No, wait a minute. That's not right. He thinks the world of your assistant.''

"Meredith? How does he know her?''

"Apparently he had to locate Nathan through her a couple of times and was impressed by her efficiency. Too bad he couldn't spare some of that praise for his brother. But that's beside the point. I didn't come over to you to talk about Nathan. We have more urgent matters to discuss. First, though, I'd like that dance I asked for.''

"Nathan went to get me champagne. I should wait for him to come back.''

"I don't think he'll be back. I saw him escaping up the gangway a moment ago.''

Abbie scanned the crowded deck below. She didn't see Nathan anywhere.

"I don't mean he was escaping from you, of course. What man in his right mind would want to do that, espe-cially the way you look tonight?''

Abbie turned toward him, and their gazes locked for a long moment. She felt as if she could stand there staring into his eyes forever. Then he took her arm gently and asked, "Would you like to dance up here or down there with the crowd?"

"Right here will be fine." Suddenly Abbie disliked crowds almost as much as she'd led Nathan to believe she did

Cal guided her into his arms. His fingers fitted into the curve just above her hip, and he pressed her close to him. His embrace was so tender it sent shivers through her, and when he bent to touch his cheek to hers, his skin felt surprisingly warm. She wondered if he might be feeling emotions as powerful as her own. She could hear the calm, steady measure of his breath near her ear, which was belied by his holding her as if he never wanted to let her go.

He was a wonderful dancer. They seemed to flow together across the deck. Any minute now, Abbie thought, she would melt into him and they'd be one forever. The sensation was both hypnotic and alarming. Abbie wasn't sure she was ready for it. She remembered what Cal had said about cautioning himself not to care for her too much because their future was so uncertain. Maybe she should be just as cautious.

"What were those urgent matters you mentioned that we have to discuss?" she asked, hoping to break the spell between them or at least lessen its intensity.

"Not now. We'll talk later," he murmured into her ear.

His voice was even deeper than usual, and a slight tremor was barely audible beneath his quiet words. Suddenly Abbie knew he was also powerfully moved by their closeness. With one last, fleeting thought about caution, she let herself surrender to that power, if only until the dance ended.

When it was over, they were standing near the base of the tall mast, just beyond the bridge-deck rail. Abbie wondered if Cal could really be as unruffled as he seemed.

She was still a little light-headed from the high emotion of their dance.

"Have you been thinking about what we discussed last night?" he asked.

"We discussed a lot of things last night." At least she could sound as cool as he did.

"I'm referring to our waterfront conspiracy."

"Do you really think that's what it is?"

"It may be a conspiracy of one, but there's some kind of plan in the works. I'd bet on it, and we have the unenviable assignment of trying to figure out what that plan is."

"Then we should concentrate on motive first." If sleuthing was what they were going to do together on this beautiful summer evening, Abbie didn't intend to be outdone.

"Any ideas?"

"Well, for one thing, I'm sure it involves more than me and my job. It doesn't make sense that someone would go to all this trouble just to get rid of a publicity consultant."

"Especially a publicity consultant who plans to leave soon anyway."

"Right." Abbie heard the pointed way he'd said that, but she let it pass for now. "So I think we can assume whatever our culprit is after has something to do with the museum in general."

"You're pretty good at this after all!"

"I read a lot of Nancy Drew when I was a kid."

Abbie also had a knack for strategy and problem solving. That was why she'd been so successful at her work. She was aware of those abilities in herself, yet she'd never felt quite as gratified by them as she did right now, in the warmth of Cal's praise.

"If I recall those stories correctly, the most popular villainous motives were power and money."

"And love," he added

'There wasn't much of that in Nancy Drew. Those were kids' books, remember?"

"Thank heaven little girls grow up eventually." He'd moved closer. "Maurice Chevalier was directly on target about that."

"Maurice Chevalier would have made a lousy detective."

"All right. I get the message." He took hold of her shoulders and pushed himself an arm's length away. "I put my money on money."

"What?"

"The motive. I say it's money," he said, stroking his thumbs along the bare skin of her upper arms.

"Why do you think that?" She reached up and lifted his hands from her shoulders.

"Because there's not enough power involved in the museum for anybody to bother with," he replied, clasping her fingers.

"Is there enough money? I understood the museum was pretty shaky financially."

"It is, except for the real estate."

He'd been easing closer again, his fingers entwined through hers. Her surprise at his words made her pull her hands suddenly from his.

"You mean the buildings the museum owns in the Seaport district?"

"Those very ones."

"They must be worth a fortune now that the area's been developed like it has."

"A bigger fortune every year, or maybe even every month, the way property values have been skyrocketing in this city."

"Do you think somebody could be after that fortune?"

"Yes, I do."

"So whoever it is sabotages the program to cut into revenues and, at the same time, makes the place look bad to discourage contributions and other kinds of funding. Before long, the museum has to sell off those properties for whatever it can get, and our villain steps in for the take. Even if he has to pay a healthy price, the value will go up fast and he'll still make a huge profit."

Cal had been advancing steadily toward her as she was thinking out loud. Abbie put her hand against his white shirtfront and stopped him in his tracks. "Who?" she asked.

"My vote goes to Lester Girard."

"But you said he's broke."

"Exactly. That's why he needs to do something like this. In fact, he's even more broke than I thought. He'd let the insurance lapse on the XKE."

"Then where would he get the money to buy up the museum properties?"

"You can always find backers for a deal like that. New York is full of silent partners looking to make a killing. With all the hours he's clocked at Dunn and Bradstreet, it's my guess our Lester knows every one of those money men personally."

"It's an interesting theory, but that's all it is. You need proof."

"That's where you come in."

Cal stepped close again and slipped his arms around her waist too firmly for her to push him away this time. She had to lean back to see his face and try to read what was in his eyes.

"What do you mean?" she asked.

"I need to have Les lured away from his office long enough for me to search his desk and files."

"I take it you want me to be the bait."

"And 'tis sure a prettier minnow there never was," Cal said in a brogue as Irish as his name.

Chapter Eignt

The first dance was bad, the second was worse, and the third was excruciating. Abbie's sandals had survived Nathan only to be sacrificed to Lester. He'd had much too much of "the bubbly," as he called it, and he was very unsteady. Yet he refused to sit on the bench near the mast, as Abbie had urged him to do.

"I have to stay on my feet," he mumbled in the vicinity of her ear as he bobbed back and forth. "I can't let any of them see this get me down. They're all waiting for that to happen. They'd get such pleasure out of it."

"I'm sure that's not true."

"It's true all right. They'd love to see me fall flat on my face." He teetered as if he might be about to do just that. Abbie made a fast step out of the range of his patent leather evening loafers, which could do painful damage no matter how chic they looked.

"They're all jealous of me," he said. "Have been from the start."

"I see."

Abbie understood that he was telling her things he would never have mentioned if he were cold sober. Ordinarily she would have discouraged him from saying more. She'd probably even excuse herself from his presence altogether, but tonight she had a mission—two missions, as a matter of fact. First, she had to keep Lester busy till Cal got back from searching his office; second, she had a suspect to investigate.

"Who exactly would like to see you fall on your face?" she asked.

"All the pompous asses down here," he blurted out, lurching forward with the emotion of his outburst.

"Do you think we could possibly sit this one out?" Abbie pleaded. "I'm a bit tired." She'd maneuvered them over to the mast, where they'd been rocking back and forth for the past several minutes in a tipsy pretense at dancing. "We'll just skip this number. Then we'll be right back up there showing them how," she said, easing him onto the bench.

"I'll show them all right." He was mumbling again.

"How will you do that?"

"I have my ways."

"Are you sure they'll work?" Abbie's detecting assignment had made her bold.

He leaned forward with a bleary grin. "Nobody knows how to make a deal better than I do, and I'm going to make a big one."

"That sounds very interesting."

"Of course it's interesting. Everything I do is interesting. But no details. Loose lips sink ships, you know," he said with a giggle and a fling of his arm to indicate their nautical setting.

Abbie smiled obligingly but couldn't manage a laugh. She wished she could get more out of him. What he'd said so far certainly sounded as if Cal's theory might be correct. Lester's big deal could very possibly involve the Seaport property. It was feasible that he might plan to get his special revenge against the people he perceived to be his enemies by slipping a fast one through right under their noses.

"I'm going back to the office now," he said suddenly. He looked as if he wasn't feeling well. "You'll have to excuse me."

The museum gossips had implied that Lester had been having trouble with his wife lately, along with everything else that was going wrong for him. Rumor had it he'd slept on the couch in his office the past few nights. Perhaps that was what he had in mind now. Somehow Abbie had to stop him.

"But you promised me another dance," she said sweetly.

"I'm sorry, my dear. I wouldn't disappoint you for the world, but I think my dancing days are over, for this evening at least. I'll make it up to you another time."

His black tie was askew, and two studs had popped open on his shirtfront. Even he had enough good sense left to know it was time for a quiet retreat. She'd have to think of some other way to keep him from discovering what Cal was doing.

"I'll come with you," she offered.

"If you're making a pass at me, Abbie, I'm afraid you've picked a bad moment."

"Cal Quinn told me to keep an eye on you."

"Quinn? Why would he do that?" Lester sounded immediately suspicious.

"He was very concerned about you tonight. He made me promise to stick with you."

Abbie told herself that none of what she was saying was actually a lie, at least not technically speaking. Even so, she didn't feel comfortable about playing this kind of game with the man who was, in reality, her boss. If he got wind of what she was doing, she'd be unemployed by morning—no job, no reference, all of her hard work to create an ımpressive professional reputation set back a giant step in one evening.

Lester weaved up off the bench. "I'd have thought Quinn would be the last person to worry about me. I'm flattered."

He let her take his arm and move into step next to him. Whether it was comfortable for her or not, the game was working. Apparently, anything that appealed to Lester's ego had a good chance of success. Abbie made a mental note of that.

"Let's go this way," she said, turning him from the direction of the spotlighted gangway and toward the less conspicuous exit at the shore end of the ship.

ABOVE WHERE THE PAIR had just been standing, a shape hung motionless, too heavy to be swayed by the summer breeze. Behind the Chart House, out of the light, the Captain drew his cape around him. He hadn't worn his scabbard tonight, so that dark folds wrapped him closely. He looked like just another shadow on the deck as he cursed the woman who'd foiled his plan.

ABBIE MANEUVERED HERSELF and Lester in such a way that she was the first to turn into the hall where his office was located. She saw the light under his door and began talking immediately in a loud voice.

"I've been researching the history of the museum, and there's something I simply have to tell you." She'd stopped walking and positioned herself so that Lester would have to face away from his office to look at her. She prayed she'd be able to distract him enough that he wouldn't turn around. "I think you've done a marvelous job of holding the line through a difficult time."

She could no longer concern herself with whether she told even the technical truth, especially since falsehood seemed to be working so effectively. Lester was giving her his full though intoxicated attention. Out of the corner of her eye, she saw the light disappear beneath his office door.

"How perceptive of you to notice." Lester beamed from ear to ear. "So few people around here have. But then they're all cretins, aren't they, my dear."

To Abbie's horror, he started down the hall, propelled into a burst of steadiness by her praise. She had to think fast or he'd be onto Cal very soon. She grabbed the silver chain at her throat, pulled it and then flung it ahead of them both. The crystal made a small clicking sound as it hit the floor and bounced, somewhere past Lester's door, along the shadowy hall.

"Oh, no! Look what I've done!" she cried in what sounded like true distress. "My grandmother's necklace—it's my most prized possession. Please, help me find it."

She rushed past his office, holding her breath to see if he'd follow. He hesitated only a moment before his sense of drunken chivalry took over.

"Don't worry, my dear. I'll find your heirloom."

He lurched after her, crouching to peer into the far corner where she was pointing. She'd read him right again. A man like Lester couldn't resist the chance to play the rescuing knight to her damsel in need of assistance. In his condition, it took only a slight nudge against his shoulder to send him toppling to his knees in the corner.

"Oh, I'm sorry," she whined, hardly able to believe she was capable of sounding like such a silly little fool. "Let me help you."

In the scramble that followed, with Abbie hauling on Lester's arm while actually tripping him up again, she saw Cal slip out of the office door and down the hall. Lester didn't notice a thing.

"Here it is!" she cried when the coast was clear. She scooped up the necklace from where she'd seen it fall earlier and cupped it in her hand so Lester couldn't see it was hardly old enough to be even a one-generation heirloom. "Thank you so much for helping," she gushed. "You can't imagine how much it means to me." She was back to part truths again.

"Happy to be of service, my dear," Lester said, staggering to his feet and brushing at the dusty knees of his black evening trousers.

The smile Abbie shone on him couldn't have been more sincerely relieved.

IT HAD TAKEN a few more flattering fibs for Abbie to get away from Lester; then she'd gone down to her office and collapsed in her chair. A few minutes later Cal slipped through the door and closed it behind him.

"You were wonderful," he said.

"You owe me one silver chain."

"It's yours."

"So what did you find?"

Cal lowered his lanky body into the worn leather chair opposite her desk. "Nothing, I'm afraid. If there's any evidence to implicate Lester, then he's smart enough to keep it somewhere other than in his office. What about you? Did you get anything out of him?"

"Several fractured toes. And by the way, add a pair of turquoise satin sandals to the list of what you owe me for letting myself be talked into this caper."

"I know this was duty above and beyond the call, but believe me, I'll make it up to you."

He'd moved forward from the chair in a movement too fluid to be disturbing, yet Abbie was disturbed by it all the same. His fingers were resting on the edge of her desk. In the circle of light from the desk lamp she could see the luster of the fine golden hairs on the backs of his hands. He bent toward her, and she felt the power of him reaching out to her like a magnet with an irresistible draw. The soft persuasiveness of his voice made Abbie think it might be difficult to deny this man anything. She leaned back out of the lamplight so the high color she felt in her cheeks would be less visible.

"Lester did some babbling that could be incriminating," she said to break the magnet's pull. She had to remember there was urgent business at hand.

"What was it?" Cal asked, settling reluctantly back in his chair.

"Nothing specific, but he was going on about some big deal he's planning that will show up everybody down here who's been against him."

"Finessing the museum out of its property would certainly do that."

"Yes, it would, but I couldn't get him to say anything specific."

"You did well. I think we make a great team."

"We're a regular Nick and Nora Charles."

"I was thinking more on the order of Jonathan and Jennifer Hart. They always end up mulling over their exploits in his monogrammed silk pajamas. She wears the tops. He wears the bottoms, at least while the camera's on them."

Cal was beyond the circle of light now, also. His eyes were dark shadows among the chiseled lines of his face.

Abbie couldn't really see his expression, but she felt what was in the air between them, strong and taut, like a wire pulling toward its highest tension.

"I have to go back down to the pier to check with my security people," he said. She could hear the quiet control in his voice, and she sensed the effort he was making to keep it there. "Why don't you come with me? Then we'll call it a night."

He stood up, walked around the desk and took her arm to ease her out of the chair. There was hardly any pressure in his fingers, yet she felt compelled to rise. He didn't try to embrace or kiss her, but she could see his eyes now. In their depths was the promise that there'd be time for that later, when his business was finished.

In silent acknowledgment of that promise, Abbie followed him out of the office. Cal didn't let go of her arm all the way down Schermerhorn Row and across South Street toward the pier gate.

"Look, there's Sam."

Cal waved at the man hurrying across the parking lot away from the far gate. It was Sam all right, in a plaid shirt and jeans as usual. He apparently didn't hear Cal and kept on going down South Street.

"I didn't see him at the party," Abbie said.

"Sam refuses to go to affairs like that. Phoebe tries to coax him into it, but he can be as stubborn as a bull moose when he wants to be."

"I heard you don't come to affairs like that either."

"That's right. I don't."

"What made you change your mind tonight?"

He turned toward her. "Tonight's gathering had special attractions."

"The chance to play Jonathan and Jennifer?"

"I don't own any monogrammed silk pajamas."

They'd reached the pier gate. Cal let go of her arm with a small squeeze that said he'd be back in a moment. Then he walked off toward the pilothouse ticket booth, which was the center of security operations for the evening. Abbie watched him go, thinking how much she liked the way he moved. She couldn't remember ever seeing anything more thoroughly masculine than the rhythm of his hips and shoulders as he strode down the dock. A few minutes later, as he walked toward her, that rhythm had turned suddenly urgent.

"They found a block and tackle hanging in the ship's rigging," he said. "It was strung to be released by a rope run down behind the Chart House. That size block and tackle could do a lot of damage if it dropped on somebody."

"Where exactly was it hanging?" Abbie could already feel the answer to that in the tightness of her throat.

"From the crow's nest of the mast near the bridge-deck rail. Right over where you were standing most of the evening."

Chapter Nine

It was Sunday morning, and Abbie was still trying to find a way to convince herself the living nightmare wasn't happening. She didn't want to believe there was some kind of murky scheme in which she was somehow involved, or that, just last night, somebody had rigged a heavy block and tackle to smash her against the deck of the *Peking*. That was why she'd kept her eyes closed long after she had awakened. She knew, once she opened them, that reality would be right here in her bedroom, waiting for her to face all of it, including what had happened last night. Then she'd have to admit she was afraid.

She'd insisted that Cal leave after he'd driven her home from the Seaport. She'd also insisted that whoever had set up the block and tackle wasn't after her specifically. He only wanted to disrupt the party and put another black mark against the museum program. She'd just happened to be standing there so much of the time last night. It was simply a coincidence. She'd insisted on that vehemently. Otherwise, she might have succumbed, right in front of Cal, to the panic she felt lurking in the corners of her bedroom this morning.

Abbie opened her eyes slowly. The white ceiling reflected pale morning sunshine in a soft glow. Nothing could have looked less sinister. She had to maintain control. She mustn't be thinking about panic or anything even vaguely related to it. That wasn't how Abigail Louise Tanner operated. She had to think her way through this, the way she always thought her way through problems, to find the logical conclusion.

In fact, she had an idea already. The museum library had files on the development of the Seaport district, the deals that had gone through and those which hadn't. Maybe there was something in the files to indicate Lester's interest in the museum properties, or somebody else's. Abbie didn't care so much who the villain turned out to be, just as long as he was caught.

She kicked off the summer-weight comforter with the blue forget-me-nots on it and sprang out of bed. After taking a quick shower, she put on her favorite casual outfit: roomy, purple fatigue pants, a tank top in a paler shade of purple, a white linen jacket and sandals. She intended to start her search of those files right away, even if it meant going to the office on the weekend. Abbie was so anxious to get there she took a cab.

She'd used the museum library extensively while researching for her publicity campaign, so she had a key to the place. The long room she let herself into smelled of dusty books with a hint of salt air thrown in. The museum's collection of ship models was stored here along with books and articles on everything related to the sea, but Abbie wasn't interested in any of that now. She hurried straight to the file cabinets along the wall. As the file drawer creaked open at her touch, it occurred to Abbie that maybe she shouldn't be here all alone, considering what had gone on lately. She forced the thought from her mind and began leafing through manila folders.

The files on the Seaport development were pretty much what she'd expected, and she didn't find Lester Girard mentioned anywhere. Everything important seemed to have happened before he became museum director, and very little since. She was more amazed than ever that he'd believed her line last night about how much he'd accomplished. She understood better now why Cal had such a low opinion of him. Still, that didn't help in terms of what she was looking for. She was almost ready to give up and go home when a yellowed clipping caught her eye.

She read the first paragraph, but it was the usual stuff about bids for area properties back in the commercial development phase of the Seaport district renovation. She wondered why she'd thought she'd be interested in this particular item. Maybe something farther down had captured her attention. She read on. She found it in the third paragraph and knew at once why she hadn't been able to pass this clipping by

"One of the most aggressive bidders for waterfront property is Calhoun Quinn, owner and president of Urban Horizons, Incorporated," she read. "Mr. Quinn's plan to purchase several properties and raze them for residential development was defeated in favor of historic restoration of those properties. Asked his reaction to that, Quinn replied, 'I'll never give up on those buildings. I'll own them someday, one way or another.'"

Abbie leaned back in the wooden library chair and let the clipping fall back with the others on the oak table. That quote certainly didn't sound like the Cal Quinn who'd sat in the Keystone Diner the other night and told her about his dedication to architectural preservation. It sounded like a businessman with big profits on his mind. Suddenly she remembered something Meredith had said about Cal's being one of a long line of wheeler-dealers. Even so, Abbie had to be sure. She put the clippings back in their folders and hurried to the cabinet to refile them.

Around the block at the museum offices, she took the stairs from the street two at a time. Once more, she was the only person in the place as she passed her own office door and went into the volunteer center instead. She located Cal's file easily among the files for volunteer personnel. Near the top of his folder was a photocopied page from *Who's Who in American Business*. From what she'd heard about the extent of his holdings, she wasn't surprised he'd be listed there.

She skipped over the statistics of birthplace and education, scanning down to the professional information. There it said his major company interest was in Quinn Enterprises Incorporated. She knew that already. What she hadn't been aware of was that Quinn Enterprises controlled a number of subsidiary companies. Abbie's finger traced down the list of names, which was in alphabetical order. Her finger was almost at the end of the column when it stopped.

"Urban Horizons Incorporated," she read out loud.

She'd been so busy with her search that she hadn't noticed the rising humidity. Her linen jacket was rumpled and uncomfortably warm, but she didn't think to take it off. She just stared at the photocopied page and wished she'd stayed under the comforter with the blue forget-me-nots and kept her eyes closed.

USUALLY, ABBIE WAS ENTHUSIASTIC on Monday mornings and eager to get started with a new week of the work she loved, but not today. She'd spent most of yesterday walking through the city, then went to a movie when she could walk no farther, just to avoid being home when Cal telephoned. But she'd had to return to her apartment eventually, and he'd called soon after she arrived. She was cool and impersonal and told him she was tired and couldn't talk very long.

"Is something wrong?" he asked finally.

"I don't want to hear another word about things hanging in the rigging and the rest of it." That was true, but she'd said it more sharply than necessary.

She could hear the hurt in Cal's silence as surely as if he'd put it into words. When he hung up a moment later, Abbie put her head in her hands and wished she weren't too tired to cry.

Now, as she trudged up the stairs to her office, the same suspicion replayed itself through her mind for what seemed like the millionth time since yesterday morning. Perhaps there was a property-grab scheme after all, but the director wasn't the mastermind. Cal had used poor Lester as a smokescreen to divert her from the truth. But then why had he led her so close? Maybe he'd thought she wouldn't be able to see the forest for the trees, or maybe he underestimated her. He probably hadn't expected her to go sleuthing on her own. Jonathan and Jennifer always worked together.

With that bitter thought, Abbie shoved her office door shut behind her. Whatever else might or might not be true, the article she'd found contradicted what Cal had told her about himself. Robert had done the same thing when she first met him. He'd misrepresented himself and what he stood for. Abbie was especially sensitive to that kind of deception now. She knew that when she next faced Cal, she'd have to confront him with his contradiction and her suspicions, too.

Yesterday's upsetting discovery, combined with the humidity and all that walking, had exhausted her; a restless night hadn't helped. Abbie preferred to postpone her fateful meeting with Cal till she felt more equal to it, so she instructed the secretary to tell him she was out if he called. Then she sat down at her desk with a sigh.

The blotter was no longer empty, as it had been on her first day of work, but Abbie had no trouble spotting the last thing she wanted to see there this already trying morning.

This time she had no illusion as to what the contents of the ivory envelope might be. She stared at it for a moment, part of her wildly wishing it would disappear. Instead, the envelope seemed to loom larger than ever against the green background. She sighed once more and picked it up. There was a sense of resignation in the way she opened the flap and pulled out the card.

"Things are going to get worse for you around here— much, much worse," it said. "You may even get hurt. Leave while you still can."

This message lacked the signature of her "Sworn Enemy," but Abbie recognized the tone. She wondered how things could possibly get worse, then cut off the thought. The card told her how that might happen. She could get hurt. Just two nights ago she very nearly had been killed. She had to do something, no matter how exhausted she was.

Going to Lester still seemed unwise. Even if he wasn't involved in some corrupt scheme to defraud the museum, he was incompetent and unprofessional, not a person from whom to seek assistance. Of course, Cal wasn't to be trusted, either.

Abbie crumpled the card in her fist. She hated all this. She couldn't remember ever hating anything so much, except maybe living with Robert. But she wouldn't need six years to get herself out of *this* situation. She pulled open the bottom drawer of her desk and hefted the thick Manhattan phone book.

"The Seaport museum will be a great jumping-off spot," said the counselor at the employment agency Abbie had called. "A good reference from there could open a lot of doors. Without it you'd probably have to start out pretty close to entry level, like most publicists who are new to the city."

Abbie hung up the phone feeling even more downhearted. She bobbed angrily out of her chair and walked to the window. How had she let herself get into such a mess? She paced to the door and yanked it open, pounding a clenched fist against the doorframe as she paced through.

"Damn it all anyway," she said out loud to the walls and overhead light fixtures in the hallway.

"Damn, damn, damn." What sounded like an echoing chorus came from behind the closed door of the volunteer office. The voice was definitely Meredith's.

Abbie opened the door to find her assistant crouched on the floor in the middle of a pile of upended files that had apparently tumbled from the shelves above.

"Oh, hello, Abbie," she said. "Sorry if my cursing disturbed you. I didn't think you were in yet."

"What happened?"

"Somebody let my dear friend Nathan do the filing, and this is the result." Meredith looked very uncomfortable with her long string of a body hunched into that position.

"Let me help you with those," Abbie offered.

"That's all right." Meredith unfolded herself from her crouch and stood up. "I've had about enough of this place already today. I think I need a little mental-health break. I'm also in the mood for mutiny. Maybe it's the weather."

"What are you going to do?"

"Absolutely nothing. First, I'm going to leave this mess where it is. That will teach the director of volunteers not to let Mr. Monkey Thumbs do the filing again."

"Are you sure you want to do that?" Abbie glanced uncertainly at the jumble of papers on the floor.

"Absolutely, positively, one hundred percent sure." Meredith strolled over to Abbie. "And then I'm going to take the rest of the day off. I've got a lot of release time coming. That is, unless you have something crucial for me to do."

"No. You go ahead. I fully sympathize with the mental-health break idea." Abbie couldn't stop the sigh that escaped her lips.

"Say, you look like you need to get away for a while yourself. What happened? Did your favorite cat run off?"

"Something like that."

"I prescribe one day of playing hooky as a sure cure for the down-and-out blues, the raging reds or whatever other color might be bugging you."

"Oh, Meredith, thank heaven for your sense of humor!"

"And my sense of proportion. Besides, you have to be back here tonight."

"I do?"

"Concert duty. Leon Russell. Remember?"

"Oh, yes. It slipped my mind."

Administrative staff, including free-lancers, had to take turns overseeing various program events after regular working hours. Abbie had drawn the concert scheduled for that evening.

"That's what it's like around here in the summer. One thing after another," Meredith remarked.

"You don't know the half of it."

"Well, I do know that both of us need a reprieve for a day." Meredith closed the door of the volunteer office behind them. "I'll even give you a ride home. Why hassle with the MTA? In my opinion, those letters stand for Most Terribly Annoying, not Municipal Transit Authority—and that's only what I call them on my more charitable days."

"I think I will take the day off if I have to be back tonight, and I'd love a ride if it wouldn't be too far out of your way."

"I've decided to go up to the old homestead in Connecticut, so I can take the Triborough Bridge. That's very near you, isn't it?"

"Three blocks away."

"All right, it's a date. I've got a couple of quick errands to attend to across the street. You meet me at the car in fifteen minutes. You know where I park in the garage on Fulton Street."

Abbie nodded. "Thanks, Meredith."

"Don't mention it. It's no fun to mutiny alone."

ABBIE TOOK THE ELEVATOR to the fourth tier of the parking garage, then had to wander around for a while before she found Meredith's car. The place was empty and nearly dark, despite the sunny morning outside. She was standing in front of Meredith's dark green Dodge when she heard tires screeching on the tier below. The car hit the ascending ramp very fast, the sound of its roaring engine echoing through the cavernous building.

A few seconds went by before Abbie considered the possibility that the speeding vehicle might be after her. By then it was rounding the row of cars where she was standing. The next moment she was looking at a large black sedan headed straight toward her. She jumped back between the parked cars with her heart smashing. She couldn't see the driver. The sedan plummeted by too fast. The man was nothing more than a blur behind tinted glass, but she could tell he was dressed in dark clothes.

Rage welled up inside her, compounded by everything that had happened to her since she'd come to South Street. Suddenly Abbie had had enough. She wasn't going to cower there with fear pounding through her veins. She was going to find out who was behind the wheel of that car and why he was after her.

She pulled up out of the crouch she'd ducked into behind Meredith's car. Then she realized she'd been hurt. She'd hit the car door hard with her foot when she leaped to safety, and now there were stabs of pain coursing up into her leg. She'd done something to her toe, sprained it or maybe even broken it. Still, she wasn't going to let that stop her.

She darted out from her hiding place, lurching slightly off the disabled foot but refusing to favor it any more than that. She could hear the car on the tier above, screeching and roaring just as it had done below. Since it had gone up there, it had to come back down. Abbie started after it in the uneven gait her throbbing toe required.

She followed the path the car had taken as rapidly as she could. She was on the next tier when she heard it barrel to a stop with one last gun of the engine somewhere against the far wall. The car door opened, then slammed shut. This guy was smart, Abbie thought. He suspected she might be trailing him, so he was going to leave the car up here and try to sneak out without being seen.

She backed up quietly, out of sight between two cars. He'd head for the elevator, which was to her left in the center of the garage. She crept to the wall and began sliding along it in the direction of the elevator. She kept herself low so he couldn't see her, which also meant she couldn't see him. Her foot was aching badly now, but she paid no attention to it.

The emptiness of the garage made the footsteps echo with a hollow sound as they approached. Abbie's heart tripped into high gear again, but more from adrenaline than from fear this time. Suddenly she remembered she was carrying her shoulder bag. She'd forgotten she had it despite the drag against her arm. She had a habit of lugging a lot of stuff around in this bag, something for almost every contingency, though she never had much occasion to use most of it. Now that habit was about to prove its worth. The bag was heavy enough to provide the perfect weapon. She wrapped the strap around her wrist, sidled up behind the car nearest the elevator door and prepared to swing. The footsteps were only a few feet away now, and she was ready.

The man was younger than Abbie had expected, and she'd never seen him before. Her blow caught him hard in the stomach, and he went down with the breath knocked out of him.

"Who are you?" she shouted, standing over him, her arm lifted to swing again.

He raised his arm to fend off a second blow, but he couldn't answer her. He could only gasp. She'd struck him with all her might, and he was obviously hurting from it.

"Tell me who you are, or I'll pound it out of you!"

The low-heeled pumps she'd worn that day had pointed toes. Perfect for kicking, she thought; it didn't even occur to her how barbaric that might be. Her anger and determination had carried her beyond such considerations. She only reminded herself that, if she did start kicking, she should use her uninjured foot.

Apparently her shouts had echoed even louder than the footsteps had. She heard sounds of help approaching from below. Someone was running up the incline from the fourth tier, and the elevator hummed as the lighted numbers clicked above the steel doors.

"There are people coming," she told the young man. "You won't get away this time."

He tried to raise himself up on one elbow, but when Abbie lifted the shoulder bag menacingly above his head, he sank back to the floor.

"Abbie, what happened?" Meredith hurried up along the roadway from the lower tier. Her gray eyes were wide with alarm.

"This man deliberately tried to run me down!"

The elevator door slid open behind Abbie as she said that, and another young man rushed out. She was vaguely aware of his being dressed like the one on the floor, in dark trousers and a dark shirt with an emblem on the pocket.

"Hey, lady, Jocko didn't try to run nobody down," he said. "He just drives fast. We all drive like that around here."

The young man on the floor nodded in agreement as Abbie began to understand what was really going on here.

"I had plenty of room to get around you," gasped the victim of her blow, raising himself up again while watching her shoulder bag cautiously. "I wasn't going to hit you. I saw you jump out of the way, but there wasn't no chance I was going to hit you."

Abbie looked from one young man to the other. They were parking attendants. They didn't have any idea what she was talking about. Nobody had tried to run her down after all. Her bag was still poised at a threatening angle over the man on the floor. She lowered it quickly, and in that moment, she saw something flash across Meredith's face.

Have you lost your mind? that look asked. Then it was gone, and Abbie was left wondering if perhaps she had.

Chapter Ten

The last thing Abbie wanted to listen to that night was a love song.

"I'll be in Sam Denicola's office if you need me," she told the staff monitor aboard the *Ambrose Lightship* as Leon Russell launched into a soulful rendition of "I'm Singing This Song For You."

The *Ambrose* had been set up to provide dressing rooms for Russell and his band. The decks were empty now except for those people who'd wheedled their way on board for a ringside seat of the spotlighted stage Sam had erected a few yards away, at the end of Pier 16. Ordinarily Abbie would have leaned against the *Ambrose*'s rail with the rest of the fans and enjoyed the concert, but she wasn't in the proper frame of mind for that. All she wanted was to be by herself for a while.

The pier was so crowded it would have been difficult for her to navigate under any circumstances; with an injured foot it was even more impossible. The scene that afternoon in the parking garage had left Abbie not only humiliated but hurt. The last two toes on her left foot were swollen and sore. She'd had to wear open sandals to be able to walk at all. She knew she'd never make it through the crowd without someone treading on her foot. The thought of pain, either physical or psychic, was more than she could face at the moment. So she skirted the mass of people and limped to the low railing that ran along the edge of the pier above the water.

It was a dangerous route and strictly forbidden, but Abbie hauled herself over the barrier anyway. She ignored the frown of the security guard as she edged sideways up the narrow apron of dock beyond. He'd have stopped her immediately if not for the administrative staff badge she was wearing; technically she was his boss for the evening. After Abbie had got past the crowd, she hauled herself back over the rail again, thinking how much heavier her body felt when she was unhappy. She smiled a polite greeting for the guard at the gate end of the dock, then hobbled toward Pier 15.

Sam's office was aboard the old, steam ferryboat, *Major General William H. Hart*. The *Hart* no longer plied the river with a cargo of automobiles and travelers but was moored permanently at the museum pier. The lower-deck car bay served as a workshop for Sam and his crew, and the upper deck had been converted to office space, with Sam's pilothouse overlooking it all.

The handrail was damp to the touch with evening coolness as Abbie went up the spiraling metal stairway from the main deck. The stairs had been added after the *Hart* came to South Street, when it no longer mattered that they blocked the wide, bay doors. At the top of the spiral was a narrow walkway bordering the enclosed upper deck. A few straight steps above that was Sam's office.

Abbie had called Sam's house earlier for permission to come here. She'd anticipated the way she'd feel tonight after the kind of day she'd had, and this was a perfect place to be entirely alone. Sam hadn't been home when she called, but Phoebe Denicola hadn't hesitated to volunteer the office in his stead.

"I know he wouldn't mind. If you can stand the mess, you're welcome to it," she said in a tone both as good-natured and ironic as her husband's. "I'm afraid Sam isn't up for any *Good Housekeeping* awards this decade."

Phoebe hadn't exaggerated. The pilothouse was badly in need of a thorough cleaning, but Abbie couldn't have cared less. She sank with a grateful sigh into a beat-up chair that smelled of machine oil.

The small room was surrounded on three sides by windows looking out on lower Manhattan. Actually, the better view was from the other pilothouse at the opposite end of the ship, with its vista of the river and the bridge lights. All Abbie could see from here was a vaulted stretch of the Franklin Delano Roosevelt Drive and, beyond that, dark buildings rising in tiers back toward Wall Street. However, among those buildings was the tower of black glass and steel where Cal had his office.

She stared at its gleaming facade as Leon launched into a blues number on the next pier. Sad piano and guitar chords drifted across the slip of water in between, and Abbie felt them wail inside her like the sad thoughts she'd had with her all day long. She'd asked herself again whether she should hand in her resignation, but that would mean giving up more than just a summer assignment. There'd be no chance of a favorable reference if she left in midproject, which would ruin her hopes of getting a desirable position with a good P.R. firm. It might even force her to relocate again to another city. For Davey's sake, she'd promised herself she wouldn't do that.

Besides, she was beginning to wonder if the rumormongers might be right. Maybe she was a little paranoid after all. Eighteen years of living with a demanding, social-climbing mother, and six with a hypercritical husband, was enough to wreak havoc with anybody's self-image. Abbie already knew that was a major reason for the way she drove herself so hard to succeed, and for doing it at breakneck speed. Perhaps the recent pressure on her had pushed her over the line into something more serious than workaholism. She couldn't deny that confusing a parking garage attendant with an assassin was definitely an example of delusional behavior.

She gave herself up to the sound of Leon's voice, letting it gradually remove her worries from her immediate consciousness. If it hadn't been for a lull in the music, she might not have heard the first footstep clank against the metal tread at the bottom of the spiral staircase a deck and a half below.

Abbie snapped out of her reverie and listened. The music had swelled again. She thought she heard another footstep, but she couldn't be sure. She told herself it was probably just a security guard and tried not to be alarmed, but she wasn't convinced. In an instant, she was out of the chair and down into the stairwell, which led to the upper-deck office area. She could see through the pilothouse windows, but she doubted anybody could see in clearly enough to make out her shadow among the others in the dark stairwell.

Her breath had turned so quiet it seemed to have stopped. Then she saw a tall, black form looming up suddenly at the window above Sam's desk. She remembered how she'd made herself look like a fool or worse in the parking garage. She was probably doing the same thing now.

"Who's there?" she called, but she didn't leave her hiding place.

The black shadow at the window was still for a moment, suspended so motionless against the murky night sky that Abbie suddenly wondered if it might be part of the backdrop and not a person at all. Perhaps this was just another delusion. She was about to call out again when the shadow swooped wider and taller, poised there for a few seconds, then ducked out of sight.

That had been no delusion. Nevertheless, Abbie wasn't sure exactly what had happened beyond Sam's dingy windows. All she knew was that this shadow man had some reason for running away. She could hear him going down the metal stairs.

Without giving a thought to whether she was acting rationally or not, Abbie bounded out from the stairwell and through the door of the pilothouse. Leon's blues number warbled to a close, followed by a crescendo of applause. Still, Abbie could hear the sound of running feet on the metal walkway that bordered the ferry's upper deck. She began to run in pursuit, moving along in a lopsided trot and ignoring the shards of pain in her foot.

At the foot of the short flight of steps leading from Sam's office to the upper deck, the man had turned to the left. Abbie wondered why he'd done that. He could have gone down the spiral stairs directly to the main deck and off the gangway to the pier. He'd have a better chance of escape by that shorter route. Maybe he wasn't familiar with the *Hart*. Yet if he was the same person who'd been plaguing the museum piers lately, and she had a feeling he must be, there was every indication he knew these ships very well.

Whatever his reason for taking this roundabout direction, he would now have to run all the way down the side of the boat, around the other end and off a long gangway to the pier. However, when Abbie reached that end of the ship herself, she heard nothing. The sheet metal of the old gangway should have been creaking with the pound of footsteps ahead of her, but all was silent.

Then she noticed that the door to the enclosed upper deck was ajar. The shadow man must have decided to run through there to Sam's office and out again. That route was even more circuitous. He was leading her on some kind of wild-goose chase. But why?

Abbie was standing just outside the doorway contemplating this mystery when a hand snaked out, locked around her wrist and pulled her inside. The door slammed tight behind her, and she was suddenly engulfed in total darkness. She could hear the ragged breathing of whoever was holding onto her, but she couldn't see a thing.

"Let go of me!" she cried.

She was about to strike out in the direction where she thought he must be when he yanked her wrist with a force of strength beyond her power to resist and flung her against the wall. She panted but couldn't regain enough breath to take any action before the iron grip whipped her around again. She stumbled but managed not to fall. Then she was hurled back against the wall a second time, with no more apparent effort than if she'd been a rag doll or a piece of flotsam tossed on the sea. She was vaguely aware of a swishing sound, like that of sweeping curtains, as she wheeled helplessly through the air.

She raised her free arm against the wall in search of something to hold on to so she could resist his next attempt to fling her around. Meanwhile, the stabbing pain in her foot had become so intense the muscles in her leg were quivering. Then her fingers closed around a metal cylinder, one of the small fire extinguishers that hung on either side of the door to the walkway. She prayed it was attached by a simple hook and could be lifted off. The cylinder was heavier than it looked and shoved her arm downward as it cleared the wall.

What she had to do next required both hands. Her attacker's breathing was labored now. He must have exerted more effort than she thought he had. He sounded as out of breath as she was. Abbie hoped with everything in her that this was true. Then she concentrated all of her strength on pulling as hard as she could against the hand that held her.

Abbie's sudden, strong movement must have come as a surprise to her captor, because he let go of her wrist. Before he could find it and grab her once more, she had lifted the fire extinguisher with one hand pressing the handle and had aimed the hose with the other, just as she'd learned to do at Girl Scout camp in Meadville, Maryland.

For a moment that felt like an eternity, nothing happened. Abbie had backed off along the wall, but she could hear him groping after her. She was almost as certain she could hear her own terror pulsing through her. Then she felt a stream of foam pour through the hose. She swept it back and forth in an arc until she heard a grunted response as the foam hit her target. Abbie trained the tube straight in that direction. The next thing she heard was the door to the walkway being wrenched open and her assailant bolting through it.

Abbie held onto the fire extinguisher and headed for the door. Maybe she could get another shot at him when she could actually see who she was aiming at. A spray of these chemicals in his face would slow him up for certain. It might even bring him down. Then she'd give him one good whack on the head with the cylinder to knock him out, and this crazy nightmare would be over for her at last. She'd know who was after her and maybe even why.

She made herself move faster despite the dragging pain in her foot. Then, suddenly, her flat-soled sandals began to slide out from under her. She'd hit a patch of the slippery foam. She lunged for the doorframe, hoping it was where she guessed it to be. Her fingers gripped rough metal and stopped her slide, but the fire extinguisher had fallen from her other hand and clattered across the floor. She didn't have time to poke around after it in the dark, so she rushed out onto the walkway unarmed.

The heavy footfalls were thudding off into the distance. Oddly enough, once again the man had taken the unlikely, circuitous route. Instead of heading down the nearby gangway to the pier, he'd gone back the way he had come, along the side of the ferry in the direction of Sam's pilothouse office. Abbie followed, though her injured foot was slowing her down now, and she knew there was little chance she'd catch him.

"Yoo-hoo! Yoo-hoo!"

Abbie almost hadn't heard that sound, but even when she did, she thought at first it might be the cry of a gull.

"Help me—oh, please, help me!"

That certainly wasn't a gull. Abbie hurried back along the walkway to the point where she'd first heard the call and looked over the ferryboat rail. Through the gloom she recognized Josie. The woman was inside a lifeboat that had been pushed out from the side of the *Hart* and now dangled by one of the curved, metal davit hooks that usually held it suspended above the deck. Abbie had been so intent on the chase that she hadn't noticed the dory was missing from its customary station when she'd run past it.

The man Abbie had been chasing was long gone now, probably even off the ferry. It occurred to her that he'd led her this way deliberately. He'd known Josie was in the lifeboat and that Abbie would be distracted from pursuing him. As Abbie gazed into the murky half-light, she could see that Josie was in real danger.

Somehow the line that held one end of the lifeboat by block and tackle to one davit hook had come loose and dropped that end of the boat downward. The upturned craft now rocked against the hook still attached above. If that line let go, as well, the boat would plummet, with Josie in it, into the water.

Josie might be spry for her age, but it was questionable whether she'd survive such a drop. The boat could come down on top of her, driving her underwater and very possibly knocking her unconscious at the same time. After that she'd be at the mercy of the treacherous undertow. Abbie was a strong swimmer, but she was uncertain how much she could do under these circumstances.

First she checked the cleat on the attached davit hook. The line from the dangling lifeboat was wound around it. She pulled at the line to make sure it was tightly cinched. To her relief, it seemed to be secure. Josie was safe for the moment. She'd wedged herself into the space between the floor of the lifeboat and the bench running across its middle.

"Help me," Josie called again. "I can't hold on here much longer." Her voice was thin and weak. If she released her grip, she'd slide down over the dangling prow and into the river.

"Hang on, Josie," Abbie yelled. "I'll get you. Just don't let go."

Josie didn't answer. Instead she began to make a keening sound. The band still crashed and wailed from the other pier, but Abbie hardly noticed that now. She grabbed the loosened line from the davit and heaved on it as hard as she could. It moved a few inches, then stopped. She pulled down on it again with all her strength, till she was nearly sitting on the deck from the effort. The line didn't budget. It was caught. Meanwhile, the jerking of the line had set the lifeboat rocking.

"Stop, please," Josie cried. "Don't do that." There was panic in her voice.

Abbie cinched the line around its cleat as fast as her hands would move. Then she reached over the side of the ship to grasp the attached rope that led to the swaying lifeboat. She clenched that line tight in her fists and held it rigid. The to-and-fro motion gradually stopped, but Abbie's heart was thumping erratically.

"No more rocking now," she said, doing her best to sound calm and reassuring. "You just have to hang on a few minutes more, Josie. I'm going to swing you closer so I can get you out of there. Don't be afraid. Everything will be all right."

"No, don't swing me." Josie started to wail.

"You have to trust me, Josie," Abbie said very firmly. "And you have to help me by hanging on as tight as you can for a little while longer."

Josie stopped wailing and started to keen again. Abbie grasped the davit above the collar near its base and turned it slowly, an inch at a time. The lifeboat began to move, almost imperceptibly, in toward the rail of the *Hart*. The davit screeched with a high-pitched, metallic sound as it turned, and Abbie prayed that Josie wouldn't panic again. Gradually the dangling craft came nearer, till it was almost touching the rail.

Josie was still wedged behind the bench. She was close enough now for Abbie to see her face clearly. Josie's eyes were large with fear. She was too terrified to climb out of the boat on her own. Abbie was sure of that. She'd have to go after her.

"I'm coming for you, Josie. Just hold on a minute more. You're almost home free."

Abbie wished she felt as confident of that as she sounded. Josie was still a crucial distance from safety, and Abbie was about to step into danger herself. Pulling Josie onto the *Hart* would be easier if she could get the older woman to let go of the lifeboat bench and grab the rail, but Josie was obviously too frightened to do that, too. Abbie would have to lean far enough out from the *Hart* to secure a good grip on Josie, then pray for enough strength to get her back on board.

For the first time during these past fleeting minutes, Abbie was fully aware of the dark water below and the darker clutch of fear in her heart. The rail of the main deck jutted just beneath her and Josie. More likely it would break their bones than stop their fall should they tumble overboard. She told herself she mustn't think about that now. A moment's hesitation could mean catastrophe.

A long coil of excess rope trailed from a nearby cleat attached to the deck. Abbie found the end of the rope, wound it around the ankle of her sore foot and secured her leg tight to the rail post. She took a deep breath before swinging her other foot over the rail. Then she inched sideways very slowly until she was directly across from Josie.

"You have to be very brave," Abbie said steadily. "You have to help me now. I can't do this alone."

Josie's face was inches from hers. She could tell that the older woman understood and was going to try. Abbie leaned forward and grasped her under the arms. Josie let go of the bench one hand at a time and took hold of Abbie's shoulders as Abbie coached her through every move. She felt the drag of the woman's full weight at the same instant that the ankle rope began to loosen. The knot was slipping.

"We have to hurry," Abbie said with an unnatural calm. "You have to climb up onto the edge of the bench for me."

She was afraid Josie might hesitate, and that could be disastrous. The ankle rope was getting looser by the second. Instead Josie responded immediately, almost too much so. She climbed onto the bench so quickly the lifeboat began to rock again.

"Step onto the ledge next to me." Abbie saw the flicker of fear in Josie's eyes. "You have to trust me. I won't let you fall."

The ankle rope was very loose now. Josie thrust one foot toward the ledge in the closest thing to a leap of faith Abbie had ever witnessed. The lifeboat was rocking harder. Abbie clasped Josie tight and pulled her to the rail. She was a lot heavier than she looked. Abbie felt tears rise to her eyes as she willed her arms not to let go. Unfortunately she couldn't impose that same will over the rope wound around her ankle. She felt it slipping rapidly out of its knot while Josie's weight pulled them both precariously forward.

The thought seared through Abbie's brain that they weren't going to make it.

"I've got you!"

As she heard those miraculous words, Cal's strong arms closed around her and Josie. He held them while they climbed back over the rail to safety. The tears that had hovered in the corners of Abbie's eyes wet her cheeks now. Whatever her misgivings about him, she would have grabbed Cal and hugged him tight right then; but Josie was still hanging on, clamped to Abbie's neck with what threatened to become a strangle hold. Cal had to pry the older woman's fingers loose before that happened.

"I'll call the guards to haul up the lifeboat," he said.

"No guards." Josie latched on to his bare arms as tenaciously as she'd been holding on to Abbie. "I don't like the guards. They always yell at me."

Cal and Abbie exchanged glances, and Abbie nodded.

"All right, Josie. I guess you've been through enough for now," Cal said. "No guards, for a little while at least. Just tell us what happened."

On the way to Sam's office, Josie told her story. She'd boarded the ferry, which she sometimes did at night, to hide out in the lifeboat and wait for the gulls to arrive early the next morning. That way she could shoo them away from the ships as much as possible.

First she'd hoisted the lifeboat up from the chocks supporting it on deck. Then she'd climbed in and pushed off the side of the *Hart*, just as she always did. She said that was a good place for getting at the birds. She had a line looped around the ferryboat rail so she could haul herself back in the morning. It was a system she'd used many times, she told them. Nothing had ever gone wrong before.

Up to that point, her story was at least believable. Then Josie started talking about something she called a gull man, and she became more and more agitated. She claimed she'd been set upon by this gull man. He'd come around the walkway from the other side of the *Hart* just after she'd settled herself in the lifeboat, swung off the ship by its davits.

"He was all black," she said, her eyes huge with fear, "and he had giant wings. He's one of them, you know."

"One of whom, Josie?" Abbie asked. She remembered Josie's talking the same way in her office.

"One of the spirits of this place." Josie looked warily around the small pilothouse, which they'd entered a few

minutes ago, as if she expected to find phantoms eavesdropping from the corners. Then she lowered her voice to
a whisper. "They come from the past, off all those ships
that used to dock here. You see, they got left behind when
the ships sailed without them, and they've been here ever
since, wandering the piers. I can feel them. But the gull
man is the only one I've ever seen with my own two eyes."

Abbie and Cal exchanged glances again.

"Errol believes me, don't you?" Josie asked Cal.

"Of course I do, Josie."

The shock of what had happened tonight seemed to have
addled the woman more than ever. Her eyes glittered,
darting back and forth between Cal and Abbie as she went
on with her story. According to her, the gull man had un-
tied the line to the prow of the lifeboat to make it fall.
Luckily Josie had been so scared when she first saw him
that she'd crawled under the bench. That was what had
kept her from tumbling into the river till Abbie came.

"He wants to kill me because I know about the spirits,
and I'm the only one who's seen him. I know you don't
believe me, but he was a gull man," Josie insisted. "He
had wings. I saw him lift them up, like this."

As she raised her arms and held them out to the side,
Abbie suddenly remembered something: a dark shape
outside the window of this same pilothouse, swooping
taller and wider for a moment, as if spreading black wings.

"A cape!" she exclaimed. "He was wearing a cape!"

"Who was wearing a cape?" Cal asked.

"I'll tell you later."

Abbie was afraid her story would only upset Josie all
over again. Josie's gull man was the same shadowy figure
Abbie had chased around the *Hart* and nearly been captured by inside the upper deck area. The swishing sound
she'd heard in the dark as he flung her back and forth had

been the whipping of the cape he was wearing. She was almost certain the pieces of the puzzle were coming together.

The part about the spirits was obviously a figment of Josie's frenzied imagination, and she'd mixed the man she saw tonight into it. Still, she *had* seen him. That part of Josie's story was definitely not imaginary. Abbie had the bruises already forming on her wrist to prove it.

"I warned you." Josie had become visibly agitated again. She crouched on the window bench and glared at Abbie with what looked like hatred in her face. "I told you not to start those crowds coming down here. They've stirred up the spirits. That's why all of this is happening."

It was true that the publicity surrounding the incident of the *Lettie* had increased attendance at the museum piers. The curious came to see the schooner that had almost made its last voyage, straight to the bottom, right here in the harbor. Then they went on to the other ships and wandered the district in general. Abbie's press-conference strategy had been a success—with everybody but Josie.

At that point, Cal called the police from Sam's phone. It took him and Abbie until the officers arrived to get Josie calm enough to talk to them.

Now Abbie told her story along with Josie's. Unfortunately, she could hear for herself how implausible it sounded; she noticed the way one officer's expression became even more inscrutable when she got to the part about the cape. He thought she was as looney as Josie.

It occurred to her that they might find out about her suspecting Les Girard of sabotaging the brakes on his XKE, as well as about her near attack on the garage attendant that afternoon. It would be very difficult to explain to a policeman or anyone else exactly why she'd thought a man who'd never seen her before in his life was trying to run her down. The revelations would go on from there, including her claims of being stalked through the streets, harassed by poison-pen notes and invaded by invisible housebreakers.

She sighed. She'd be lucky if the police didn't end up accusing her of trying to murder poor Josie. In fact, Abbie had to admit she probably wouldn't believe her story herself, considering the circumstances. For an instant she even wondered if there was a chance none of it had happened at all—but, of course, it had. And an explanation as simple as paranoid delusion or wandering spirits would not satisfy anyone.

"I THOUGHT WE WERE SUPPOSED to be working together," Cal said.

They'd taken Josie home and were on their way to Cal's office suite in the tower of steel and black glass. He'd invited Abbie there for a brandy and because he said he needed to talk to her. He insisted it couldn't wait till tomorrow. Since he'd probably saved her life earlier, she could hardly refuse. At least, she told herself that was her reason for going with him.

"Last thing I knew, we were partners," he went on, "smoking this thing out as a team. Then I call you at home last night and you're cold as ice. This morning your secretary tells me you're not in, and I hear through the grapevine that the truth is you just weren't in if I was the one calling. I went back to Boston thinking I might never see you again. When I got home tonight there was a message from Phoebe, who tells me you broke your toe in a garage today where somebody was supposedly chasing you in an Oldsmobile. If she hadn't let it slip that you were in Sam's office, I'd never have come to the *Hart* looking for you, and you and Josie would be feeding the fish out past the Verazzano Narrows right now.''

"News certainly travels fast around here, doesn't it?'' Abbie was referring to the story about her in the parking garage.

"Sure it does. Especially when it's about how I'm getting the brush from the first woman I've given a tumble to since I started hanging around this place ''

Abbie had never heard him sound so obviously from Brooklyn. She guessed his old speech habits recurred when he was upset. And she could see he was very upset now. She wished she had a better explanation than the one she was going to give him, but she didn't want to tell him the rest of it just yet. She'd had enough confrontations for the time being. They could discuss the unpleasant subject of her suspicions about him later, maybe even another day.

"Remember at the *Lettie* when you told me Meredith needed some time by herself to sort things out?'' she asked.

"I remember.''

"I've started to feel that way myself.''

He glanced skeptically over at her. "And you had to get away from me to do it?''

"That's right.''

The brightness of his blue eyes was clouded as he studied her. "I suppose I'll have to accept that answer for now.''

Yes, you will, she thought.

They left the express elevator at the thirty-fifth floor and walked along a dark marble hallway. Each doorway was a well of shadow in the eerily striated stone. Abbie was glad to have Cal at her side. The events of the evening had left her feeling shaky and easily spooked. Even Josie's crazy story about the spirits had gotten to her. Abbie could almost sense some of those ghosts lurking in this hallway.

The ghosts of millions spent, she told herself wryly to dispel the strange sensation that had crept over her for a moment.

As for her doubts about Cal, there was a chance she'd been too easily spooked in that department, also. After all, the article she'd found was yellow with age. Maybe he really had changed his way of thinking since then. Besides, she needed to be with him tonight. After what had happened to her today, she knew he was the only one who could make her feel everything was all right. For now, her doubts seemed far less important.

Halfway down the long hall, Cal unlocked a door, and Abbie walked past him into the most beautiful office she'd ever seen. The mauve carpet was deep and luxurious beneath her feet, enveloping her in a soft, safe cocoon of elegance; she knew at once that she'd been right to come here with him.

Across the wide room was a raised tier and, beyond that, a glass wall stretching the length of the room. In the center of the tier stood a long desk table made from a thick slab of Plexiglas mounted on cylinders of shiny chrome. The chair behind it had a scooped-out, modern shape and was covered in a dark mauve suede that looked almost purple. Abbie was surprised. She'd expected a much more traditional setting for Cal.

"I'll show you the way I like this room best," he said.

Suddenly even the subdued lights had been extinguished. The glass wall revealed the starry summer night. Abbie hadn't seen the stars since she came to New York. The city had a way of drowning them in its twenty-four-hour glow. Cal's office was up high enough to be nearly beyond that glow. Almost to heaven, she thought.

She walked toward the window, as if drawn by the magnetism of the stars. The night sky was velvet dark. When Abbie reached the glass, she stared out into that darkness that seemed so endless and inhaled a deep breath.

"I'm angry with you about something else, too." Cal had come up from behind and spoke softly into her ear.

"You don't sound angry."

"This is my nice-guy act."

"What are you angry about?" She didn't turn around, and it was too dark to see his reflection in the glass. She couldn't tell if he was serious or not.

"Chasing after caped villains can be a risky business. You should have called for help. You should have called me."

"There wasn't time to call anybody." She could feel his breath on her neck, warm and very close.

"I can't help worrying about you. You're so accident-prone. You smash into windows. Now you're limping around on a broken toe."

"It isn't broken. Whoever Phoebe talked to was obviously exaggerating."

"I still think you need somebody to take care of you."

Abbie sighed. She didn't like to think of herself as vulnerable, and she certainly wasn't helpless. Still, being taken care of suddenly sounded very appealing.

"Promise me you won't chase after any more men in capes without calling me first." His voice was softer now. He touched her bare arms and slid his fingers up them.

"No promises. Promises ruin things."

"How?" His hands cupped her shoulders. The tips of his fingers were under the edges of her sleeveless blouse.

"Promises get broken. Then everything changes."

He turned her toward him. She sensed more than saw his gaze travel over her, from her hair to her eyes to her lips.

"I won't break any promises to you," he whispered.

His well-memorized features were as clear to her in the dark as they would be in the brightest light. He was moving closer still. Abbie put her hand against his chest to stop him. "Then promise that everything you've told me about yourself is true."

He drew back slightly. "What's wrong?"

"Just promise me that you've always told me the truth.'

"I have." His voice was a whisper again. She felt it against her face as he moved close once more. She didn't stop him this time, though the thought flickered through her mind that if he'd been lying all along, his promise was worthless now. Then his mouth found hers.

The kiss wasn't hard or insistent. Abbie almost wished it were. The instant their lips touched, she knew. Ever since that night in her hallway, she'd been waiting to be with him like this.

He brushed her lips with his, then covered them, then brushed them again, pressing her closer to him each time. His kiss might have been gentle, but his body was less so. He wanted to make love to her. She could feel it. When the situation finally got that far, she wondered if she would resist. She wasn't going to have her answer just yet, because he was pulling slowly away.

"Let's have that brandy now," he said.

"All right." She understood that he wanted to savor this moment, to make it last as long as possible. She felt the same.

"I have some special vintage in the next room. I'll be right back."

He walked away from her, and she immediately wished he were in her arms again. He'd gone to a door that looked like part of the wall till he opened it. He touched a panel near the doorway, and subdued lights came on once more.

Their glow was golden and dreamy and very much in tune with what Abbie was feeling.

She hadn't thought about moving. Then, suddenly, she was wandering through the deep hush of carpet, along the tier toward the Plexiglas desk. She stopped behind it and ran her fingers over the luxurious suede of Cal's chair. A flush of warmth spread inside her as she anticipated running her fingers over his naked body.

She glanced down at the desk, which was strewed with papers, and her hand trailed to the topmost sheet. Her glance didn't focus intentionally. Abbie was still caught up in her desire for Cal. She had no idea how much time had passed before she realized that she was looking at something she didn't want to see. By then it was too late. Her hand moved of its own volition to the gooseneck lamp and snapped it on. The truth on the page in front of her was as unavoidable as her compulsion to read it over three times, till there could be no mistake in her mind of its dread meaning.

Chapter Eleven

Thank heaven I didn't tell him that.

This was the first thought that popped into Abbie's head the next morning. She'd slept only an hour or so because she'd stared at her bedroom ceiling most of the night. She was glad she hadn't revealed her doubts about her mental stability to Cal. She felt vulnerable enough to him already without having trusted him with her secret fears. She knew now that he wasn't to be trusted.

For what must have been the thousandth time since she'd run out of his office last night, she remembered what he'd said before she discovered the papers on his desk. He had sworn that he'd always told her the truth. He'd promised that and vowed never to break that promise. Then she'd seen those papers on his desk and known he'd been deceiving her all along.

The papers were price estimates for a list of properties. They compared the purchase price of each building with its much higher real market value, beginning with the year 1974 and updated annually to 1980. To the right of the typed columns was another column, added by hand in what was unmistakably Cal's writing. It listed the present year's buying price for each of the buildings and their projected resale value five years from now. The profit margin was immense. What Cal had estimated on those pages was a real estate deal that would make a fortune for the company named at the top of each sheet. That company was Urban Horizons, Incorporated, and the addresses of the buildings in question were those of properties presently owned by the Seaport museum.

Abbie had stared at the pages for several minutes, unable to move her glance away no matter how much she wanted to. But she couldn't deny their meaning; the evidence was too blatant.

She hadn't waited for Cal to come back with his special vintage brandy. She'd simply fled. She hardly remembered the cab ride home or what she'd done afterward, except that she'd run into the shower and stood for a very long time beneath the cleansing spray.

Now she didn't struggle to keep her eyes shut, as she had done the other morning. With her eyes closed, columns of figures in all their painful reality played over and over across the insides of her eyelids as if imprinted there with indelible ink. Abbie turned back the comforter to its plain blue underside; she couldn't bring herself to look at forget-me-nots this morning.

She sat on the edge of her bed, listening to a stiff summer breeze rattle the narrow-slatted blinds at the windows. Her feet rested on top of her backless bedroom slippers instead of inside them. She sat like that for several minutes. The edge of the bed felt like neutral territory right now, halfway between burrowing back under the comforter to hide and standing up to start a day she'd rather not face.

Along with what she'd discovered about Cal, someone had nearly succeeded in killing Josie last night. That made the situation at the Seaport even more serious than it had been. She could sit on the edge of the bed from now till doomsday, but that wouldn't change the fact that she—as well as others—was obviously in danger. Even so, what was really causing her paralysis of will was her discovery about Cal.

He hadn't changed his mind about what he was quoted as saying in that yellowed clipping. He was still after the museum properties. In fact, he'd been working on the deal so recently, the files were on top of everything else on his desk. He might even have been busy with them last evening, just before he'd come to the *Hart* for his gallant rescue of her and Josie.

Suddenly something horrible occurred to Abbie. It sickened her so, she had to reach forward and grasp the border of the mattress for support.

What if Cal was the man she'd chased last night, the man who'd left Josie dangling over the river?

Then she realized it couldn't be true. She'd been close to that man in the dark upper-deck area, close enough to smell him and get a sense of how he moved. If he'd been Cal, she would have known it. Her awareness of Cal and everything about him was too strong for Abbie to be fooled about something like that. Of course, her mind perversely insisted, there was still the possibility that Cal could have hired somebody to do the job for him.

A blast from the door buzzer postponed the continuation of that upsetting thought. Abbie reached for her robe, then changed her mind and grabbed her jeans instead. She should be dressed to go to the door. She stuffed her short nightie into the jeans before zipping them and added a sweatshirt on top. The buzzer blared again. She hurried barefoot out of the bedroom and across the living room carpet to the hall.

"Who is it?" she called through the intercom.

"It's Mr. Dee from the hardware store," a raspy voice shouted a little louder than was necessary. "I'm here to install your new lock."

Abbie had almost forgotten having ordered the extra-protection, tamperproof lock the day after she found her apartment door open. She pushed the button to let Mr. Dee into the lobby and peered through the peephole until she saw the stocky, gray-haired man. Then she turned the dead-bolt and undid the chain lock above it. She already had barricaded herself in like Fort Knox, and now she was going to have a third lock installed. She'd decided that if it made her feel safer, it was worth the trouble.

She opened the door to find Mr. Dee studying the dead-bolt already in place.

"You know what, lady?" he said. "This lock you got here is the same kind I brought you. It's about as tamperproof as they come."

Abbie stared at him for a minute until the meaning of what he said sunk in. "You mean nobody could have picked it?"

"It's real hard to pick these babies." He patted the lock cylinder with affection. "You pretty much have to have a key to get through one of them."

Nobody had a key but Abbie. Not even the building superintendent was allowed to have access to individual apartments unless the tenant let him in.

"They're not supposed to make copies of these keys without seeing identification and checking the filed registration number of the lock to find out who it was sold to," Mr. Dee went on.

"You're saying that even if somebody got hold of my keys, he couldn't have them copied?"

"I'm saying no one's supposed to be able to have them copied. That doesn't mean they can't do it. You can get just about anything you want in this town if you're willing to pay for it."

You can get keys illegally. You can have people chased and scared out of their wits. You can even have somebody killed. Abbie didn't say those things. She only thought them.

"Did somebody break in through this lock you got?" Mr. Dee asked.

"Yes, as a matter of fact."

"Then he most likely had a copy of your key. If I was you, lady, I'd think back who I gave my key to."

"I didn't give it to anybody. I have the only one."

"Then you better think back where you had that key around the time you got broken into. Because somebody probably borrowed it when you wasn't looking. Now, do you still want this other lock I ordered? I can sell it to somebody else if you don't want it. I mean, you already got one on here. Two's probably overdoing it for this neighborhood."

"Put it in anyway."

"Whatever you say, lady. You're the customer. Far be it from me to turn business away."

Abbie puttered around the kitchen while he drilled a hole for the new lock. She knew he thought she was strange for wanting so much security in a neighborhood that took pride in its low crime rate. He'd looked at her and shaken his head a couple of times since he started working. Abbie pretended she hadn't noticed. Anything that made her even just psychologically more at ease was important to her right now. Still, she was a little embarrassed to seem so neurotically squeamish in his eyes. Also, the high-pitched whine of the drill was starting to give her a headache.

A few minutes later Mr. Dee called out that he was missing a tool and would have to run across the street to get it. Would she buzz him in when he returned? Abbie said she would. As soon as he left, she went into the bedroom to dress herself properly, then began to brush her hair. Usually she found that particular activity soothing, but not this morning. There were degrees of tension that couldn't be brushed away.

When the doorbell rang again, Abbie put the down the brush and went to answer it without bothering to clip back the froth of curls that surrounded her face. Since she assumed the caller was Mr. Dee, she didn't bother to ask him to identify himself through the intercom. She didn't want him to think she was any more obsessed than he already thought she was. So she pushed the button to release the lobby door and went into the kitchen to refill her coffee cup.

Abbie didn't realize that Mr. Dee had left her apartment door unlocked. She should have known he didn't have a key for the original lock, and the new one was only half installed. He'd had no way of locking up when he left.

It wasn't until she walked back into the hall that she saw the large, broad-shouldered figure in her open doorway. He stood against the light, and for a moment his features were indistinguishable. Abbie was so shocked to see him standing there that his identity didn't register with her at once, even though he happened to be the person most on her mind.

"I'm here to find out why you ran out on me last night," Cal said as he stepped into the light from the kitchen window.

Abbie held herself very calm, but the grim set of his handsome face threatened to destroy her facade. For an instant all she could think of was the feel of his lips moving softly over hers. The answer to his question seemed to have escaped her. Why would any woman run out on such a man?

Three blasts from the doorbells in the lobby, one to her apartment and one each to the neighbor on either side of her, brought Abbie out of her stupor. She heard the buzzer sound as one of her neighbors responded, and Mr. Dee let himself into the building. She was relieved to see his portly form bustling toward them. She didn't want to be alone with Cal right now. Especially not with so many uncomfortable questions between them.

Mr. Dee looked from Cal to Abbie and back again. He must have sensed the heavy tension in the air. "I can finish this job another time," he said. "The lock you have already will do till then. That is, unless your intruder still has a copy of your key."

Abbie thought about that, distracting herself from her problems with Cal for a moment. "I imagine he does have a key," she said.

"Then I can change just the cylinder in the old lock and give you a new key."

"Why don't you do that?" Cal stepped between Abbie and the hardware man. "But we'd appreciate it if you could continue the job in an hour or so."

Mr. Dee peeped around Cal to see how Abbie was reacting.

"Mrs. Tanner and I have some business to finish that can't really wait," Cal added. He looked back at her with an expression that said he'd have it out with her whether anyone was there or not.

"It's all right, Mr. Dee. I'll call you later," Abbie said.

"You're the customer, and the customer is always right," the stocky man told her, "whether she's right or not." He gathered up his tools and left, shaking his head in disbelief.

"Now I want an answer to my question," Cal demanded as soon as Mr. Dee had closed the door behind him.

"What question was that?"

"You know very well what question. Why did you run out on me last night?"

They were facing each other across Abbie's white tile kitchen floor. She took a deep breath and decided to do this fast and have it over with.

"I found out something about you that I don't like at all."

"What was that?"

"You own a company named Urban Horizons, Incorporated, don't you?"

"Yes, I do."

"And you're planning to use that company to acquire museum properties for private development. Isn't that right?"

"No, it isn't." He didn't elaborate. He just stood there watching her, his expression unreadable.

"You planned to have Urban Horizons buy museum properties a few years ago. That much you can't deny."

"I never had any such plan, either now or in the past."

His clipped, noninformative answers were making her more irritated with him than ever. "Look, Cal, there's no point in trying to lie to me any longer. I've seen the proof."

"What proof is that?"

Abbie breathed an exasperated sigh. "Well, first of all, there was an article in the museum files with a direct quote by you."

"What am I supposed to have said?"

"You said you'd get hold of the museum buildings one way or another someday. Those were your exact words, according to the clipping I found."

"I don't suppose they mentioned whether Cal Quinn junior or senior was doing the talking."

Abbie hesitated. She felt a little like a stranded traveler who saw rescue in the distance but was afraid to believe in it because it might be a mirage.

"My father and I have the same name," Cal continued. "The clipping you found was probably about him."

"But the firm involved was Urban Horizons, and you just said that's your company."

"Until a few years ago my father owned it. I bought him out at the same time I convinced him to do business in Florida instead of New York."

Abbie sat down on one of the dinette chairs. She wasn't sure what she should be thinking right now. Meanwhile, Cal was staring past her through the window to the fence covered with honeysuckle across the way. He looked as if he'd pinched his face tight in preparation for some pain he was about to be inflicted with.

"You thought I was a crook, didn't you?" he asked.

"That's not how it was." But she'd thought exactly that about him.

"Well, let me set your mind fully at ease."

"You don't have to do that. I—"

"My father likes to refer to himself as a shrewd man of business," Cal went on as if he hadn't heard her speak. "That's an accurate description of him as far as it goes. What you read in that article was the kind of thing he said all the time. He was always vowing to do everything one way or another no matter what, and the truth is he didn't really care much which way it turned out to be. His ethics weren't what you'd call ironclad by any stretch of the imagination."

Cal smiled without mirth, his strong features set firm in the wash of morning light from the kitchen window. He still wasn't looking at Abbie, and she had a feeling that was because he was ashamed. She would have liked to reach out and touch him, but even though he was less than an arm's length away from her, she understood he was actually much farther away, in a place where he didn't want her to go.

"You really don't have to tell me any more, Cal."

"You're wrong about that. I do have to tell you. I need for you to know. My dad used Urban Horizons in a number of real estate schemes. They all went approximately the same way. He'd buy in, usually on some arrangement that skirted the border of legality without a millimeter to spare. Then he'd turn the buildings over fast, without a qualm about whom he was selling them to or what the new owners intended to do with them or to them. Remember when I told you about my old neighborhood being turned into a shopping mall?'

Abbie nodded.

"That was one of my father's deals. He made a lot of money on that one. He made a lot of money on all of them. I don't have anything against making money as such. I've done some of that myself. It's the way he did it that I can't stomach, whether he's my father or not."

This time Abbie did reach out to him, laying her fingers gently against the fine down of golden hair just above his wrist. She no longer cared if his cool distance made her feel uneasy. It only mattered that these things were difficult for him to say, and she wanted to spare him what she could. He must have understood that, because he looked away from the window and into her eyes, and his strained expression moved into a smile that now had some real warmth in it. He seemed to have just remembered she was there and was glad of it.

"Then he went after the Seaport buildings, and I decided I had to stop him. So I blocked the deal in a way that nobody but the two of us knew where the opposition was coming from. Then I made him an offer he couldn't refuse."

"What kind of offer?"

"I proposed a more than fair price for Urban Horizons, and I also promised to block every land deal he made till he agreed to get out of town." Cal looked down at her and put his hand on top of hers. "You see, I have some of him in me after all."

Abbie drew him closer and down into the chair next to her. "There's nothing wrong with being shrewd when it's in the right cause," she said.

"Well, right or not, it worked."

"Was that when he went to Florida?"

Cal nodded. "He made it sound like it was his idea, of course. We couldn't swim in the same pond was the way he put it. He was right for once about that. I had a hard enough time even after he was gone. People kept mistaking me for him because of the name. His reputation wasn't an easy thing to live with, especially in the business world. Nobody wanted to trust me."

"Why didn't you change your name?"

"I thought it was my responsibility to clear it, not run away from it."

Abbie realized she should have known that was what he would say.

"I thought I *had* cleared it, until now." His smile was bittersweet.

"I'm sorry, Cal."

"I don't blame you for what you thought. I just wish you'd asked me about it sooner."

"I was going to last night. Then I saw some papers on your desk. I still don't really understand what they were about—a bunch of figures on the sale value of some museum properties."

"Oh, those." Cal laughed. "Now *I* understand." He took both of her hands in his. "I may pride myself on being an honest man, but I never said I wasn't human. I was reviewing that file because of what we'd discussed about Les. I'm afraid I couldn't resist figuring out exactly how much my honesty was losing me. Quite an impressive amount, isn't it?"

The good-natured, blue twinkle was back in his eyes. Abbie couldn't have been more relieved to see it.

"Very impressive," she agreed.

"Tell me something. If you already thought I was such a lowdown character, why did you come to my office with me last night?"

"None of that seemed to matter right then."

"Does it matter now?"

"Not in the least."

"I'm glad to hear that." Cal reached across the short space between them and lifted her easily from her chair to his lap. "I dreamed about you all last night. Now here you are."

He drew her closer, slowly and deliberately, as if he were still in the hypnotic movement of his dreams. She was pressed against his broad chest as he cradled the back of her neck in his hand and brought her lips to his. This kiss was what she'd been eager for last night, tender yet insistent, loving but intense with the demands of desire. Abbie yielded completely, moving her lips against his, savoring him and each new sensation he aroused in her.

She felt the wakening begin within her and knew she'd been waiting, possibly all of her life, for someone to make her feel exactly the way she did right now. She'd sensed all along that she'd recognize that feeling if and when it finally happened. Now there could be no mistake. She wanted Cal Quinn as she had never wanted a man before, and she had to tell him.

She pulled gently away from his kiss. "I'd like you to make love to me," she said, and the words came simply and directly from her heart.

His hand moved from the nape of her neck to her cheek, and he caressed her face. "I've wanted to do that since the first minute I saw you."

Cal slipped one arm around her waist and the other under her knees. Then he stood up and carried her out of the kitchen, through the living room and into the bedroom. She'd put her head on his shoulders and her arms around his neck.

The comforter was in rumpled folds across her bed, and a lively breeze still rattled the blinds, which were closed to subdue the morning light. He laid her down gently, then swept the comforter aside. "I'm glad it's daylight," he said, his voice hushed and deep with emotion. "I want to see every inch of you."

His hand moved to the top button of the blouse she'd put on to replace the sweatshirt. She remembered the mesmerizing trail of his fingers down the buttons of her suit that first day in the office and knew she couldn't wait so maddeningly long this morning to open herself to him. As he undid the first button she was doing the same to the second. Their fingers raced together till her blouse fell back from her breasts.

"You're even more beautiful than I imagined," he whispered.

He fell across her and took her mouth more avidly this time. His tongue and lips discovered hers and made them his own as sounds of hunger and desire began to rise from both their throats. He was more insistent now, and Abbie matched his eagerness with her own. Their fingers grazed each other's palms and raked sensuous trails up each other's arms.

They came together for quick, urgent kisses. Yet still they were holding back, prolonging the moment in a delicious torture of delay. She seemed to know without a doubt what he wanted most at that moment, and he seemed to know the same about her. They plucked the pieces of clothing from each other's bodies like petals from flowers and cast them with abandon onto the floor.

Their sudden heat touched the cool sheets and turned them instantly warm and disarrayed from rolling back and forth, first one on top, then the other. All the while, they touched and fondled and stroked as if their hands had become as insatiable as their mouths ever since his naked body had covered hers.

Abbie had never experienced such lovemaking. It sang along her skin and through each nerve and sinew to the very center of her being. Her mind was emptied of all former doubts and problems. There was nothing in her thoughts now but Cal and her yearning to be entirely his. At this moment she lived only for his flesh against hers and their passion mounting like the wind outside.

He rose above her, looking down for a long, hushed moment at her pale body. His strong thighs straddled her, and she could see the ripple of muscles in his shoulders as he lowered himself slowly toward her. This was the most exquisite torment of all. He held himself away from her, gazing down, taking in every inch of her, as he'd said he would. He strained against their frenzy as the passion surged between them, controlled at trembling point by his hovering just above her until she couldn't stand it any longer. She reached for him and pulled him suddenly close.

"Love me now," she pleaded, the sound coming from deep in her throat. "Please."

Her words seemed to ignite a power in Cal too intense for him to restrain. He slid his hands beneath her hips and lifted them to where his body waited. Then they were back into frenzy again, then beyond it, past the fever of impatience to conflagration. For just an instant Abbie was afraid. Her body seemed about to blow apart with the fury of what she was feeling.

Then the explosion came, but she wasn't destroyed. Instead it burst over and through her, with a soul-deep release of all the tension she'd been feeling these past trying days. The aftermath of release brought a peace more complete and satisfying than anything she'd ever known. Her limbs had turned liquid and drifted up to wrap themselves around him.

Abbie had never been able to sleep in a man's arms. She'd always been too restless for that. Today was different. She fell off to sleep, not only in Cal's arms but entwined with him, their bodies pressed so tightly together it seemed they were defying the effort of their separate skins to keep them apart.

Much later, she awoke, more profoundly refreshed than she'd have thought possible after so many nights of troubled tossing. The torpor of their lovemaking still slowed her movements to a fantasy pace as she luxuriated in the tangled sheets. She looked lovingly along the length of her own body. She'd never known she was capable of such joy. Till now she'd lived mostly through her mind and instincts, planning every move and acting very consciously in the manner that would advance her the fastest toward her goals. Today Cal had introduced her to a different world entirely, and she knew she would never be the same again.

The shadows had deepened into late afternoon. Somewhere in the last levels of her sleep she'd felt Cal slip from her arms and cover her gently with the sheet. Now she was suddenly aware that he wasn't beside her. A pang of disappointment nearly shattered her reverie as she realized that he might have left without waking her. Then she heard the sound of a rich baritone singing its way across her living room, extolling the virtues of the beautiful morning.

Abbie smiled and hugged the pillow she'd rolled onto. It smelled like Cal.

"It's hardly morning," she said as he came through the door.

He was carrying a tray, and he was completely nude. She noticed how his smallest toes curved slightly under the others at the edge of each foot, and she felt a sudden urge to kiss them both.

"Were you wandering around my kitchen like that?" she asked with a fleeting, amused thought of the neighbor's yard on the other side of the honeysuckle-covered fence.

"I closed the blinds to avoid a scandal," he whispered with a playful leer.

The tray he carried was the wooden one she kept on a shelf over the stove; he'd found cups, saucers and the makings for the coffee that steamed aromatically from her white ceramic pot. He'd also discovered the croissants in the back of her refrigerator, and she could tell he'd heated them because a pat of butter was melting over each one.

"I see you got to know your way around the place already."

"Do you mind?" he asked as he smoothed a space on the comforter and set down the tray.

"Not at all. In fact, I think I like it." She moved over so he could sit next to her.

"I had to do something to keep myself occupied while you slept the clock around."

"I didn't really do that, did I?" Because of all the weekend time she'd been working, today had been her day off. Had she really slept through it somehow? Should she be back at work right now?

"No, of course not." Cal laughed at the flicker of panic across her face. "We still have hours and hours left of this beautiful day."

"Oh, good." Abbie sighed with relief.

"You're right about one thing, though. It's definitely no longer morning."

"My stomach's telling me that in no uncertain terms," she said, eyeing the tray at the end of the bed.

"Well, if you want me to give you a chance to eat, you'd better let me do this." Cal pulled the sheet up gently where it had slipped off one of Abbie's breasts.

"You, too," she replied, tucking the white material around his body and thinking she might not be hungry only for food after all.

He passed her a croissant on a saucer, then settled himself against a pile of pillows as she poured coffee for them both.

An hour later they'd eaten and talked about nothing of great importance and then just stayed quiet for a long while in each other's arms. They turned together almost at the same moment, their hands exploring more slowly than they had in those frenzied moments several hours ago. This time their loving was more in tune with the dreaminess of their refreshing sleep. They took the time to learn about each other, where to touch, when to kiss, in the first lesson of a study that Abbie hoped would last a very long time.

She'd been certain nothing could be more intense than their earlier rocketing together to climax amid moans and tangled sheets. Yet this tender probing, as they sought out the deeper tremorings beyond the clamor of need, transported her still further into her own capacity for sensation and love. They mounted gradually this time toward the crescendo that broke over them finally and left her totally content in his arms.

Abbie ran her thumb slowly, gently, along the ridge of his eyebrow and marveled that nothing had ever seemed so precious in quite the same way as touching him did now. Davey was endlessly dear to her, but he moved a different part of her. What Cal had brought to life was the woman beyond not only the mother, but everything else she'd ever been.

"How do you feel?" Cal asked, propping himself up on one elbow so he could look at her.

"Wonderful."

"And?"

Abbie thought a moment. "A little guilty."

"Guilty?" Cal straightened up more. "For what?"

"For feeling so wonderful when everything's so terrible." She hadn't realized she felt that way till he asked her.

"I understand what you mean." Cal cupped her cheek in his hand. "This bed is an island, and the waters around it are troubled."

"Very troubled."

"What do you think we should do about that?"

Abbie sighed. "I think I should close my eyes, then open them up again and find out none of it ever happened." She didn't want to think about the problems at the Seaport.

Cal's fingers stroked through her hair, easing out the tangles. "I wish I could make that true for you, but I can't. So maybe we can do the next best thing."

Abbie wound herself in the sheet and sat up next to him. "What's that?"

"Solve the situation ourselves so it won't be happening any longer."

"You mean play Jonathan and Jennifer?"

"Something like that." He picked up her hand and kissed her fingers gently. "Since you're so good at it, where do you think we should start?"

Abbie sighed again. She supposed this was inevitable. She thought a moment, her fingers tracing his lips. When she finally answered, it was in a decisive tone. "At the scene of the crime."

Chapter Twelve

This wasn't the same nighttime Seaport of crowded events. The place was deserted, and the guard at the gate was nervous. Abbie had to show two forms of identification besides her staff card and answer a number of questions before he would let her on the pier.

"I hope you understand I have to be extra careful right now," he said. "We've been having some trouble down here."

"Yes, I heard."

The plan was hers. Cal hadn't liked it from the start. He'd said it was too risky, but Abbie had kept after him. She reasoned that the shadow man had attacked Josie because she'd seen him and he was afraid she could identify him. In that case, he might be thinking the same thing about Abbie. He couldn't be certain she hadn't got a look at him, too. Her idea was to use his fear to draw him out of hiding long enough for her and Cal to capture him.

Since he seemed to spend so much of his time skulking around the museum piers at night, Abbie wanted to try to lure him into going after her there. Cal had finally agreed on the condition that he would be watching every minute. They'd waited until dark and then put the plan into motion.

The problem was how to get Cal on the piers without anybody, especially the shadow man, seeing him. Abbie's solution was for Cal to pick up the powerboat he kept moored at the Seventy-ninth Street boat basin and come into the Seaport from the river, with the motor low so no one would hear. They'd coordinated their timing to the minute; Cal was scheduled to be drifting up to the dark side of Pier 15 just as Abbie passed through the gate.

Abbie had decided to show herself along the two more lighted piers first. That way, if anybody was indeed around, he'd be sure to see her. Of course, anyone out there besides her and the guards at this hour was there without permission, because the museum areas of the Seaport were officially closed. Abbie didn't see anybody, but the shadow man could still be lurking about. There were plenty of places in which to hide and not nearly enough lights to illuminate them all.

She walked directly down the center of the pier and made some noise. Then she wondered if she was being too obviously conspicuous. She started pushing at her hairpins, then remembered Cal had convinced her to wear her hair down. That was one reason she'd had trouble getting past the guard at the gate. She didn't look like the picture on her staff ID card.

She moved over to the darker Pier 15, which was only partially open to the public even in the daytime. She felt less at ease there because of the many shadowy corners out of which someone could leap. She looked around for Cal and saw no sign of him; but, of course, he was supposed to stay out of sight and just watch. Still, she wished she could call out to him and hear his reassuring voice call back.

"Psst. Over here."

Abbie spun around. That hadn't been Cal's voice. It was low and raspy; and at first she had no idea whose it might be.

"Who is it?" Her own voice rasped a little from the tension she was suddenly feeling.

"Over here. I have to tell you something crucial."

This time there could be no mistaking the identity of the person. It was Josie, for whom everything always seemed to be crucial. Abbie sighed. Then she recalled that Josie's alarm had been very much justified about the *Lettie* and when she'd been on board the *Hart*.

Abbie saw the woman's familiar, frizzled head of hair peeking out from behind a pile of deck planking covered with tarpaulins. Josie's eyes were large and fearful, as they'd been when she was in the lifeboat. It crossed Abbie's mind that such an experience might have unstrung the sea-gull lady permanently. Right now she was beckoning furtively and casting glances from side to side as if she expected an attack at any moment.

"You have to believe what I'm going to tell you," she said when Abbie reached the hiding place Josie refused to leave.

"What is it?"

"Shh." Josie lifted her finger to her lips in an urgent gesture and glanced to both sides again. "You have to be quiet as a mouse."

"All right, I'll be quiet," Abbie whispered cooperatively. "Now, what's happened?"

"I saw him by the *Pioneer*."

"Who did you see, Josie?"

"I saw Captain Blood. He was even wearing his sword."

"I see." The gull man, Captain Blood. It was difficult to tell whether Josie was imagining things or not. Then it struck Abbie. "Errol Flynn played Captain Blood!"

"Did he?" Josie was wearing one of her vague looks again.

"Yes, he did."

Josie must have seen Cal, whom she was constantly mistaking for Errol Flynn. That meant he was here somewhere after all.

"His sword scared me, so I hid," Josie said. "But I'd have known him anywhere It was Captain Blood all right."

"I'm sure you thought it was, Josie."

"I didn't just think it. I *saw* him." She was suddenly indignant, and Abbie sensed one of her mood changes coming on.

"All right, then, Josie. You saw him."

"I know you don't believe me, but I swear it's true. He had on a wide sash and the sword was stuck through it, just like in the movie. He passed right by me. I had to hold my breath so he wouldn't know I was there."

This was a full-blown hallucination for sure. Josie might have seen Cal, but he certainly wasn't dressed like that.

"I saw that one fifty times, you know," Josie went on.

"What?"

"The movie, silly. *Captain Blood*. I saw it fifty times, maybe more. It's one of my all-time favorites." She said it with a real sense of accomplishment.

To Abbie, Josie sounded as if she were tripping along the edge of sanity. She probably should be taken to a doctor, but Abbie knew what would happen if Josie were examined now. The doctors would put her in a psychiatric ward somewhere. She'd be scared and bewildered, and she wouldn't understand. Abbie couldn't bear the thought of that. She took Josie's arm very gently and asked, "Have you told anybody else about this?"

"Nobody. I just saw him a little while ago, right after I saw Sam…or did I see Sam this afternoon?" Josie looked puzzled. "I could tell Sam. I told him about the gull man and about the other time I saw Captain Blood, too."

"You've seen him before?"

"Yes, and that time he spoke to me."

"What did he say?"

"He said, 'Beware the spirits.'" Josie made her voice sound solemn and eerie, like something out of an old Bela Lugosi film. "He said it just like that."

"I see." More hallucinations. What else could it be? "I want you to do me a big favor, Josie."

"Anything," she chirped, sprightly and eager once more.

"I don't want you to tell anybody else about seeing Captain Blood. I want him to be our secret."

A grin broke across Josie's face. "I love secrets. If we have a secret just between the two of us, does that mean we're special friends?"

Abbie reached around the older woman's shoulders and gave her an affectionate squeeze. "Very special friends," she said over the sudden lump in her throat. She hoped she could keep Josie's fantasies between the two of them. Some other people—Lester Girard, for example—might not view those fantasies as harmlessly as Abbie did.

Meanwhile Abbie had been sidetracked from her original purpose. She was about to try to think up some way of getting Josie off the pier when she heard a motor launch roaring toward the slip. Abbie hurried to the side of the pier. She recognized Cal's boat immediately, since she'd left him at it in the marina before she'd taken a cab the rest of the way downtown.

Obviously he hadn't gotten here when he was supposed to, though there'd been plenty of time for him to do so the way they'd worked it out. Nor was he coming in to the pier either slowly or quietly. Abbie wondered what could have happened to make him abandon their plan.

She ran toward the spot where he was about to dock. Josie was right behind her. Suddenly something occurred to Abbie. "Is that Captain Blood, Josie?" she asked, pointing to Cal. He was clearly visible now as he maneuvered the launch alongside the pier.

"Of course not, silly," Josie said with one of her very lucid looks. "That's Cal Quinn."

Abbie didn't have time to wonder what it all meant, because Cal was motioning her over to the boat.

"Get in," he said tersely. "I spotted the *Pioneer* docked up on the Hudson River. Someone must have stolen it, and I think it could be our man."

UNFORTUNATELY, IT WASN'T "their man" who'd taken the *Pioneer*. It was Sam Denicola. Even more unfortunately, Cal and Abbie weren't the only ones to find out. Stealing an iron cargo schooner, now converted to a tour boat, in New York harbor without being noticed wasn't an easy thing to do. Calls had gone out, and Seaport security was aboard the *Pioneer* before Cal and Abbie got there. Luckily, no one had called the police. The matter would be handled internally.

The next morning Sam was called to Lester Girard's office. Lester was definitely sober, which didn't seem to help his disposition any.

"What kind of clown stunt was that?" he was asking Sam as Abbie walked in.

When Abbie had arrived at work a few minutes earlier, Meredith had told her to get to Girard's office right away. "I think your friend Sam's about to go down for the third time," she'd said.

The looks on the faces of the two men convinced Abbie that her assistant hadn't exaggerated.

"Come in, Mrs. Tanner," Lester said with mock sweetness as Abbie made her uninvited entrance.

She hadn't stopped to talk to the secretary or knocked. She didn't want to take the chance that someone would stop her from being here to support Sam. He must have had a good reason for taking the *Pioneer*. Neither she nor Cal had been able to get to him last night to find out what the reason was. Still, she had no doubt about standing up for him this morning. She wondered why Cal wasn't here yet to do the same.

Lester's complexion was more florid than usual. Abbie guessed that anyone on Sam's side wasn't very popular with the museum director right now, and it would take more than some stroking of his ego to change that. Sam sat staring out the window with his mouth set in a hard line.

This is definitely one of those you-can-cut-the-atmosphere-with-a-knife moments, Abbie thought.

"Your friend Mr. Denicola isn't talking," Lester said in the same nasty tone. "If he doesn't tell me something soon, I just might call in the police and see what they can get out of him."

Light from the window glinted in Sam's wire-rimmed glasses. He stared out a moment longer, then slid his gaze past Lester to Abbie. She'd never seen him look this way before. His expression was granite firm, as if it had been chiseled onto his face. Then the granite crumbled for a second.

"Good morning, Abbie," he said. "I hear you and the mighty Quinn tried to join me for a sail last night. Maybe some other time."

"You won't be having any other times on this waterfront if you don't answer my questions and do it fast," barked Lester, who was growing more red in the face by the minute.

The office door opened and Cal was standing there, his tall, broad frame nearly filling the doorway. "I think we have the answers you want right here, Les."

He stepped aside to reveal Donna Gelfand, the captain of the *Pioneer*. She walked past Cal and into the office with a no-nonsense glance that swept over them all.

"I don't know what everybody's so excited about," she said to the room in general as she strode over to Sam. "I gave Denicola permission to take the schooner last night."

"You did what?"

Lester had come out from behind his desk when Cal and Donna walked in. Now he moved quickly out of Donna's way. He was smart enough not to try to stop her when she had something on her mind.

"I said I told Sam to take the *Pioneer* out on the river last night, and I'd like to know what all this foolish fuss is about. With so much else to do around here, it seems to me our time could be better spent."

Donna's hair was streaked silver and waved almost to her shoulders. Long hours under sun-washed sails had bronzed her skin beneath the open-collared shirt and windbreaker she was wearing. She was the only female schooner captain on the river, but she looked more as if she should be off for a turn around the back nine of a Westchester country club. Only her walk gave her away. There was a sway to it with the rhythm of a rolling deck.

"Why did you tell him to do that?" Les wasn't as indignant now. He was no match for Captain Donna.

"I needed to get some kinks out of a new sail, so I asked Sam to do a late run for me last night after the evening tour. Then he got becalmed up on the Hudson, and some idiot jumped to the conclusion that somebody had stolen the *Pioneer*."

"What new sail? I didn't hear anything about a new sail." Les was still trying, but he'd lost considerable wind himself.

"Come now, Lester, you haven't heard about most of what's going on at the piers. You have to visit them once in a while to do that, and I understand you don't go anywhere that doesn't have ticker tape all over the floor."

Donna said this without belligerence, but everyone in the room, including Lester, knew how much she resented his lack of interest in the ships. Still, Abbie hadn't heard anything about a new sail, either, and she'd have thought Donna was the type to run out her own kinks. She glanced at Cal, but he was wearing his unreadable face at the moment. She couldn't tell whether he was buying any of this or not.

"Listen, Lester," Donna went on, "I've got other things I should be doing right now. In case it's slipped your mind, the *Wavertree* fund-raiser is tomorrow night, and the Harbor Festival is just a few days away. Thanks to this lady's publicity, we're going to have half the town down here watching fireworks and falling into the river for that one." She nodded toward Abbie. "So we need to get to work yesterday. Now, if you've finished with your version of the Spanish Inquisition, Sam and I have some genuinely important business to take care of on Pier 16."

"All of you get out of here," Lester said with a burst of false bravado as he marched back to his chair. "I've got work of my own to do."

Donna turned and walked out of the office. Sam, Cal and Abbie were right behind her.

"Would somebody like to tell me what just happened in there?" Abbie asked when Lester's door had closed behind them.

"Not here," Cal said in a secretive tone. "The walls have ears."

She remembered Meredith's telling her the same thing once and waited till they were out on the street.

"I've got to get back to the *Pioneer*," Donna said as they walked toward Schermerhorn Row.

"Thanks, friend. I owe you one," Sam told her.

"Anytime," Donna answered with one of her serious-eyed smiles. "And good luck with the *Wavertree* bash, you two," she added to Cal and Abbie. "Keep them greenbacks rolling in. We can use 'em."

Then she was off across the brick walkway toward the waterfront, her seaworthy gait carrying her swiftly along.

"You still haven't told me what happened," Abbie said. "I feel like everybody's in on a secret but me."

"Sam did steal the *Pioneer* last night, just as Lester thought." Cal had spoken so matter-of-factly as they strolled along that Abbie wondered if she'd heard him correctly.

"Now I have the feeling it's a joke everybody else is in on instead of a secret. I suppose I shouldn't mind as long as the joke's not on me," she said.

"Actually, part of this one is."

"Cal, what *are* you talking about?"

"It seems that our buddy Sam here thought you and I might be the ones sabotaging the ships. He got it into his head that maybe we unplugged the pump on the *Lettie*, and rigged the block and tackle on the *Peking* and even set up that little drama with Josie on the *Hart* as publicity stunts to bring out the curiosity seekers."

"Well, look for yourself," Sam said. "If that had turned out to be your plan, you could certainly call it a success this morning."

He was referring to what was going on across South Street, at the gate to the museum piers. The crowd that had gathered was at least twice the usual size for this time of day. Beyond the gate, the ticket booth had a line in front of it stretching back to the dock apron.

Abbie nodded. This was what she'd been hired to accomplish. "I just wish it were my work that had brought them here," she said half to herself.

"I'd say the way you've handled the coverage of what's been going on has a lot to do with it," Cal said. "You've managed to keep the public from thinking there's anything suspicious happening."

"Even though there just might be," Sam added.

"Is that why you took that voyage up the Hudson?" Abbie asked him. "Because you thought something really bad might happen aboard the *Pioneer*?"

"You could say that."

"Did you actually think Cal and I could be involved in something that might hurt people?"

"Not intentionally. But things like publicity stunts can get out of hand. Then there was also what Josie told me about seeing someone dressed like a pirate on board the *Pioneer*. I know about her loony habit of confusing Cal with Errol Flynn. Everybody knows she does that."

"You mean you actually believed Josie?" Abbie was astonished.

"Josie has moments when she knows exactly what she's saying."

"Sam's right. She does," Cal agreed.

"I'm not sure how many of those moments she has these days," Abbie said, remembering how Josie had carried on last night at the pier.

"Anyway, I could have sworn this was one of the times when she was perfectly sane," Sam went on, "and I didn't want to take a chance with the *Pioneer* or any of her passengers. I planned to stash her up the Hudson so I could go over her very carefully, engine and all, without raising much fuss. I figured I'd have her back here by this morning. Obviously it didn't work out that way."

Cal shook his head. "No, it didn't."

"I suppose I shouldn't talk about Josie being crazy after I had that nutty idea about the two of you. Right?" Sam looked a little sheepish.

"Right," Cal and Abbie responded in emphatic unison.

"But you're forgiven," Abbie added. "Now, what about that story Donna told Lester?"

"She understood that Sam was just trying to protect the *Pioneer*," Cal said. "She thought the yarn about the sail would be more believable than bringing Josie and her pirate into it. Also, both Donna and Sam were concerned about not implicating you and me."

"Thanks," Abbie said, squeezing Sam's arm. "But what about Donna's claim of having a new sail on the schooner? I have a feeling Les might check up on that."

Cal grinned. "A new sail will be there shortly. That's what Donna was in such a big hurry to get to."

"Compliments of the generosity of Quinn Enterprises, I might add," Sam said. "And I think I'd better get over there and give her a hand rigging it. That is, if the two of you think you can get along without my brilliant schemes for a while."

"It looks like tragedy's been averted," Cal said.

"Let's hope it's not just tragedy postponed. You've still got that *Wavertree* thing coming up."

Sam didn't smile as he said that, and neither did Abbie. There'd be a lot of reporters at the fund-raiser, especially those from the society beat. Nobody loved a juicy, mean story better than they did.

"Then there's the Harbor Festival to get through," Sam added.

Abbie couldn't worry that far ahead. She already felt her stomach starting to churn at the thought of tomorrow night's bash.

Chapter Thirteen

Abbie wore her favorite dress to the fund-raiser, a royal-blue Norma Kamali. The wide shoulders emphasized the length and grace of her neck, which she'd always thought of as one of her best features. The line of the dress, tapering down to a narrow hem at the knee, made her look even slimmer than she already was. Abbie called it her confidence dress. She wore it whenever she was feeling a little nervous, which would definitely describe her state of mind tonight.

The reception table had been set up on the pier next to the *Wavertree*'s gangway, and the canopy over the table was striped red, white and black to match the colors of the gracious, full-rigged ship. The plate-steel walkway down the center of Pier 15 had been cordoned off with red velvet ropes; black tarpaulins covered the rubble of the usually closed dock beyond the walkway. The gangway rails were strung with chains of red and white carnations, and the deck was arrayed in flowers, soft lights, and lovely canapé and cocktail tables.

Abbie had spared no expense in designing the decor. Tonight's guest list included some of the most prestigious names in New York. She'd learned long ago that a cut-rate show never got such people to open their checkbooks quite as wide as a little understated elegance could. So she'd insisted on the best of everything, from French champagne to foie gras, and the result was worth it. This would be an event long remembered in Manhattan society.

Meredith was behind the reception table, and Abbie was grateful for that. If her current agitated state caused any detail to go unattended, her superefficient assistant would be sure to notice and take care of it. Meredith was very good at filling in whenever necessary.

Nathan was there, too, in the same baggy suit he'd worn to the party on the *Peking*. Meredith kept chasing him from underneath the canopy, but he'd return all the same and ask if there was anything he could do. Abbie was aware of how out of place he looked at such an elegant affair, but she couldn't hurt him by asking him to leave.

The guests had begun to arrive. Lester Girard scurried past in the wake of Hatcher Benjamin Baxter IV, one of tonight's wealthier notables. Abbie looked up from the gilded guestbook a few minutes later to find Cal headed toward her. Seeing him made her relax a little; she felt as if nothing could go very wrong as long as he was nearby. As always, his movements were composed and casual, but something in the set of his shoulders told her he was especially on the alert tonight. She smiled as he walked straight up to her, but she was surprised when he took her firmly by the arm and propelled her from behind the table with an insistence she couldn't very well resist.

"If you'll excuse Mrs. Tanner," he said to Meredith, "we have some important business to attend to."

"Take over for me, Meredith," Abbie said. "I'll be back in a few minutes."

Cal leaned across the pile of museum brochures with a mischievous grin. "Don't count on that," he said, and planted a comradely kiss on Meredith's cheek.

Her gray eyes popped wide open to match her gasp as Cal hurried Abbie away.

"You shouldn't tease Meredith," she said. "She takes things very seriously."

"I can't help it. You bring out the leprechaun in me."

She looked up and saw he really was wearing a very impish grin.

"I think it's got something to do with being uproariously happy," he added, letting go of her arm with an affectionate squeeze. "It doesn't look right for me to be dragging you along. So why don't you just follow me."

"Where are we going?"

"To take care of that business I mentioned."

He moved off toward the gangway without another word. She mounted the incline behind him and kept track of his crisply tailored white suit through the crowd to the cabin area at the stern of the ship. He ducked into one of the small cabins on the pier side of the long hallway, waited till she had entered, then shut the door.

"Now for our business," he said, and pulled her toward him. His free arm clamped itself around her, and she was dragged hard against his chest with an urgency that told her he could hardly have waited another minute to hold her.

"Cal, what if someone comes in?"

"They won't," he murmured very close.

Then her open lips were covered by his as his tongue tasted her hungrily. There was fierceness in this kiss, and Abbie felt a rising need to meet it. He caught the back of her neck in his powerful fingers and held her there, but she would have stayed nonetheless.

His other hand began to travel down her side, and he bent to reach the hem of her dress and slide his fingers underneath. Abbie moaned as the warmth of him touched her skin and slipped up the silken smoothness of her stockings. The loose tunic dress moved cooperatively out of the way, allowing his hand to edge along her thigh, over her hipbone and past her waist, until it found her breast in its wisp of lace. He was savoring her body, and she had never felt as completely desirable as she did at this moment.

His hand swept down again and out from beneath her hem, and he smoothed away any wrinkles he might have caused in the resilient jersey of her dress. With one last taste of her lips, he moved his mouth a few inches away.

"I had to do that," he said, his voice deep from the sensuous moment that had just passed between them. "All day I've been dying for the touch of you."

Abbie drew in a long breath, then let it out again before she could speak. "I've missed you, too."

She was still slumped against his chest, but suddenly she noticed he wasn't holding her as tightly any more. She looked up to see that he was staring past her with a startled expression on his face. Abbie followed his gaze to the porthole but still didn't understand the cause for his alarm.

"I don't believe it," he said.

"What's wrong?"

He drew her along with him to the porthole and gazed out. "We're moving," he said, and Abbie could see he was right.

The *Wavertree* was a stationary exhibit ship, moored permanently to the museum pier. She hadn't moved in several years, other than being hauled to New Jersey for repairs; and they weren't headed for Hoboken now. Somehow the old, iron-hulled vessel had come unmoored and slowly, steadily, was headed into one of the busiest shipping channels in the world.

All the way down the hall to the deck, hurrying behind Cal, Abbie tried to tell herself there must be some simple, safe explanation. She brushed her dress smooth once more and ran a hand through her hair before emerging onto the main deck.

The *Wavertree* wasn't equipped to be anything but an exhibit. She was lashed to Pier 15 by thick lines looped over high pilings. She had been seaworthy once, but it was questionable how she would fare in open water now. The ship had no motor or sails, and there were a lot of people on board tonight. Abbie was instantly aware that if they really got into the shipping channel, the consequence could be a disaster worse than all the unfortunate events of the last weeks combined.

Cal was already headed up the steps to the bridge deck, taking them two at a time. Abbie hurried behind him but tried to move at a less attention-getting pace. Once on the bridge, however, she recognized the futility of her efforts at discretion. There'd be no way of preventing everyone on board from knowing exactly what was going on. The *Wavertree* was definitely moving, no matter how slowly, and some of the guests were gazing curiously over the side and wondering aloud what was happening.

"What is it?" she asked Cal, who had rushed to the rail and was staring over.

"I'd say someone either cut the mooring lines or managed to push them up over the pilings. The lines are trailing in the water. I can't tell anything for sure except that they're not holding the ship to the pier any longer."

"How could this have happened with all the security around?"

"I have no idea. It could have been Josie's gull man for all I know, sweeping down out of the sky." Cal had already turned to head toward the steps. "I'm going to look for some heavy line belowdecks. Maybe we can hook her back onto one of those pilings before she gets into the current at the end of the pier.''

"What if you can't?'' Abbie asked, keeping pace with him as well as her narrow dress would allow.

"Unless we can secure her to the wharf, we'll be adrift in a strong current downriver toward the ocean,'' he answered over his shoulder. "Maybe she'll drift stern first, maybe sideways. There's no way of telling what she'll do.''

"What about the guests? Is there any chance of getting them off?''

"Definitely not. That would put them in more danger than keeping them on board. They'd all be tumbling over one another into the river, trying to get to shore ahead of everybody else. You'll have to do your best to keep the panic at a manageable level.'' He was at the bottom of the steps now, with Abbie a few steps above him. He looked up at her for a brief moment, his eyes filled with concern. "Be careful,'' he said.

"You, too,'' Abbie responded softly, but he was already gone.

She drew in a quick, deep breath. There was no time to think of Cal or even of her own fear right now. There was only time to act. She stepped down the first tread from the landing; the tight hemline of the designer dress caught at her knees, restricting the length of her stride.

She didn't have to consider what to do for more than an instant. She reached down for the hem and ripped as hard as she could till the seam was open halfway up her thigh and her legs could move freely. Then she followed Cal's example and bounded down the steps two at a time to the main deck.

An off-and-on, stiff breeze had been gusting all day long. There'd been a lull for a while, but Abbie could feel the wind picking up again. The garlands of carnations fluttered vigorously along the gangway rails. That was the last thing they needed, a good wind to carry them more rapidly into the channel.

Abbie understood exactly what the danger was out there. She could picture the line of freighters lying at anchor under the Verazzano Bridge, waiting for the harbor pilots to come on board. Then they'd move on into the center of the channel, right where the *Wavertree* was headed. Cal had said the ship might even drift sideways, and a target 293 feet across would be easy to hit.

Meanwhile, their predicament was becoming general knowledge among the guests. The level of conversation on the main deck had risen in pitch, and Abbie heard rapid, startled voices all around her. The mass of people at the center of the deck had suddenly grouped together and was moving as a unit toward the rail on the pier side of the ship. Abbie remembered Cal's remarks about them tumbling over one another, trying to save themselves. The image gave her momentum.

She tore across the deck and dashed up to the middle step of the short flight leading to the gangway. She was there ahead of the pack, but it kept advancing. She gripped a stair rail on either side as the crowd bore down on her.

"Stop!" she shouted in a voice so filled with steel she hardly recognized it as her own. "You can't come up here. It's too dangerous."

The mob hesitated, but she knew she hadn't stopped the people for good. They were merely hovering for a moment while they filtered her words through their collective, terrified mind. Then they'd probably charge over her and up the steps to send themselves, by sheer force of action, over the side.

Abbie could hear the metal gangway prongs groaning off to her left. They wouldn't hold much longer as the huge ship moved steadily riverward. This crowd, converging onto the already precarious walkway, could send the whole thing crashing down. They'd all be in the water, in danger of being crushed between the heavy ship and the pier pilings.

"If you try to get off the ship now, you could very possibly be killed," she said coldly, so they could hear she wasn't dramatizing. "The gangway is about to break loose."

"I have to get out of here!" shouted a portly man, launching himself toward Abbie.

She recognized Hatcher Benjamin Baxter IV, the man who'd come aboard with Lester. If he got past her, the others would follow—and he was too big for her to hold back very long. The crowd watched, but no one came forward to help when he began pulling at her arm to break her grip on the rail. She felt a jab of pain as a fingernail tore, but she didn't let go.

"Take it easy now, Bax. Everything's going to be fine." The voice belonged to a man Abbie hardly expected to come to her rescue.

Lester Girard had forced his way through the press of people and taken Baxter's arm. He tugged the portly man gently but insistently off her, and his usually pompous tone took on the soothing quality of a parent easing a child out of a nightmare back to safety.

"Just come along with me," he said to Baxter, his voice loud enough to reach the rest of the mob, as well. "This situation will be taken care of shortly."

His manner was so wonderfully reassuring that, for an instant, Abbie almost believed him herself. She watched in amazement as, like a pied piper, he led the lot of them back to the center of the wide deck and began urging them to sit down on the planking. She was beginning to suspect that Lester had the makings of a director after all.

Still, no matter how calm he kept the guests, there was no minimizing their peril if the *Wavertree* should collide with another vessel in the channel. There were no life jackets on board, and the maybe half a dozen life rings were used for decoration. It would be literally sink or swim for all of them, and the East River current was known for being treacherously powerful.

Abbie was about to experience her own moment of the same, mindless terror that had gripped the crowd. Then she heard a thin, familiar voice off the side of the ship.

"I'm coming to help."

It was Nathan, and he was halfway up the gangway from the pier before Abbie saw him.

"Nathan, go back." she shouted. "Don't come any closer."

The groan of the steel gangway against the iron ship had risen to a metallic scream. The prongs couldn't hold much longer, and Nathan was still advancing. He was almost to the top now.

"Go back!" Abbie hollered above the screeching metal.

Nathan was looking straight at her, his mouth open to call out something back, when he glanced down into the space of dark water a considerable drop below. Abbie saw the lines of his face set instantly into rigidness. She shouted to him again, but he didn't respond.

Nathan had forgotten his fears for one bold moment in his eagerness to help, which was so typical of him. Now he stood, frozen, at the top of a gangway that was about to wrench loose and pitch him into the river. Abbie had no choice. She had to do her best to save him. There wasn't time for more attempts to shout through his paralysis.

She clambered up the few remaining steps to gangway level. One prong had sheared almost all the way through, and the other was splitting under the weight of the enormous vessel as it moved relentlessly down the pier. The rolling trolley at the dock end of the gangway had followed along as far as it could.

Electric cables had been strung overhead to accommodate the extra power needed for tonight's reception. Now those cables had begun to spit and spark. They were about to tear apart and fall almost to where Nathan was standing. Live wires on a metal gangway. He'd be electrocuted instantly, if he wasn't flung into the river first.

Abbie could think of only one thing that might work. She'd hurl herself onto the gangway, directly into Nathan. She'd grab hold of him and try to roll the two of them down to the pier before the moving ship tore loose or those hot wires hit the metal. It was a crazy idea. There was a good chance both she and Nathan would topple into the river with the heavy gangway on top of them. Still, she had to risk it.

She slipped off the flat-heeled shoes she'd worn for comfort behind the reception table and prepared to jump.

"Nathan, get off that gangway!" Cal's voice boomed from above and behind her. He was leaning over the bridge-deck rail. "I said move it, Nathan. Do what I'm telling you, this instant."

His was the voice of command, and Abbie prayed it would get through the fog of Nathan's phobia. Meanwhile she was ready to leap. She'd give Cal's tactic a few seconds, but if it didn't do the trick, she'd have to act.

For a moment there was no change. Nathan stood poised across from her, frozen stiff. Then in the soft lights, now flickering from the deck, she saw something, like a

fissure on the stone surface of his face. First there was a
ripple of response, then a twitch. He'd heard.

"Run, Nathan!" she cried as loud as she could.

Nathan turned and stumbled down the gangway, half
running, almost falling, just as a crack of metal signaled
the final severing of the second prong.

Abbie was lifted off her feet. For an instant she thought
the jerk of the gangway letting go had thrown her off the
platform. Then she realized Cal had tossed her up into his
saving embrace as easily as if she were a twig on the rising
breeze. For the second time during these past terrible
weeks, his strong arms whisked her clear of catastrophe.
He carried her to the bridge-deck stairs as all hell broke
loose around them.

The wires above the ship rail crackled and danced fire at
the ends. One falling wire touched a trail of carnations torn
from the newly detached gangway. The string of flowers
sizzled in a chain reaction toward the ship's rail, then went
out. A breath of something like carnation incense wafted
through the air for a moment before the breeze blew it
away.

The gangway careened backward on its rolling trolley
and slammed down to hang, half on shore and half out
over the water, at the edge of the pier. Hot wires crackled
along it, electrifying its surface, exactly as Abbie had
thought they would. Thank heaven, Nathan had run off
just in time. The chaos on deck was no less alarming. As
the last of the power cables ripped free from the bul-
warks, the ship plunged into darkness. The wrenching of
the vessel as it ejected the gangway sent cocktail tables
sliding. Glasses smashed, and silver hors d'oeuvre trays
clattered onto the deck.

Abbie heard squeals and exclamations from the circle of
guests crouched around Lester. She hoped with all her

might that the continuing drone of his assurances could keep them huddled there. The situation was impossible enough already without panicking people dashing every which way, maybe even hurling themselves over the side.

Abbie wasn't certain at what instant Cal had let her go. She only knew he was gone. Then she saw him running toward the foredeck at the other end of the ship. He had several coils of thick, heavy rope slung over his shoulder. She scrambled after him. By the time she reached the foredeck, her heart was racing. She'd had to shake off the clutching fingers of guests along the way as they shouted frantic questions for which she had no answers.

"What can I do?" she asked as she ran up behind Cal.

He whirled around in the half-light from the pier. "You can get back down on the main deck where you're safe and I won't have to worry about you."

"There's no safe place on this ship right now."

His face was only inches from hers. Suddenly all she could think of was how much she wanted to kiss him again, maybe for the last time, and she knew he was feeling the same.

"Yes, that's true," he said more softly. "There's no safe place."

"Then I'm staying here with you."

Cal didn't repeat his protest. He turned back to what he'd been doing with the rope and spoke to her over his shoulder in a low, determined monotone. "We're on our way into the channel with no lights. That means there's very little chance an oncoming ship will see us in time to avoid a collision. If we drift sideways, which is a good possibility, we'll be struck broadside."

"The *Wavertree* has an iron hull. Couldn't she survive a collision?"

"She might not break apart, but the impact of a large freighter hitting midships could heel her over."

"You mean she might capsize?"

"Yes, and then she'd probably sink."

Abbie looked out across the channel. There were no large ships in sight. Traffic must be light tonight. Only the graceful sails of the *Pioneer* jutted above the shoreline near the row of docked cargo vessels over on the Brooklyn side of the river. Donna must have stopped to give her evening passengers a last look at the nightlit skyline of lower Manhattan. From way over there, she couldn't see the trouble the *Wavertree* was in, especially with the big ship as dark as it was.

"Is there any way to get help?" Abbie asked.

"The people on shore probably called the coast guard, but it could take them as long as fifteen minutes to get here from Governor's Island. We don't have anywhere near that long."

Abbie could see that was true. More than half the length of the *Wavertree* was already past the end of the pier and headed toward the channel.

"What are you doing with that rope?"

"I'm going to try to throw a loop over one of the pilings. I tried it at the stern, but it didn't work. The ship moved by too fast. This is our last chance."

"Then please, let me help."

"All right." Cal gestured toward the wide bar attached to the deck around which he'd just finished winding one end of the rope. "You watch the line as it plays out to make sure it doesn't catch."

Abbie nodded but didn't answer. She waited, tense and ready, as he adjusted the coil in his hand, raised it over his head and began to swing. It whistled like a lariat, around and around in the air. Cal had taken off his white suit jacket and snatched open his collar. The hard muscles of his back and shoulders strained against the fine fabric of his shirt. Then he let the thick line fly.

It sang over the side while Abbie kicked and pulled out kinks as the rope snaked from the coil on the deck. Then she ran to the side just in time to see the loop overshoot its mark and land beyond a tarpaulin-covered pile of deck planking.

"Damn!" Cal exclaimed and began jerking the line back in.

The loop caught on a jagged corner of the mound of planking, and the rope wrenched suddenly taut with a jolt that lifted Cal off balance for a moment. At the same instant, a wind gust gave the ship just enough of a shove to pitch him out from the rail with the rope still yanking at his grip. Cal was on his way overboard.

Abbie dived after him. She locked her arms around his legs, then plummeted herself as hard as she could onto the deck, pulling him down with her, back over the side to safety. She'd bruised and scraped her knees against the rough decking, but she hardly noticed. She was too busy helping Cal to his feet.

"Are you all right?" she cried.

"Thanks to you, yes, I am." Then he was back at the rail, flipping and wriggling the line free from its snag and hauling it back on board. "We have time for one more try," he said over his shoulder.

The ship was closer to the pier at this point, almost raking the corner of it. He had more hope of hooking on now, but the *Wavertree* was about to pass the last piling at the end of the pier. There wouldn't be a chance for another toss if this one didn't work.

Cal leaned over the bulwark, and Abbie leaned with him. They held the loop wide open between them. From this angle, with luck, they might be able to drop the rope over the top of the piling instead of trying to lasso it. The ship drifted steadily toward their mark. Even the slightest jar of the vessel, which was scudding perilously close to the dock now, could bounce the loop from its target. Then they'd be off into the shipping channel with nothing to stop them. Suddenly the drift of the *Wavertree* slowed, just enough for Abbie to notice.

"The wind has shifted!" Cal exclaimed.

Abbie glanced up to see the decorative pennants on the mast stays flapping in the direction of the shore. That meant they were drifting against a head wind for the moment. They wouldn't pass this piling quite as fast as they had the others. Now if the wind would only hold for just a few seconds longer!

Abbie leaned even farther over the side and readied herself for the drop. Every muscle in her body felt as if it had been twined as tight as the strands of the rope, and she could see the long branches of bulging sinew above Cal's gripping hands. She and Cal seemed suspended, with the pier inching by below, like exhibits caught in amber. For an instant Abbie had a terrible vision of them frozen there, as Nathan had been, unable to perform the act that was their last remaining hope.

Then the piling was directly under them, gray and beaten silvery by wind and river. The loop poised a second, then two.

"Now!" Cal shouted.

Abbie's fingers opened at exactly the same moment his did, and the rope fell. The moment stretched, breathless and heart-still, while the loop settled over the piling and slid downward.

Abbie had been unaware of faces lining the rail on either side of them or of the people in cocktail finery staring up from behind a cordon of security guards on the pier. A cheer broke forth with a volume and exuberance she wouldn't have thought possible from such an ordinarily subdued and proper crowd.

"We're not out of this yet," Cal murmured as he stared off across the *Wavertree*'s bow.

Abbie was surprised to hear no elation or even relief in his voice. Then her eyes followed his gaze, and she understood why. The *Pioneer* had crossed the channel under sail. Donna obviously intended to stop near the museum piers and furl canvas there, then dock the rest of the way under power. Her passengers would get an extra treat that way, running cross-river ahead of a gusting wind.

Ordinarily that wouldn't cause any problem. Ordinarily the *Wavertree*'s darkened hull wasn't jutting beyond the end of Pier 15, straight into the schooner's path.

The shifted wind, which had been salvation a few moments ago, was now driving the *Pioneer* toward their stern. Most of the people on the pier were latecomers to the fundraiser who'd watched the *Wavertree*'s plight with gaping stares. There'd been nothing they could do to help. Not even the security guards could be of much assistance, other than to disconnect the spitting wires and keep the onlookers away from the edge of the dock. If they'd tried to catch the line when Cal cast it, they could have been pulled into the river themselves.

Now the guards saw what was happening with the *Pioneer* and hurried as a group to the end of the pier. Standing side by side with socialites in summer furs and silk suits, they all began jumping up and down, waving their arms and screaming to get Donna's attention above the whip of wind and canvas.

The ruckus worked. The *Pioneer*'s engine rumbled to life, and even with half its sail still aloft, the captain turned the schooner hard-to just in the nick of time and headed back into the channel a safe distance from the *Wavertree*'s jutting hull. Since Donna had no more trouble saying what she thought than she did navigating the river, Abbie was sure she would have some very pointed remarks to make about what went on here tonight.

"Only a few more crises to go," Cal said with an edge of irony in his voice.

The heavy ship was still attached to the dock by the single line he'd managed to secure, and that line had zinged tight now and was groaning toward snapping point. Meanwhile the *Wavertree* was moving in an arc on the fulcrum of the line, her long bowsprit headed straight for the *Peking* across the docking slip. Cal was already on his way across the deck when Abbie recognized this new predicament.

Suddenly sirens screamed out of the wind and two spotlights cut through the gloom. Just like the cavalry riding over the hill in a John Wayne movie, the coast guard had arrived, and not a moment too soon. Two cutters were coming in fast from the channel. They could be thrown a line from the *Wavertree* bow, then tow her around before her sprit slammed into the *Peking*. The question was, would there be time?

Cal and Abbie clamored up on the foredeck to discover they weren't the only ones who knew what was needed now. Lester Girard and Hatcher Benjamin Baxter IV were hunched over a cleat near the bow, lashing a line to throw overboard as the first cutter came alongside. Amid shouted instructions from a midshipman into a bullhorn below, the *Wavertree* was secured to Pier 15 once more, and the crisis had passed.

Cal and Abbie turned, moving as one, and fell into each other's arms.

Chapter Fourteen

No one could talk of anything but the *Wavertree* for the next two days. The police were all over the piers, and few still disbelieved Abbie's stories about harassment or Cal's theory of a conspiracy. The fund-raiser sabotage had been brilliantly executed by someone who knew what he was doing and was very intent on his purpose. The mooring lines had been sawed nearly through, then patched with gum and paint so that nothing showed, even to the closest security check. It was inevitable that the weight of the huge ship would sever the remaining strands sometime during the evening.

The saboteur had probably planned the disaster to happen a little later than it did, when all of the guests would have been on board; but the stiffness of the wind had hurried his timetable. It was possible that he had even been aboard himself when the ship broke loose, thinking he'd have time to escape but getting caught there instead. The police weren't discounting any possibility. They'd even come to the office to check the files of present and former Seaport employees, especially those who'd left under questionable circumstances.

Abbie could hardly believe how good she felt. She certainly shouldn't be feeling good under the circumstances.

There was a real madman on the loose who'd jeopardized the lives of a shipload of people. Because of the threatening notes and other incidents, she had reason to believe he had singled her out for some special punishment. As if that shouldn't have been enough to ruin her frame of mind, the society press had crucified the *Wavertree* reception in every edition, comparing it to the *Titanic* because there'd been so many aristocrats on board.

Still, Abbie felt wonderful, and the only explanation was what had happened between her and Cal. They'd struggled together, side by side, to save the *Wavertree*. They'd proved they really were a winning team, and she was certain now that there was no problem they couldn't lick as long as they attacked it together.

She'd even reached a kind of acceptance of the terrible situation at the Seaport, as if a climax point were approaching and there'd be some kind of solution soon She'd decided to stick it out till that solution appeared. That night on the *Wavertree* had made her aware of how much she cared about this place and these ships. She wouldn't run out on them now. Consequently, when the phone call came from Boston, she knew at once what her answer would be.

"We've heard about your work through our New York office," said the personnel officer for the Boston branch of the prestigious public relations firm. "We'd like to offer you a position up here."

"I can't leave New York," she said quickly.

"It would most likely be only a temporary move. If you do as well as we anticipate, you could be transferred to our New York office eventually."

"I'm sorry, but this is my home," Abbie said. "I couldn't leave it even temporarily."

She smiled at the receiver. She was grateful to her caller for helping her realize that she'd settled down at last.

The personnel officer hadn't given up yet. "You don't have to decide right now. We'd just like you to think it over for a few days. We'll get back to you."

"All right, but I doubt that I'll change my mind."

Abbie had hung up and was still thinking about what she'd said when she heard the sound of raised voices through the wall. Usually Abbie couldn't distinguish what was being said in Meredith's office next door, unlike the volunteer office on the other side, where people sounded as if they were in the same room with her when they talked. Right now, Meredith and whoever was in her office were speaking so loud Abbie couldn't help but hear.

"Listen, sister," shouted a female voice Abbie didn't recognize. "You owe me."

"I don't owe you a thing," Meredith shouted back.

"You mean you think you can weasel out of this without paying up? Well, sis, you got another think coming."

There was silence for a moment. "All right, all right. Keep your voice down," Meredith said finally, still upset but resigned now.

Those were the last words Abbie understood clearly. The women lowered their voices, as Meredith had suggested. Still, she'd heard the agitation in her assistant's tone and wondered whom Meredith could be arguing with so vehemently. A few minutes later Meredith's door was pulled open and closed with a bang as someone stomped off down the hall.

Abbie couldn't help but worry about what was going on and if there was something she could do. She went to her own door and looked out just in time to see a remarkable-looking woman turn to go down the stairs to the street. She was tall and blond, but the most extraordinary thing about her was the way she was dressed. She wore a tight sweater and an even tighter skirt. If either had been a fraction smaller, they'd have exploded off her body. She had very round hips and bust and a fairly small waist. The woman's hourglass figure was emphasized by her very high heels, which made her hips switch in an exaggerated roll.

After Abbie heard the sound of those heels click down the stairs, she went to Meredith's door and knocked. "Are you okay?" she asked.

There was silence inside, and Abbie was beginning to think she should mind her own business.

Then Meredith answered. "Come on in. I'm fine."

Abbie opened the door and saw that Meredith was anything but fine. Her hair was tousled, as if she'd been raking her fingers through it, and there were spots of red in the center of her usually pallid cheeks.

"I couldn't help hear some shouting. I was worried about you."

"You heard?"

"Only a little. Was that your sister?"

Meredith stared at her for a minute. "How did you know that?" she asked.

"I heard her call you sis."

"She's my sister all right," Meredith said, settling back in her chair. "But we've never gotten along very well."

"That happens, I guess. I never had any brothers or sisters myself."

"Consider yourself lucky." Meredith seemed a little less agitated now. "I hope we didn't disturb you. Could you hear what we were arguing about?"

"Not really."

"Did you hear us yelling about money?"

"Well, yes." Abbie was feeling a little awkward now, as if she'd been eavesdropping the way everybody else seemed to do around here. "But that was all I heard, that she wanted you to give her some money."

"She was putting the bite on me as usual, but I guess that's what kid sisters are for."

"I guess so."

"I think I'll take a walk and cool off. She has a way of getting me very steamed."

As Abbie watched Meredith trudge off down the hall, her stick-slim shoulders hunching even more than usual, she thought it was no wonder that the sisters didn't get along. They were so different from each other. Only their tendency for tough talk was the same.

The phone ringing on her desk drew Abbie back into her office. Her joy at hearing her former mother-in-law and friend on the line lasted only a moment. The tone of Victoria Tanner's voice immediately told Abbie that something was terribly wrong.

"What is it, Victoria?" Abbie's throat was suddenly tight. "Has something happened to Davey?"

"Not in the way you're thinking." Victoria's cultured, Southern-lady accent was strained. "But something has happened nonetheless, and I believe Davey should come back to you immediately."

"What are you talking about, Victoria?"

"This is very hard for me, Abigail. After all, Robert is my son, but I just can't stand by and watch him do what he's planning to do."

"What is he planning?" Abbie's knuckles were white from her gripping the phone.

"Robert doesn't realize I know about this, but I still have allies on staff at Tannersfield. They tell me he's about to institute a new custody suit against you, and with Davey down here he'll have a much better chance of winning. So he's not going to let Davey return to New York. He's going to keep him here."

"I'll be there as soon as I can get a flight out." Abbie had already pulled the Yellow Pages from her desk drawer. She began leafing through it in search of the airlines section.

"That may not be soon enough," Victoria said. "I understand Robert is putting his plan in action this afternoon. My lawyer says if Robert gets to the right judge while Davey's still here, he'll probably rule for him to stay at Tannersfield till the case has been heard in court. With a shrewd delaying strategy that could be many months from now."

"Oh, no. What can I do?" Tears stung Abbie's eyes.

"Don't worry. If we move fast we can catch my crafty son by surprise. He won't expect us to have a strategy of our own. He has a tendency to underestimate women. I've often told him that would be his undoing someday. Meanwhile, Davey's with me, and I have him all packed. I'm putting him on the next shuttle flight to New York. I'll stall Robert off for a while by telling him Davey's on a picnic with friends in Alexandria."

"I appreciate your doing this, Victoria. I understand how awkward it must be for you."

"Quite awkward indeed, but I must err to the side of what I know is right. Robert isn't really interested in being a father to his son."

"Then why is he doing this?"

"I think he's been waiting to get back at you ever since you left him. He was very humiliated by that, you know."

"But that was five years ago!"

"We Southerners can carry a grudge a long time. We still haven't forgiven the Yankees for the Civil War. You should know that, but we'll discuss history another time. I must get Davey to the plane now.''

"Victoria, I don't know how I'll ever be able to thank you for this.''

"You're a wonderful mother to my beloved grandson. I consider that thanks enough.''

"Are you sure you'll be able to handle Robert? He can be very nasty when he's crossed.''

"Don't worry about me, my dear. My great-grandmother held off a platoon of Yankee raiders for two days single-handed. I think I'm more than a match for one ill-tempered Tanner.''

"Yes, I'm certain you are.''

As soon as Victoria had hung up, Abbie was pushing the buttons of a now-familiar number.

"Cal, I can't explain on the phone," she said when he answered, "but I need to get to LaGuardia Airport right away.''

THEY ARRIVED AT THE AIRPORT far too early, but Abbie had insisted they leave the Seaport immediately. She didn't want to take even the slightest chance that she'd miss Davey's plane. All the way there she'd stared out the car window without seeing anything. Her thoughts were absorbed by threatening visions of Robert in Washington, concocting schemes to take her son away. She might have foiled him this time, but she had no doubt he'd try again.

She'd explained everything to Cal when he picked her up at the office. He hadn't said much in response. He didn't have to. She had felt his disapproval of what she was doing. He'd agreed to take her to LaGuardia, but she could tell it was against what he thought was his better judgment. She'd had to accept that, because her first priority was getting to Davey. Still, she'd felt much farther from Cal than the width of a car seat. How ironic that such a short time ago she'd been thinking that together they could lick anything. They definitely weren't together in this.

The Eastern Airlines Shuttle Terminal was in its lull period between the morning and afternoon rush of business commuters to and from Boston and Washington. Even so, the cafeteria had a line for the salad and sandwich bar. Abbie didn't really feel like eating, but Cal insisted she should. Then she noticed his being waved ahead in line by a pretty woman behind the counter who smiled sweetly and called him by his first name.

"I'm here so often everybody knows me," he explained. "I go to Boston two or three times a month, remember. In fact, I should be there now, but I don't want to leave New York till this mess at the museum is cleared up and I'm sure you're safe."

"I see." That was just about the first thing Abbie had said since they left Manhattan.

"She got your attention, though, didn't she?" He smiled and jerked his head toward the young woman still watching him from behind the sandwich counter.

"She's very attractive."

Abbie had to admit, if only silently and to herself, that she'd experienced a twinge of jealousy.

"Can't hold a candle to you," he said.

Abbie managed a brief smile. She knew he was trying to lighten the atmosphere between them, and she wished she felt more like cooperating.

They took a table at the back of the room that adjoined the cafeteria. Cal had picked out a seafood salad in pita bread for her. She hadn't eaten breakfast today, and the shrimp and crabmeat mix looked good. Still, she only stared at it as Cal opened the small can of V-8 juice, which had been the one thing she'd chosen for herself.

"Davey's going to need you to be ready to listen to hours of stories about his trip. You won't be equal to that unless you fuel up first."

"Hours of stories about how his father tried to bribe him with promises of trips and presents he knows I can't afford."

Cal poured the juice over the ice in her Styrofoam cup but didn't say anything.

"Sorry. I'm not a very good lunch companion today." Abbie picked at a piece of shrimp with her plastic fork "I'm just worried about Davey."

"Then why didn't you let him stay in Washington like you planned instead of wrenching him back the same way you wrenched him out of here?"

He hadn't bothered to hide his disapproval now. Abbie glanced up sharply from the indentations she was making with the fork in her Styrofoam plate. "I told you about Victoria's call and what Robert intends to do."

"Are you sure your mother-in-law isn't overreacting about all this?"

"Victoria isn't the overreacting type, and neither am I."

There was a long silence between them, during which Cal appeared to be studying the geometric pattern of the airport lounge carpet with intense concentration. Abbie stared at the television set that was perpetually on at the other end of the room. A soap opera was playing, and Abbie thought how much like a soap opera her life seemed to have become.

Cal finally turned his attention from the carpet. "I've told you how I feel about kids and their parents in situations where there's been a divorce," he said.

"And I think I've told you that my son's circumstances are nothing like yours were." She'd said that louder than she meant to.

The surrounding brown Formica tables were occupied mostly by groups of businessmen. The only exception was a table with two pilots. Each had his feet up on the red vinyl chair next to him and was gazing half-attentively at the daytime drama on television. Both men must have preferred the real-life variety, because when Abbie made her loud remark, they put their feet down and turned around.

"I think we might be about to make a scene," Cal said, but he didn't sound too concerned.

"Am I to understand you're on my ex-husband's side in this?"

"I'm not on anybody's side in this, except maybe Davey's."

Abbie stood up abruptly. "Speaking of my son, I'm going to wait for his flight." She flounced her bag over her shoulder.

"Maybe it would be best if I stayed in the main terminal while you go down to the gate."

"Maybe it would."

Abbie turned and walked out of the lounge. She let her glance slide with cold disdain over the two pilots, who made no attempt to hide the fact that they'd been listening to every word she and Cal had said. She didn't really care who'd heard them. All she cared about was that Robert was up to his usual manipulative tricks, and the man she loved wouldn't believe that.

She stopped short just outside the cafeteria door. This was the first time she'd thought of herself and Cal in those specific terms. She sighed. Why did it have to happen when they were in the middle of having a fight—and why were they fighting anyway?

Because, she told herself, there are some things we have to be together on, or we can't be together at all.

She didn't like the sound of that, but she knew, for her at least, it was true. She was tempted to go back and tell Cal exactly that. The two pilots would probably love to hear another installment of their saga. Instead she hurried toward the concourse and the gate at which Davey was scheduled to arrive. She had her son to worry about and take care of now. Maybe she'd been a fool to have thought she'd found someone who would understand how she felt about that.

She waited in the dismal, brown corridor, feeling just as dismal herself. She wanted Cal to be there with her, but she didn't want to argue with him any more. So she waited alone. Then the intercom announced the arrival of Davey's flight, and she felt a little better. A few minutes later she saw his auburn head peeking out from behind the woman in front of him on the ramp from the plane.

"Mommy, Mommy!" he cried. "I missed you so much!" He leaped into her arms, nearly knocking her over. He seemed so much heavier than she'd remembered.

"I missed you too, sweetheart," she said. As she hugged him, she knew just how very true that was. She wished more than ever that Cal could share their happy moment.

"David Tanner. Please come to the Eastern Airlines ticket counter on the lower level."

Abbie took a few seconds longer than Davey to register the meaning of the unexpected intercom message. By then he had darted out of her arms.

"That's me," he said as he started down the concourse at a run.

"Davey, wait!"

Abbie ran after him. Something told her he was in danger.

"I can't wait, Mom. They're calling me," he shouted back, eager and excited as always. Everything was an adventure to Davey. Being paged on the intercom was no exception.

He'd already streaked to the end of the concourse. He looked to the right and left, spotted the ticket counter and took off in that direction. Abbie was in pursuit, but she was no match for his sprint. Her foot was still tender from the incident in the parking garage, and she'd banged her knees up pretty badly on the *Wavertree*. Still, she ran as hard and fast as she could. As she dashed out of the concourse, she saw Davey straining up to talk to the woman behind the ticket counter. She handed him a brown-wrapped package just as Abbie came running up.

"I'll take that."

It was Cal's voice over her shoulder. He reached past her to grab the package from Davey, then headed for the nearest exit.

"That's the man who drove us to the airport when I went to visit Daddy. Why did he take my present, Mommy?" Davey's green eyes were wide and bewildered.

"It's all right, honey. Cal wants to make sure the package is, uh . . ." Abbie groped for an explanation, then settled on there being none. "He'll be back in a minute."

"Ma'am, is something wrong?" The woman behind the ticket counter looked almost as bewildered as Davey.

"I'm not sure," Abbie said as she watched Cal hurry through a revolving door and out of the terminal, cradling the package carefully in his hands.

"Are you the boy's mother?" the ticket agent asked.

"What?" Abbie's attention had been on the door through which Cal had just disappeared. "Oh, yes. I'm David's mother."

"Well, I wanted to explain that we checked your son's package when it arrived. We do that with all deliveries. It's a safety precaution."

"I understand." Abbie's attention was fully on the revolving door once more. Cal was just coming through it again, back into the terminal.

"I just wanted to say that the item was broken before we checked it," the ticket agent added.

"Broken?" Abbie was suddenly reminded of those moments Josie had when she wasn't sure exactly what was going on.

"What happened to my present?" Davey wondered.

Cal was beside them now. The brown-wrapped parcel, which he'd opened, contained a badly smashed replica of the *Peking.* Looking from the package to the solemn expression on Cal's face, Abbie couldn't help feeling almost as shattered.

A hastily improvised story about mail damage appeased Davey, especially after Cal gave him carte blanche at the airport gift shop to buy anything he wanted as a replacement. According to the ticket agent, the smashed ship model had been delivered to the airlines parcel service by a New York cab driver. Cal pointed out that it would take considerable time and police involvement to trace the driver. Even then, the sender probably was shrewd enough to have used a gypsy cab rather than one from a regular fleet, and that would make tracing even more impossible.

"Of course, we'll report it," Cal said. "But maybe we should concentrate our energies in other directions."

"Maybe I should concentrate my energy on getting Davey back to Washington where he's safe," Abbie answered.

"I don't think you need to do anything that drastic just yet."

"I thought you were the one who told me to let Davey spend more time with his father."

"You're Davey's mother, and you know what's best for him. I shouldn't have interfered."

"Thank you," Abbie said, and she meant it.

"In the meantime, I know a place where both you and Davey will not only be safe but very welcome."

PHOEBE DENICOLA WAS as terrific as Abbie had expected her to be. She scurried about making tea, finding Davey things to play with in the next room and generally enfolding the Tanners into her home. On the way to Sam and Phoebe's Brooklyn apartment, Cal had stopped off at the museum office to pick up some files and leave a message for Sam to join them as soon as possible.

"It's time we all put our heads together," Cal said as they sat over tea and Phoebe's muffins.

"Well, mine's frosted over some from living with Sam, but you're welcome to it." Phoebe's wry wit was as similar to her husband's as the round, wire-rimmed glasses they both wore.

"I hear we have a houseful for the duration," Sam said when he came in a while later.

"I hope you don't mind," Abbie said.

"I can't imagine minding less."

It was unusual for Sam to leave the waterfront in the middle of the day. The fact that he had was an indication that he took their discussion very seriously.

"How's it going at the piers?" Cal asked him.

"I'm still everybody's favorite suspect, if that's what you mean. Now it's what they call my expertise they're holding against me, but isn't that why you've gathered us all here today? To clear my good name?" His tone was cynically amused, but his expression was grave.

"I can tell them Sam couldn't be their villain," Phoebe said. "He could never keep enough details straight to tell so many lies. He's too absentminded for that." She reached for Sam's hand under the table. There was no mistaking the affection on her small heart-shaped face when she looked at him. They were together in this all the way, no matter how it turned out. Watching them, Abbie understood that was exactly what she wanted for herself and Cal.

"So tell us what you two Sherlocks have up your sleeves," Sam said.

"I think we have to review all the possible suspects," Cal told him. "We'll take Phoebe's word about your absent-mindedness and leave you out of the running."

"I've forgotten what she said already," Sam quipped.

"Meanwhile I've commandeered some information that might give us a starting point." Cal drew a pile of files from the package he'd picked up at the museum. "The police just finished going over these. They're the records of employees who left the museum staff in the past two years. The police apparently didn't find anything, but I thought maybe you might have some insights they wouldn't know about, Sam, having been around the place so long."

"I've known 'em all, that's for sure."

"Have we given up on Lester as a possibility?" Abbie asked.

"We haven't given up on anybody," Cal answered. "I just tend to think Lester wouldn't have been anywhere near the *Wavertree* if he'd known she was headed for the channel, and he wouldn't have tempted fate, either, by coming on board even for a little while that night."

"I second you there," Sam said. "I wouldn't necessarily put it past Les to sacrifice somebody else, but he's too much of a narcissist to take a chance on hurting himself."

"Exactly," Cal agreed.

"So what about these files?"

"What I'd like you to do, Sam, is give us a character sketch of each of these people as you remember them. You know, the stuff the files leave out."

"Sort of thumbnail the lot?"

"That's right."

"Okay, if you think it'll do some good." Sam looked a little skeptical, but then he often looked that way.

"It just might shake something loose."

Abbie hoped Cal was right. Unfortunately, an hour later, their hopes appeared to have been dashed. There was one file folder left, and nothing had shaken loose yet. The files had been in alphabetical order, and the name on the final tab was Katrine Zaigo. She'd been a bookkeeper at the museum for a while, then left for a better position uptown a year and a half ago.

"Ah, yes." Sam sighed, leaning back in his chair. "I'm a red-blooded boy from the West Side. I wouldn't be likely to forget her." If he was concerned about their lack of leads so far, he hid it well. "She was a real tall drink of water with blond hair. The bright, yellow kind that only comes in a bottle. She wore her clothes so tight you'd have had to sandblast her to get them off, and she had a walk that reminded me of my sixth-grade teacher who had to stay two feet from the blackboard so her hips wouldn't knock the chalk off the tray."

"Sam," Phoebe protested with mock indignation.

"Obviously, I prefer the mere slip-of-a-lass type myself, my love." Sam gave her a wink and a loving smile.

"Wait a minute." Ordinarily Abbie would have told Sam how sexist his description of Katrine Zaigo had been, but she was too busy with the associations coming suddenly together in her mind. "Did she also wear very high heels and talk kind of tough?"

Sam nodded. "The toughest. That one was an honors graduate of the truck drivers' school of English vocabulary. Why?"

"I think I might be onto something." Just then the phone began to ring, and Sam got up to answer it.

"I hope you're right about being onto something," he said when he returned a moment later. The concern he'd been hiding was in his eyes now.

"What's happened, Sam?" Phoebe asked, hurrying to his side.

"That was one of my men at the Seaport with a timely tip for me to take it on the lam." He put his arm around his wife and squeezed her with an urgency that belied his tone. "It seems the cops are on their way over here with a warrant for my arrest."

Chapter Fifteen

Abbie had never realized Cal could be so determined. His friend was in trouble, and he was going to do something about it immediately, if not sooner. She could see now that loyalty was a large part of his character. If he stood by his friend this staunchly, he'd hardly do less for the woman he loved. But then, did he love her?

There wasn't time for wondering about that now. Cal made it very clear there was only time for helping Sam, and not enough time as it was. That was why he'd decided to take Sam's motorcycle instead of the car to Katrine Zaigo's address in Sunnyside, Queens. Cal said he wouldn't get stuck in the rush-hour traffic on a bike.

As they sped between the lines of bumper-to-bumper, workday-end traffic on the Brooklyn-Queens Expressway, Abbie clutched his waist and prayed her helmet was on tight enough. She hadn't told him she'd never been on a motorcycle before. In the neighborhood where she'd grown up, no one had been allowed to drive a motorcycle on the streets. Her mother would be absolutely scandalized if she could see her now. At the moment, that was Abbie's only consolation.

Of course, she couldn't very well object to their mode of travel, since Cal hadn't wanted her to come along in the first place. It was his friend who was in trouble, he'd said; she didn't have to stick her neck out.

"Sam's my friend, too," she'd replied. "And my neck is already stuck out, a mile at least."

So there she was, with the wind blowing her heart from her mouth into her throat with every horn blast. Yet she knew she'd been right to come. Cal was too angry now to be trusted alone with a situation that might demand some diplomacy. But she understood his anger. As far as Cal was concerned, the Seaport saboteur had taken one step too many. He, or she, had planted incriminating evidence in Sam's workshop aboard the *Hart*, the worst kind of incriminating evidence: the makings of a bomb. The police were going to hang on to Sam, one way or another, until there was rock-solid proof of his innocence.

Abbie just wished Cal hadn't let his anger shut her out. He was as encased in it now as he was by his black-visored helmet and zipped-up leather jacket. She even suspected he'd chosen to take the cycle partly because they wouldn't be able to talk to each other on it the way they might have in a car. She had to admit she'd done almost the same thing herself earlier, when she'd been all wrapped up in her worries about Davey. Obviously she and Cal had a lot to learn about sticking together when the chips were down.

The police had already noted from Katrine Zaigo's file that she still lived at the same Sunnyside address.

"But what if she doesn't come home tonight?" Abbie had asked Cal as he put on his helmet in front of Sam and Phoebe's building. "What if she goes out to dinner or something?"

"Then I'll wait on her doorstep till she comes back."

They parked down the street from the high rise in which Katrine lived. Abbie watched the entrance. She had no doubt she'd recognize the woman if and when she arrived. Abbie tried not to be restless, but Cal and Sam weren't the only ones with a lot at stake. She'd pretty much decided that if they couldn't find out who'd been doing all these deadly things, especially to her, then she was going to accept the Boston job offer after all. She'd have no choice. She couldn't keep Davey here while a maniac was after her, and she couldn't hide out with Sam and Phoebe forever, either.

Forever was how long it felt they'd been waiting before Katrine showed up. Abbie recognized her instantly as the woman she'd overheard in Meredith's office. Katrine smiled very wide as Cal approached her. A fast glance flicked down his body and back again, and Abbie could tell the woman liked what she saw.

"Are you Katrine Zaigo?" he asked.

"That's right. *Miss* Katrine Zaigo."

"I'd like to talk to you about some problems we've been naving at the Seaport Museum. I understand you used to work there."

Her red-lipped smile faded. "Look, I talked to you cops already. I don't have nothing more to tell you."

Abbie had hung back till now, to see how far Cal's masculine charms would get him; but obviously Katrine wasn't being charmed any longer. Abbie stepped forward from behind the parked car where she'd been listening.

"We aren't the police, Katrine," she said, "but we can get them here pretty fast if you'd prefer to talk to them. Then we can have them ask you about your relationship with Meredith Stanfield."

Katrine looked from Cal to Abbie, then back again. "If you're not the cops, then what are you after?"

"Why don't we talk about that inside?" Abbie suggested.

They followed Katrine up to her apartment. Once they were inside, Katrine said belligerently, "I didn't do a damn thing, and you can't prove I did. I just asked my old buddy Meredith for a loan."

"The police might call it something else. Like blackmail maybe?" Abbie knew she was fishing now. She had nothing to go on but the beginning of a hunch.

"On the other hand, if you help us, we might be able to help you. It's no skin off our noses either way." Cal sounded as streetwise as Katrine. Abbie was impressed. She was also relieved to see that he wasn't letting his frustration show.

Katrine hesitated, obviously considering Cal's proposition.

"The truth is going to come out eventually, Katrine," Abbie said in a friendly, supportive tone that was the perfect contrast to Cal's hard-boiled one. "I know there must have been some real problems between you and Meredith. It would really help if you'd tell us your side. I'm sure Meredith is telling hers." Abbie was still fishing, but this time, she caught something.

"I'll just bet she is." Katrine's face had turned into a hard mask of overbright makeup. "Problems? I'll say we had problems. That broad tried to railroad me out of my job."

Abbie caught the flash of Cal's glance at her over Katrine's shoulder. "Come on now," he said. "You expect us to believe a tough cookie like you let herself get pushed around by a little girl from Connecticut?"

"Little girl, my eye. She broke into my apartment. Stole my keys out of my purse, had them copied and broke in— and that was just the beginning. She left me notes at the office. She even threatened to kill me. In fact—" Katrine leaned forward with a look on her face that said she was about to deliver a delicious shock ''—she even tried to hire somebody to set this place on fire.''

Unfortunately, Abbie wasn't shocked. The pattern Katrine was describing was painfully familiar.

''Can you imagine that? She tried to hire one of the waterfront boys to torch my apartment. Luckily, most of them guys were buddies of mine, so I found out about it. I'd been just about ready to quit my job before that happened. And do you know why she did it?''

''No, why?'' Abbie asked.

''Because I was dating this tour-boat captain from the Circle Line. I guess he had a drink with her or something once, and she got it in her head he liked her. Can you believe that? She actually believed a boyfriend of mine could go for a scarecrow like her. Then when I faced her with it she went on and on about always being passed over. How her parents always liked her younger sister better and how she was always ignored on the job. I'm telling you, she was nuts over that stuff. She's crazy all right. I wouldn't be surprised if she's the one behind all that trouble down at the piers.''

Abbie didn't say anything. She couldn't speak just yet. She needed a few minutes to get used to the idea that she'd been betrayed.

''Don't you think your theory is a little farfetched?'' Cal asked.

''Farfetched?'' Katrine laughed. ''That's a good word for Stanfield. She's about as farfetched as they get, but I showed her.''

''How did you do that?''

''I made her pay. I made her pay through that long, skinny nose of hers. I told her she'd better make it up to me for all the trouble she caused, or I was going to the front office with my story. Then we'd see how much longer she got to hang around her precious ships. She's just goofy over those boats, you know."

"What did she do to make it up to you?" Abbie had found her voice again, even though she could no longer manage a friendly tone.

"Gave me some cash and got me the job I'm in now." Katrine looked furtively at the two of them again. "Say, are you going to screw this up for me?"

Abbie stood up from the chintz couch where she'd been sitting. She didn't want to hear any more, and she wasn't going to promise this horrid woman anything, either.

"We'll see what we can do," was all Cal said as they walked out the door.

"Do you believe her?" he asked Abbie when they were down in the street again.

She sighed. "Yes, I do."

"So do I."

CAL DROVE DOWN Tenth Avenue, on the far West Side of Manhattan, heading for Meredith's apartment. Abbie was surprised to see how shabby the area was. She'd have thought Meredith lived someplace nicer. She remembered hearing about how much money Meredith gave the family that supposedly gave her little in return. Maybe that was why she had to live in this neighborhood. Still, Abbie could feel no sympathy. She'd been filled with too many other emotions in the forty-five minutes since she left Sunnyside: hurt, depression, anger. Now, as the cycle rounded the corner onto Meredith's block, Abbie began to experience yet another emotion. This time it was dread.

An ambulance stood in front of the five-story tenement building where Meredith lived. White-uniformed attendants were bringing a stretcher down the steps as Cal and Abbie pulled up.

"She coulda blowed up the whole building," said an indignant tenant from the steps. He had a heavy Spanish accent. "Gas. Crazy gringa took gas."

THE GAS HADN'T KILLED Meredith. A neighbor had kicked the door in and got her out before that could happen. However, she was in a coma, though the doctors said she'd be out of that soon. In fact, she'd been drifting in and out of consciousness for some time. She was lucky, if you could call somebody lucky who was facing criminal charges, including attempted murder.

She'd left a note confessing to being responsible for everything, and she said Abbie was the reason she'd done it.

"I can't see how she could have hurt the ships," Abbie told Cal the morning after Meredith's near suicide. "She loved them."

"Her letter explains that. She got it into her head that she'd been passed over for you because she wanted your job. She was so furious about that, she decided to bring the whole place down. I have to confess, I'm probably more to blame for her feeling cheated out of the job than anybody else."

"Why is that?"

"Because she came to me once, saying she'd be interested in heading up the museum's publicity department. I never took her very seriously. She was so unsuited for the job. It takes an idea person, like you. Meredith was very efficient, but she didn't have an ounce of imagination that I could see."

"Please, don't talk about her in the past tense." Abbie didn't like the thought of Meredith's almost dying, no matter what she'd done.

"Sorry. Apparently I was wrong about her lack of imagination after all. She certainly turned out to have a very active one."

"Yes, she did."

Cal had kissed Abbie then and left. He had to get to the airport. He was flying to Boston again. With everything straightened out here, he felt he could leave for a couple of days. He'd invited Abbie to come along, but she had her own hands full with preparations for the Harbor Festival. Still, she hated to see him go, and she knew she'd miss him terribly.

Chapter Sixteen

The eve of the Harbor Festival found Abbie working very late. Without Meredith she had more to do than ever. She had brought Davey with her to the office, thinking she'd be finished long before now, but it was well past dark when she left to take her last tour of the *Peking* exhibits to make certain everything was in order.

The night was warm and soft, much like it had been for the party aboard the *Peking*. Davey ran on ahead to peer over the rail at the end of the peer, while Abbie remembered dancing in Cal's arms. She wished she could relive that night now, without all the suspicions and scheming. She certainly wouldn't waste it by having her sandals trounced all over by Lester again. She and Cal would dance till dawn. Then he'd carry her off somewhere and they'd make passionate, tender, incredible love, with only the morning star as witness.

As her thoughts drifted through that beautiful fantasy, her feet drifted up the gangway toward the *Peking* deck, where the lanterns had glowed pink-gold that night.

"Mrs. Tanner."

The voice came from behind her on the pier. Abbie turned to see Nathan hurrying along after her at an awkward half run.

"When am I going to get you to start calling me Abbie?" she asked as he reached the bottom of the gangway, panting for breath.

"I don't know," he answered. He looked as if the question bewildered him.

Abbie laughed. "Was there something you wanted me for?"

"What? Oh, yes. I have a message for you, but I see you must have gotten it already."

"What message, Nathan? I didn't get any message."

"Oh, I'm sorry. I thought, since you're on the ship, you must have got the message, because it said to go to the *Peking*."

"Who wanted me to do that?"

"Mr. Quinn."

"Cal?" Abbie's heart tripped gaily. "Is he back?"

"Well…" Nathan looked bewildered again. "I guess he must be, because he said for you to meet him in the crew quarters. He said he has something to show you."

"Really? That's wonderful." Abbie scrambled down from the gangway to the deck, then peeked back over the rail. "Thanks, Nathan," she said before hurrying to the aft end of the deck.

She opened the door to the crew cabin area and stepped into the corridor that divided the small living quarter cubicles now used mostly for storage. It was darker here than on deck. Only a small light in a sconce at the end of the corridor illuminated the gloom. It was also very quiet. The sounds of the night and the river had been silenced by the heavy hull, and the only scent on the air was a slight suggestion of mildew. She wondered what Cal could have to show her in here. Then she remembered that he'd talked about restoring some of these old cabin areas as had been done on the *Wavertree*. He'd sounded very enthusiastic about it. He probably wanted to show her what he had in mind.

Sure enough, a pale line of light was barely visible beneath one of the doors ahead and to her right. Abbie hurried toward it. An alcove with a kitchen-style sink set into it was just beyond the door. These had been officers' quarters back in the days when the *Peking* was still under sail. If Abbie remembered correctly, this cabin was listed as "Miscellaneous Equipment" on the ship's diagram. She smiled at the thought of the jumble of odds and ends that euphemism must signify.

She lifted the latch handle and, finding the door unlocked, pushed it open. She was totally amazed by what she saw inside. Far from being a catchall for waterfront junk, this compartment had been transformed into something she recognized immediately from pictures she'd seen in the museum library. It was an exact replica of a nineteenth-century ship's officer's cabin.

Abbie gazed around her in wonder. The narrow berth was made up with what had to be a feather bed covered by a blanket and sheets so old the embroidered crest on the hem had yellowed against the aged linen. The washstand next to the bed held a brass bowl and pitcher, both polished bright and strapped down to prevent spillage on a rolling sea. There was even water in the pitcher. Abbie walked over and dipped her fingers into it, then lifted them to her lips. She smiled. It was fresh water. Cal had thought of everything. By the wall near the door stood a writing desk with a ledger-style book open on top of it. A quill pen lay beside the ledger and a bottle of ink.

How wonderful. Cal had obviously done this as a surprise gift to the museum, and he wanted her to be the first to see it. She couldn't have been more pleased.

She walked to the desk and leaned over to examine the open page in the light from the hanging oil lamp that swayed and flickered above her. The book was an officer's log and very old, judging from the brittleness of the pages. Yet, strangely enough, the entries she was looking at were in dark, unfaded ink. They couldn't have been more than a few weeks old. She looked closer and was startled to read her name and Cal's, as well.

She skimmed the page, then flipped back to the one before it and skimmed that, too. Back several pages more, the entries were still in fresh ink. The dates of the entries covered the past month and told a story that was quite different from the one outlined in Meredith's suicide note. According to this version, the bizarre events on the *Lettie*, the *Hart* and the *Wavertree*, as well as the block and tackle in the rigging of the *Peking*—in short, everything involving a threat to life and safety—were the work of someone referred to only as the "Captain."

Abbie leafed back to the front of the book and the title page. The ink here was faded to near transparency, making her think the date of 1856 was probably authentic. However, it was the name of the log's author that caught her eye. The title page clearly stated in a florid hand that this ship's record was the work of the Honorable Captain Hezekiah Mallory.

"I see you've found my book."

The voice was not altogether unfamiliar, as if she'd heard an echo of it sometime in the past but couldn't quite place it. When Abbie first looked up, she thought she must be mistaken about the voice. She'd never seen this man before. Even without his unusual costume, she was sure she'd have remembered him.

He was tall and stood very straight. He carried his head thrown back like that of a bullfighter, but his dress was definitely not a matador's. Two items of his outfit captured Abbie's special attention, and her alarm—a black cape draped over his arm and a sword in a scabbard thrust through his wide sash. The man standing before her was Josie's Captain Blood.

Abbie knew he was supposed to be a sea captain; she sensed, rather than truly recognized, that he was also Nathan Mallory. What made him so very much unlike Nathan was his manner. Aside from his arrogant, matador stance, there was something in his face that was the exact opposite of Nathan's quiet vulnerability. For a moment Abbie wondered if he might be the other Mallory brother Cal had mentioned. No, this was Nathan all right, or a caricature of him. But as Abbie looked into his eyes, she understood that he was too dangerous to be amusing. He was the "Captain" of the recent pages in the ship's log, and he had performed all the evil deeds written there. She was certain of it.

"I've composed a fascinating document, wouldn't you agree?"

"Yes, fascinating," Abbie answered softly.

She wasn't exactly sure how she should handle him, but she suspected she had good reason to be afraid, especially when he gestured toward the logbook and the folds of his cape fell forward to reveal the handle of a revolver protruding from the other side of his sash.

"It tells of my work here on South Street in great detail. It will be an invaluable record of what I have accomplished. I must make certain it survives."

"Survives what, Nathan?"

The minute she said the name, she knew she shouldn't have. He grabbed her wrist in a painful grip she recognized immediately from that night on the *Hart*.

"Don't mention that sniveling fool in my presence again."

"No, Captain. I won't," she said, keeping her voice respectful.

His hair was slicked back with a greasy substance that smelled unpleasant at such close range. Everything about him was unpleasant and menacing as well. Abbie knew she was going to have to be very careful. This wasn't Nathan. This was a perversion of Nathan, twisted by sickness into something brutal and ugly. There was nothing in this Captain of the gentle, endearing young man she knew.

Meanwhile he was deliberately hurting her wrist and enjoying it. She imagined he wouldn't hesitate to do much worse. He'd done much worse already. He'd threatened many lives. He probably enjoyed that, too, his only disappointment being that his potential victims had been saved from him each time.

He sneered down at her, his free hand resting on the hilt of his sword. Suddenly it struck her that he thought of himself as a superior being, so superior he had license to do whatever he pleased. In that instant she realized how truly dangerous he was. She'd try to play for time, as cautiously as she could.

"I'd like to read more if you wouldn't mind," she said.

He flung her wrist away from him as if it were a trifle and strode to the bunk where he threw down the cape.

"I can describe my deeds even more impressively in person than in writing. Ask me anything you wish to know. Though my most spectacular feat is yet to be written or spoken of because it is yet to be performed."

"What feat is that, Captain?"

"We'll let that remain a mystery a while longer, my dear. Of course, I'll have to make the log entry in advance for obvious reasons. I'll tell you about it then."

Abbie sat down on a stool as she listened closely to every word he said, trying not to miss any clue he might give her, intentionally or not. She could think of only one reason that he would so obviously have to record this climactic act of his in advance. He didn't plan to be around after it was over. He'd also mentioned making certain the log survived. Could that mean nothing else would? If so, would she also be destroyed?

And what about Davey? Where was he now? She prayed he'd gone to the guard at the gate by the parking lot. Maybe the guard was looking for her at this very moment. She hoped so, because she was comprehending more clearly by the second just how insane Nathan, or whoever he'd become, actually was.

Fear clamped down on her throat as tightly as the Captain had clamped his hand on her wrist. Abbie knew she had to overcome that fear, or she wouldn't have a chance of overcoming him. She had to be governed by her mind now, not by her emotions. Her strategy must be planned more carefully than she'd ever planned any project before. Her life could depend on it.

"Captain, you said you'd tell me about what is written in this log."

"Gladly, my dear. All the world should know. And they shall know, very soon. All of them." He made a sweeping gesture with his arms that reminded her of a dark form outside the window of Sam's pilothouse office. "They'll know, all right, after my work here reaches its crescendo tomorrow."

"It's crescendo?"

"You won't get me to tell you that until I'm ready." He laughed. It sounded almost melodramatic, like the laugh of a villain in an old-time movie. "All I will reveal now," he went on, "is that this will be my most glorious achievement. It cannot be stopped now, since that cowardly friend of yours is gone forever."

"What cowardly friend of mine?"

"That spineless fool, Nathan." He said the name as if he hated the sound of it. "He held me back those other times, but I've destroyed him. He won't return. I even threw his clothes in the river. He won't be needing them."

What Abbie saw glinting in his eyes could only be described as evil—cold, deadly evil. She realized he could be right. There was certainly no trace of Nathan visible in the man who postured before her. That meant there'd be little chance of reasoning with him on any human level. Till now, she'd hoped there might be.

"Of course, the little worm did come in handy at times. For example, he got you to come in here."

It sickened Abbie to see the self-satisfied smirk he was wearing and, even more so, to think of what he was saying about poor Nathan, whom her heart had gone out to with such compassion.

"He was my hiding place all those years," the Captain said. "As long as they saw only him, they thought I was gone."

"Who thought that?"

"All the people who feared me, especially his brother."

He sneered those last words with such venom that Abbie cringed. He was a maniac, pure and simple. She had to get away from him before it was too late. If reasoning was out, she'd have to get through the door somehow or grab the gun. She'd keep him talking and wait for an opening.

"What did Nathan do to hold you back?" she asked.

"He made me plug the pump back in on that old tub before it sank. He made me leave before I could push that crazy old woman all the way into the river that night on the ferryboat. Then he made me lead you to her so you could save her worthless hide from falling. He even tried to help all of you out on the *Wavertree*. That would have been my most brilliant accomplishment so far if it hadn't been for you and your boyfriend and a slight miscalculation of the wind.'' He loomed closer to Abbie with an ugly, twisted grin on his face. ''But you'll pay for that interference soon now, very soon.''

He waved his arms dramatically and paced the cabin while he talked, but he also watched her every minute. There'd been no chance for either a dash to escape or a lunge for the gun. Abbie could hardly look at his glittering eyes without panicking. She was having a difficult time carrying on so calmly, especially now that she'd become the subject of his raving.

''Don't worry, my dear, your Nathan won't stop me this time, and neither will that man Quinn. You'll get your just reward.'' He reached down and pinched her cheek, and she had to hold herself rigid to keep from shrinking instinctively from his touch. ''And don't think I'm not aware of what you're doing. You think if you keep me talking, I'll drop my guard eventually, but you're wrong. You're not dealing with Nathan now. He was out of control. I'm quite the opposite.''

He pinched her cheek again, much harder this time. Abbie knew he was right. She wouldn't be able to take him by surprise from just encouraging him to talk. He was too cunning for that, and she had to be equally so. She had to jolt him out of the control he was bragging about. She had to make him angry enough to forget himself, if only for a moment. It was very risky, but she had to try.

''You're Nathan all right, and you're the coward,'' she said in the most derisive tone she could muster. ''I saw you at the top of the gangway that night on the *Wavertree*. You were so scared you couldn't move. I never saw anything so pathetic in my entire life. That was you up there. Don't try to pretend it wasn't."

His eyes widened considerably, making them look nearly all white for a moment with dark points at the center. He was about to attack. Abbie could almost hear the message being telegraphed from his twisted brain to his tensed muscles. She was tensed herself, ready to grab the revolver from his sash as soon as he came at her. Then he pulled himself up straight, and she understood that the message had been short-circuited.

"You're very clever, my dear," he said, his voice a surly growl, "but not quite clever enough. Your assistant tried to be clever, too, and look what happened to her."

"Meredith? What do you mean?"

"She also thought she could manipulate me. She tried to get me to save her precious ships for her. She figured out what I was doing. She knew about Nathan and his problems from that brother of his."

"What problems?"

"About his being in the hospital once, several years ago. His brother paid your assistant to keep an eye on him, and she thought she could do the same with me. But I was too clever for her. I let her believe there was only that fool, Nathan. I never let her see that there was more of me and less of him all the time. Until the other day, after the *Wavertree*, when she said she was going to tell the police."

"What was she going to tell the police?"

"That Nathan was responsible. Can you imagine that?" He sniffed his disgust. "She really believed that fool could do what I have done. But there was too much danger that someone might make the connection, so I took care of her."

"What did you do?"

"You know very well what I did, my dear. I made her write it all down, blaming herself to throw everyone off my trail. Then I held a cushion over her face until she was unconscious, and finally I turned on the gas. Unfortunately, she survived. But she won't be telling anyone anything until it's too late to stop me. You see, it's already too late for that, my dear."

"Why are you doing this?" Abbie asked.

"To show them all who I really am, who I've always been. That family of his, that brother, the ones who mistook me for that sniveling nobody all these years. Do you know how long I've waited? How long I've saved this revenge?"

Abbie was reminded of Victoria telling her about Robert waiting all this time to get back at her. Suddenly Abbie knew why she and Cal hadn't been able to figure out who the guilty person was. They'd been looking for rational reasons where there was only wrath and insanity. Now she was making the same mistake again, trying to use reason to outwit this man when reason had absolutely no place here.

Without thinking, using only her instincts and the power of surprise with which the beast attacks its prey, she leaped from the stool and grabbed the revolver from his sash. The look of amazement in his eyes showed this was the last thing he'd expected of her.

"Get back against the wall," she said in a voice as surly as his had been a moment before. "Put your hands above your head where I can see them."

"Mommy, is that you? I've been looking all over for you."

The Captain was nearer to the cabin door than she, and hearing Davey's voice had made her falter. He was in the Captain's clutches before she could do anything to stop it.

"I'll take that, my dear," the Captain said, reaching for the gun.

Abbie had no choice but to give it to him.

DAVEY HAD BEEN ASLEEP in the bunk for what seemed a long time. Abbie had managed to convince him they were just playing a game about going on a sea voyage and he had to obey the rules. The Captain hadn't contradicted her little charade. In fact, he seemed to be less and less aware that she and Davey were even there, though she was sure he'd notice if she made a move for the door. He'd warned her not to do that and had promised to take out his punishment on Davey if she did.

The Captain was writing in his log and talking to himself. Abbie listened but could understand little of his jabbering as he continued to mumble. He was also growing more visibly agitated.

At one point he shoved the log at her and motioned for her to read. She didn't dare refuse. According to what he'd written, he'd planted charges of black powder all along the piers and on the ships. He intended to set them off tomorrow during the fireworks display, when there would be thousands of people crowded together watching. This was the feat he'd bragged about earlier. He laughed and laughed while she read, its manic sound reverberating through the cabin. She didn't dare ask what he planned to do with her and Davey. She didn't dare talk to him at all. He seemed too volatile for her to risk setting him off even more.

Consequently, she was terrified when Davey opened his eyes and started talking immediately to the Captain before she could intervene.

"Are we leaving on the voyage yet?" he asked.

"It won't be long now," Abbie answered, hoping the Captain hadn't heard.

"I guess you don't believe that superstition." Davey was still addressing himself to the Captain, who seemed to have begun to listen. "I read about it, but my mommy says it isn't true. You know the one, about how you can't have ladies on a ship because they'll make everything go wrong."

Almost before Abbie knew what was happening, the Captain had dragged her out of the cabin and set the latch in place to lock Davey inside.

"I'll hit her over the head and toss her over the side," he kept muttering like a chant as he forced her out on the deck and up the steps to the poop deck. Abbie thought his revolver would dig a hole in her side.

Once again there was no rational way out of her predicament. In a few minutes she'd probably be drowning, so she had nothing to lose by taking whatever action she could. He was on the step below, pushing her ahead of him. She plunged downward with all her might onto his foot, twisting her body away from the gun at the same moment. Then she grabbed his wrist and sank her teeth into it as hard as she could. He let out a yelp, and the gun clattered onto the deck. Suddenly, she felt him being yanked back down the stairs with her on top and realized a third person had joined the fray.

"Get the gun, Abbie," said a voice that sounded like a gift from heaven.

"Cal!" she exclaimed.

Then she was on her knees, groping over the rough decking for the revolver in the dark. She saw the Captain wrench himself away from Cal and run for the gangway. Cal was after him at once. Finally she felt the metal of the gun and was able to join in the pursuit.

By the time Abbie reached the pier, Cal had caught up with the Captain. They were grappling together at the far rail. She heard the guards coming from the other end of the pier at the same time that she saw the Captain pull the sword from its scabbard in a flash of steel and lift it above Cal's head. Abbie aimed the gun, but the men were too close together to allow her a clear shot. She might hit Cal.

"Look out, Nathan. You're going to fall." The words burst out of her with the force of pure inspiration.

The hand holding the sword froze halfway through its swing, and for an instant the Captain was as still as a statue, staring down at the water below. Except that he wasn't the Captain any more. Abbie was close enough now to see his face more clearly. It was the face Nathan had worn at the top of the *Wavertree* gangway.

"Drop that sword!" Cal shouted in the same commanding voice he'd used that night.

The steel clanged against the deck as two guards ran up. A few moments later it was Nathan Mallory, not the Captain, who walked quietly away between the security men. By then Abbie was already back at the cabin, letting Davey out and trying to explain to him what was going on.

"Cal saved us," she said as he came hurrying up. "By the way, how did you manage that?"

"I'm not exactly sure. I stopped at your office when I got in from Boston. The lights were on, so I figured you were still around. I came over here, but I couldn't find you anywhere. I was about to leave when I spotted this line of bread crumbs..."

"You followed my trail," Davey said with obvious glee.

"What trail?" Abbie and Cal asked in unison.

"There was this nice, old lady at the end of the pier. She told me all about the sea gulls, and then she gave me a bunch of bread crumbs. After that I went looking for you,

Mom, and I thought you might be looking for me, too. So I made a trail, just like in the story.''

Abbie hugged her son very tight.

"Did I help save us, too?" he asked.

"You certainly did," Cal said, and hugged them both.

A BURST OF COLOR spun up at the sky, then broke into points of light that drifted down like brilliant rain. Record-breaking crowds had thronged the museum piers all day without so much as a hint of an unpleasant incident. Everyone had a wonderful time, especially Davey. Right now, he was watching the fireworks from the deck of the *Pioneer*, where Captain Donna had officially christened him with the newly created rank of Smallest Mate. Sam and Phoebe were there, too, celebrating what Sam called "the end of the world's shortest criminal career."

Nathan's powder charges had been dismantled long before the Seaport had opened for business that morning. He was in the psychiatric ward at Bellevue Hospital now. Farther uptown, in another hospital room, Meredith had regained consciousness and agreed to psychiatric evaluations of her own. She'd also revealed one last piece of the puzzle. She was the one who had convinced William Mallory to engineer the Boston job offer for Abbie in another effort to get her out of town.

"Were you thinking of taking off again?" Cal asked.

He and Abbie were standing behind the window wall of his office with their arms around each other. The dancing fire from the sky flickered beyond the glass. No one had objected when they sneaked away from the celebration a little early so they could be alone.

"Not unless I had to," she answered.

"Maybe we should hire you for that promotion director's spot fast, before you get the wanderlust again."

"At least it would get Robert off my back."

"You'll hear no arguments about that from me."

Abbie looked up at him, and they both laughed.

"Well, whether you take the promotion job or not, we're still partners. Right?" Cal asked.

"I hope so."

"And partners have to have a uniform. Right?"

"What are you talking about, Cal?"

"This."

He flipped open a large box on his desk and pulled out a pair of silk pajamas. The top was monogrammed "Hers," and the bottom was monogrammed "His."

"Just like Jonathan and Jennifer?" she said with a loving smile.

"No. Just like Cal and Abbie."

Then they were in each other's arms. Before the night was over, they'd be making fireworks of their own. They wouldn't be needing pajamas, either.

Janet Dailey

Americana

A romantic tour of America with
Janet Dailey!

Enjoy two releases each month from this
collection of your favorite previously
published Janet Dailey titles, presented
alphabetically state by state.

Available NOW wherever paperback books
are sold.

Take 4 best-selling love stories FREE
Plus get a FREE surprise gift!